Camy Tang continues v ___ Lancaster in her next Prote ___ bines
technology, intrigue, and ___ ws to
create a very entertaining ___ and flawed and one
tough lady. Don't miss this ___ ies!

—RACHEL HAUCK, award-winning,
bestselling author of *The Wedding Dress*

Camy has crafted a story with beautifully quirky characters caught
up in trying to elude an assassin. It's a story of love and faith and
sacrifice. A story that reminds us that it's never too late or too early
to tell someone about the love of Christ. Definitely a one-day read
because you won't want to put it down.

—LYNETTE EASON, award-winning,
bestselling author of the Women of Justice series

I always love a Camy Tang novel! With characters so real you think
they're real and prose so real it makes you forget you're reading,
Camy excels at romance, suspense, and humor.

—TOSCA LEE, *New York Times* bestselling author
of *Havah: The Story of Eve* and the
Books of Mortals series with Ted Dekker

Camy Tang mixes action, romance, and the Japanese mafia in
a fast-paced story that will take you on a thrill ride through the
streets of San Francisco. Buckle up and hang on. Tessa Lancaster is
one hard-hitting heroine!

—LISA WINGATE, award-winning and national bestselling author
of *Dandelion Summer* and *Blue Moon Bay*

Begin reading *A Dangerous Stage,* and you'll be pulled at once into Tessa Lancaster's intense, action-packed world. And that's just the first chapter! Camy Tang delivers a tale that taps into our modern culture and our common fears. And she delivers to the contemporary romantic in us all.

—TRISH PERRY, author of *The Midwife's Legacy,*
Tea for Two, and *Unforgettable*

Camy Tang round-kicks tension up on every action-packed page of *A Dangerous Stage*. Rife with witty prose, sassy dialogue, and ethnically rich scenes, Tang's vibrant writing takes us on humorous but meaningful trips into Tessa's fun career where we experience the hilarity of her dysfunctional family, clever twists of mystery, and the romantic saga with Charles. Everyone needs a Tessa Lancaster in their life.

—CHERYL WYATT, author of award-winning inspirational
action-romance

No one does Asian-American comedic suspense like Camy Tang. *A Dangerous Stage*, book two in Tang's Protection for Hire series, has it all—intrigue, humor, romance, and faith, as well as a feisty, excon heroine who will steal your heart and prove, once again, that Camy Tang's writing is *ichiban*!

—DEBBY GIUSTI, author of *The Captain's Mission*
and *The Colonel's Daughter*

A breakneck plot, a gutsy heroine who can roundhouse kick right off the page, characters I wish I knew personally (and a few I hope I never to meet), sharp wit, and sizzling romance—Camy Tang delivers an action-packed read that doesn't skimp on depth. Loved it!

—ERIN HEALY, author of *The Baker's Wife* and *House of Mercy*

PROTECTION FOR HIRE

A DANGEROUS STAGE

A NOVEL

BOOK TWO

CAMY TANG

ZONDERVAN®

ZONDERVAN.com/
AUTHORTRACKER
follow your favorite authors

ZONDERVAN

A Dangerous Stage
Copyright © 2012 by Camy Tang

This title is also available as a Zondervan ebook.
Visit www.zondervan.com/ebooks.

This title is also available in a Zondervan audio edition.
Visit www.zondervan.fm.

Requests for information should be addressed to:

Zondervan, Grand Rapids, Michigan 49530

Library of Congress Cataloging-in-Publication Data

Tang, Camy, 1972-
    A dangerous stage / Camy Tang.
        p. cm. — (Protection for hire series ; 2)
      ISBN 978-0-310-32034-0 (softcover)
      1. Bodyguards—Fiction. I. Title.
    PS3620.A6845D36 2012
    813'.6—dc23   2012016766

Any Internet addresses (websites, blogs, etc.) and telephone numbers in this book are offered as a resource. They are not intended in any way to be or imply an endorsement by Zondervan, nor does Zondervan vouch for the content of these sites and numbers for the life of this book.

Scriptures taken from The Holy Bible, *New International Version®, NIV®*. Copyright © 1973, 1978, 1984, 2011 by Biblica, Inc.™ Used by permission. All rights reserved worldwide.

Published in association with the Books & Such Literary Agency, 52 Mission Circle, Suite 122, PMB 170, Santa Rosa, CA 95409-5370, www.booksandsuch.com.

Cover design: Jeff Gifford
Cover illustration: iStockphoto® SUPERSTOCK
Interior illustration: Dreamstime®
Interior design: Katherine Lloyd, The DESK

Printed in the United States of America

12 13 14 15 16 17 18 /DCI/ 20 19 18 17 16 15 14 13 12 11 10 9 8 7 6 5 4 3 2 1

A DANGEROUS STAGE

Chapter **1**

Tessa Lancaster checked in her car's rearview mirror and spotted the headlights of the slightly battered black pickup truck again. Yup, they were definitely being followed.

And the person doing it was really bad at it.

He'd nearly crunched into her rear bumper when he'd had to jam on the gas through an intersection in order to keep up with them after the light turned from yellow to red. It had given Tessa a good view of his face—coarse and red, almost as fiery as his short, spiky hair, with a mean sneer that curled the thin mustache on his upper lip. A second man was in the passenger seat, but Tessa had only gotten a fleeting glimpse of a broad face and dark hair.

She turned to Erica, who was sitting in the passenger seat. "Don't turn around to look, but I think your ex-boyfriend is behind us."

Erica bit her lip and paled so much Tessa worried she might throw up. "How'd he find us? How'd he know we were going to the bus station tonight?"

"I don't think he knew," Tessa said, switching lanes aggressively and causing a cacophony of car horns behind her. "He might have followed us from Wings."

"How did he know we were at the women's shelter? Wings didn't tell him we were there, did they?"

"No, they don't do that." Tessa yanked hard on the wheel of her ancient Toyota, nicknamed Gramps, and sent the car into a tire-squealing left turn just in front of a wave of traffic from the opposite direction.

"Ohmygoshohmygoshohmygosh!" Erica grabbed onto the door handle with both hands.

As they zipped away, they heard another blare of car horns, but Dan's black pickup was left stranded in the left turn lane, unable to follow them.

The rather neat maneuver—if Tessa did say so herself—had awakened Emily, who was strapped in her car seat in the back, and she sent up a wail. Erica turned to soothe her daughter. "It's all right, honey. Tessa's just trying out for the Indy 500."

A flash of headlights made Tessa glance in her rearview mirror again. "I don't think we lost him though." Dan had managed to swerve his left turn between two oncoming cars—making one driver slam on the brakes—and now roared down the street trying to catch up with them. Subtlety was not Dan's middle name.

"What are you going to do?" Erica's voice had a low tremor, a remnant of her fear of Dan and his flying fists. The young hairstylist still had yellowing around her cheek and left eye from the last time she'd seen him.

"Erica, I am going to get you and Emily on that bus tonight," Tessa said firmly. "I promise you that."

She considered the situation. Dan had possibly figured out they were heading to the bus depot, since she had left Wings domestic abuse shelter heading northwest. But when she'd begun suspecting they were being followed, she'd pulled four right turns in a row to confirm. Dan had followed each turn.

After that last left turn, they were now heading southwest. Right toward the Caltrain station.

Perfect. That's where Dan would assume they were heading.

But first Tessa had to make sure Erica and Emily were safe.

She could totally see Dan charging into a wild car chase in the middle of San Francisco, but she didn't want her passengers in the car if that happened. Yet this was the middle of the city. Where could she drop them off where they'd be safe?

"Erica, get into the backseat with Emily," Tessa said, "and unbuckle her from the car seat."

"What are you going to do?" Erica's elbow clocked Tessa in the temple as she scrambled between the front seats.

"I can get far enough ahead of Dan to make a right turn." Tessa checked out the street signs. Yes, she was now on Fourth Street. "It'll give us a couple seconds where he won't be able to see us. When I stop the car, I want you to get out fast—and I mean *fast*—and run into the In-N-Out with Emily. Hopefully by the time Dan turns the corner, you'll be inside the restaurant, and I'll be driving down the street, and he'll never know you're not with me in the car."

Tessa floored Gramps's accelerator, and he responded with a hack and a wheeze from his ancient engine before picking up the pace. She wove in and out of the cars on Fourth Street, a wide, straight shot toward the Caltrain station. Dan tried to catch up, but his larger truck had a harder time maneuvering into the small spaces between the cars. He attempted to muscle his way in a few times, but the drivers were reluctant to let him in, so he had to move slowly in order to not take out someone's front bumper. Tessa zipped Gramps farther away from him.

"Are you ready?" Tessa glanced in her rearview mirror at Erica's tense face. She'd dragged Emily into her lap.

"Yes." Erica reached for the door handle.

Tessa cut across two lanes of traffic and swerved right toward the new In-N-Out Burger, which flashed bright and new since it had opened off of Fourth and Brannan a few weeks ago. She slammed on the brakes, earning her a car-horn blast from the SUV behind her who had to swerve around her to continue down the street. "Go!" she shouted to Erica.

Erica was already out the door, her daughter in her arms, before Gramps even came to a complete stop. She slammed the door shut behind her and raced toward the bright lights of the building, which was filled to the brim with people. She instantly blended in with the other twentysomethings who were grabbing a quick bite in the late evening.

Tessa threw Gramps in gear and jerked away from the curb. About a second and a half later, she saw Dan's pickup turn the corner onto Brannan and head toward her.

Showtime.

She cruised down the street, making a few turns to head toward the Union Square Park area. As she drove, she dialed 9-1-1 on her cell phone.

"Nine-one-one, what's your emergency?" The woman sounded faintly bored.

Tessa injected as much theatrical fear as she could into her voice. "Please, help me! I think someone's following me. I'm nearing the corner of Maiden Lane and Grant Avenue." She didn't disconnect the call but tossed the prepaid phone onto the passenger seat so she could concentrate on her driving.

She turned onto Maiden Lane, a narrow one-way street bordered by tall buildings that housed boutiques and art galleries, heading toward the Gambit, a small nightclub and bar that opened a few months ago. She passed the restaurant, which was fronted by a line of people waiting to get in. Colored lights flickered out from the open doorway. The deep bass of a dance beat made Gramps's steel frame shudder as Tessa drove by.

She slowed as Dan's pickup turned onto Maiden Lane. When he was only a couple car lengths behind her, she sped up toward the intersection of Grant and Maiden.

Then she swerved the car sideways in the middle of the street and came to a halt.

Dan was too close to stop. His brakes squealed a split second before his truck rammed into the tiny Corolla.

The impact made Tessa jolt in her seat while her seat belt sliced into her torso like a sword blade. She couldn't breathe for a few seconds, her stomach crushed with pain.

She came to her senses before Dan did. She was staring at the steering wheel and out the front window, where she could see she'd hit a lamppost at the corner of Maiden and Grant. The white steel pole looked a bit slanted from where it rose out of her car's front bumper.

But she remained in the car, waiting.

Dan seemed to take forever to finally get out of his car. Tessa grabbed her head, pretending to be dazed, as she heard his car door open and then slam shut.

Then she heard a second car door slam. That's right—a

second person was with Dan. She'd been so focused on her driving she had forgotten he'd had a passenger.

No problem.

Dan yanked open her car door so hard it rocked on its squeaking hinges. He grabbed at her shirt to pull her out of the car, but her seat belt was still firmly fastened, and it dug into her already bruised stomach with a sharp snap. She winced.

Cussing, he hit her, a jab to her cheek.

But she had seen him crank his arm back and had been able to roll with it, reducing the impact so that it felt more like a hammer than an anvil. Regardless, it still made her cry out as his fist crunched into her face. Breath hissed between her teeth as the pain radiated out from her cheek.

Dan reached across her and hit the button to unfasten her seat belt, untangling her from the strap to drag her out of the Corolla. "Where is she?" he roared, spit flying in Tessa's face.

"Hey," said a man's voice over his shoulder.

Oh no. Tessa glanced over to see a young man dressed in black slacks and a silk shirt, obviously one of the people who'd been in line to get into the Gambit. He approached Dan warily. "Let her go, man."

Tessa wondered if Dan would let her go to engage with the Good Samaritan, but his fists tightened on the fabric of her T-shirt, and he glanced back toward his truck.

It didn't look like the collision had done much damage to the front of his truck, aside from a frowning front bumper. Tessa got a look at Dan's passenger now and saw not one but two people.

One was a burly man, black goatee and long black hair that he flipped out of his eyes. She noted the gesture.

The other was a woman who sported a gigantic black eye,

cut lip, and hair mussed as if it had been grabbed by a meaty fist. What was surprising was that she was dressed in a cream-colored business jacket and matching skirt, a crumpled white silk blouse underneath. She limped on Italian leather heels next to the burly man, her thin arm firmly in his grasp.

They'd beaten this woman up. And brought her with them in the truck. Tessa's jaw clenched tight.

The burly man tossed the woman aside onto the street, where she lay exhausted on the asphalt. He then approached the Good Samaritan and shot his hand out to punch the guy in the nose.

Blood spurted as the young man whirled away, staggering and grabbing his face.

No, Tessa wasn't going to stand for this. She grasped at Dan's hands, which were still full of her shirt.

He removed one hand to slap her across the face.

The blow, coming on top of the other blow to the same cheek, rocked her more than she expected. Maybe because she hadn't been sparring as much for the past sixteen months as she had when she was in prison. She'd gotten soft. She blinked away the stars in her vision and took advantage of the opening Dan gave her by slamming the heel of her hand into his nose.

His other hand released her shirt, and he jerked back a half step. She followed up with a knee to his groin, a fist to his kidney, and an elbow to the back of his exposed head as he folded in half. He dropped to the ground.

Her elbow stung from where it had collided with his skull. She shook it off and turned to face Dan's sidekick.

He approached her with more caution than Dan had, his fists up. He moved like a boxer, and he had the shoulders of one. She brought her fists up as he took a swing at her, testing her, and she easily dodged him. He took another swing, this time more forceful, and she ducked, feeling the air whooshing against her skin as his knuckles just missed her temple.

He took a third shot at her, a beefy uppercut, but as his hand retracted, his long hair fell over his eye. Tessa took advantage of his impaired vision and snapped her leg up in a front kick that slipped between his upheld hands and collided squarely with his jaw.

He reeled backward, his eyelids already starting to fold as her blow knocked him for a loop. She advanced with him, swinging in a reverse roundhouse kick that caught him hard in the temple. He was unconscious even before he dropped to the ground with a satisfying smack, his entire body limp.

Tessa's hands shook with adrenaline, and the entire left side of her face was a swollen mass of throbbing pain. She stumbled as she walked toward the woman in the business suit. "Are you all right?"

The woman looked up at her through her one good eye and nodded numbly.

"You're okay now." Tessa looked up as a few people from the crowd that had been gathered in front of the Gambit approached her.

"Are you okay?" asked a young blonde woman with a short silver skirt and glittery purple top. "The police are on their way. People called 9-1-1 as soon as the cars crashed."

Tessa remembered the 9-1-1 call on her phone—which was probably somewhere on the floorboard of the wrecked car—and figured they'd probably be here soon. "Did anyone call the club manager?"

"I saw the bouncer head inside," the woman said.

At that moment, a short, stocky Japanese man pushed his

way out of the club doors and rushed toward them. His black Hugo Boss suit made him almost invisible in the darkness of the narrow street, but Tessa recognized him.

"Itchy," she said as he drew near, "I was hoping you would be here."

Especially since the Gambit was owned by her uncle Teruo Ota, leader of the San Francisco yakuza—the Japanese mafia—and her cousin Ichiro always liked going to their uncle's newest clubs. She'd deliberately avoided her family connections in the twelve months since she'd gotten shot by a Chinese Triad assassin, because she wanted to be legitimate and didn't want to be dependent on her uncle's money or resources. But right now, she could use Itchy's help.

"When the bouncer told me about an Asian girl taking on two guys, I knew it had to be you, Tess." Itchy's deceptively sleepy eyes took in Tessa's aching face and the woman's black eye. "What happened?"

"Those two guys were tailing me."

"Oh, that completely explains why your face is purple and you wrecked my dad's car in front of the Gambit."

"I wrecked the Corolla in front of the Gambit because I knew there would be at least one *kobun* here who could lend me a car." Tessa hoped none of the onlookers knew that *kobun* was Japanese for a yakuza member.

Itchy rolled his eyes. "You really think someone's going to lend you a car after you did this?" He flung his arm out toward the smashed Corolla.

"I've got a single mother and her daughter stranded at the In-N-Out on Brennan. I have to go get them so they can make their bus tonight."

"Erica Parker," the woman croaked.

Tessa regarded her with narrowed eyes for a long moment. "Who are you?"

"Charlotte Quilly. I'm Joseph Tucker's admin."

"Wait a minute. Joseph Tucker? Erica's lawyer?" Then the pieces fell into place. "You're the one who messed up and sent those papers to Erica's home address rather than to the Wings shelter."

The woman drew in a sharp breath, looking offended. "How was I to know it was going to be an issue?"

This Charlotte Quilly was the reason Erica had to escape on that bus tonight. Erica's abusive ex-boyfriend, Dan, had opened the envelope from her lawyer, which contained copies of documents Erica had signed a couple weeks ago, and discovered that his girlfriend—formerly his punching bag—had inherited a cool ten thousand dollars from a great-aunt. He'd been scouring San Francisco trying to find Erica ever since.

"It wasn't my fault," Charlotte insisted. "I've sent papers to the wrong addresses before, and it's never been a problem."

"They beat you up to get you to tell them where Erica was staying," Tessa said, her voice neutral. "Then they followed us from Wings."

Tessa supposed she shouldn't blame the woman. Most people who had been tortured this way would give up the address of anyone, even a single mother staying at a domestic violence shelter. Tessa's new faith in Christ demanded she give grace the way grace had been given to her. She had beat up plenty of people for her uncle, and God had still forgiven her.

And she guessed that Charlotte wouldn't mess up an address again anytime soon.

The police finally arrived with flashing lights and solemn

beeps from their squad cars. They parked a few feet from the accident and the men's prone bodies.

Itchy groaned. "You had to wreck in front of Uncle's club, didn't you?"

"They're not going inside the club. All the witnesses are out here. Besides, Erica's and Emily's lives were in danger. I had to take care of these guys somehow."

While waiting for the police to take her statement, she crawled onto the seat of her totaled car and rummaged for her cell phone, which had disconnected after the dispatcher ended the 9-1-1 call at some point. She straightened, tugging her shirt down over her briefly exposed lower back. She then called to check on Erica.

"We're fine!" The young woman had to shout a little to be heard over the noise inside the In-N-Out. "We're snacking on fries at an inside table."

"This might take a few more minutes," Tessa said, "but we'll make your bus tonight."

"Okay."

The policeman who talked to Tessa was young, too young to remember her face from when she and Itchy had been involved in shady dealings in San Francisco more than eight years ago. He took her statement but didn't seem to believe her when she said she'd thrown a few punches and kicks to get the two men to leave her alone. The policeman obviously thought the Good Samaritan, not the slender girl in leggings and a long-sleeved T-shirt, had been the one to dispatch the men.

The Good Samaritan talked to another officer and seemed to be feeding their impressions, mimicking punches in between dabbing at his broken nose.

Tessa was relieved, truth be told. The street was a bit dark, and maybe the other witnesses would give only vague accounts of the fistfight. She just wanted to fade away as a hapless victim rather than be drawn into anything that would bring her family connections to light.

Dan and his boxer friend were handcuffed and sulking in the backseat of the squad car. When the officer turned his attention to the two men in the car, Tessa nagged Itchy into letting her borrow his car, a brand-new black BMW coupe, then left to pick up Erica and Emily and drive them to the bus depot.

ه

Standing in front of the waiting bus, Erica folded Tessa into a hug, holding her tight to convey her gratitude.

"Remember the tips I told you for staying off the radar. Just in case Dan gets out of jail faster than we expect."

"Thank you for setting all this up and helping us to get away. I wish you'd let me pay you, especially now that I have my aunt's money."

Tessa shook her head. "You'll need it soon enough. Emily will probably want to go to some expensive private college."

Erica laughed and gave her another strong hug. "I'll keep in touch."

"You can email me or write to me through Wings. I volunteer there twice a week, usually." Tessa gave Emily a smacking kiss on her round, soft cheek, making the little girl giggle. "Good-bye, sweetheart."

"Bye-bye."

Tessa sent them off, waving at them as the bus drove off into the night. The satisfaction of helping Erica warred with the empty feeling of another person moving out of her life. Tessa's clients came and went. Her old yakuza mafia connections had been severed when she stepped away from the family. And Charles was gone.

She felt a small stab in her heart. She had been proud of herself for only thinking about him once a day now.

Tessa drove back to the Gambit, where Itchy was pacing outside the club, waiting for her. He circled the car as she drove up, inspecting it for scratches.

"This wasn't here before," he accused her as he fingered an almost invisible scratch along the car's left rear panel.

"Yes, it was," Tessa shot back. "What, like there are any bushes for me to drive through on the streets of San Francisco?" She tossed him his car keys. "Thanks for the ride."

"It's only because you could kick my butt if I said no," he groused.

"And don't you forget it." She gave him a quick peck on his clean-shaven cheek. "It's good to see you, Itchy." She thought back and realized that the last time she'd seen him had been ten months ago when she'd gone to her uncle's house for Christmas. She hadn't made it to Uncle's annual Fourth of July barbecue.

He nodded toward Gramps, now a crumpled heap being loaded onto a tow truck Itchy had called for her. He gave her a sidelong look. "Not that I intend to be your personal car supplier, but you need a new one now, right?"

She gave him an evil grin. "Why, thanks, Itchy, I'd love to take your Beamer off your hands — "

"No, no, no," he said hastily. "Keep your paws off my new baby. But Dad just got a 1991 Suburban from a friend of his for cheap."

"Really?" Tessa couldn't help but be interested. A '91 Suburban was built like a tank. With her new bodyguard business, Protection for Hire, the extra protection of solid steel would make her — and her clients — feel more secure.

"I'll have Dad call you."

"Thanks, Itchy."

He waved at her, already circling his car to get into the driver's seat so he could find it a nice safe parking spot. She waved back as he drove away, then dialed Wings on her cell phone.

"Hello. Wings Domestic Violence Shelter. This is Karissa." Karissa's voice sounded as young as she was, a perky twenty-two years old.

"Hi, Karissa. It's Tessa. I didn't know you were still there tonight."

"I was just about to leave. What's up?"

"I hate to bug you, but could you pick me up near Union Square Park?"

"What happened to Gramps?" Karissa asked, surprised.

The sound of a motor filled the air as the Corolla was slowly lifted from the street onto the tow truck. "Um ... he finally retired."

Chapter 2

What happened?" Tessa's best friend and old cell mate, Evangeline, asked as Tessa entered Wings thirty minutes later.

"Oh, just another day on the job." Tessa's cheek, swollen from the blows she'd received from Dan, made her words come out a bit muffled.

"You know, that gets old after the twentieth time you say it." Evangeline gave her a dry look.

"It's true, sad to say." Tessa's stomach was still bruised from the truck colliding with her and the seat belt cutting into her torso. She winced as she sat down on a couch in the living room. It was empty, since most of the inhabitants of Wings were asleep in the rooms at the back of the old Victorian house.

Tessa tentatively touched her swollen face, but Evangeline slapped her hand away. "Karissa, would you please get me some ice from the kitchen?" she asked, then started cleaning up Tessa's face.

"I wouldn't think you'd normally get this beat up," Evangeline said as Karissa returned with a bag of ice.

"This time, I was trying to start a fight." Tessa winced as Evangeline dabbed alcohol on a cut.

"Why?"

"I managed to crash Dan's truck in front of a nightclub with people outside it, so I wanted them to see Dan beating me up. Someone was bound to call 9-1-1 or at least go get the nightclub manager."

"Wait a minute. Dan? As in Erica's abusive psycho ex-boyfriend? How'd he find out you were taking Erica to the bus depot?" Evangeline's brown eyes were sharp as they studied Tessa's face.

"Joseph Tucker's admin accidentally sent inheritance paperwork to Erica's home address, not to Wings. They tracked down the admin and beat where Erica was staying out of her. They were probably watching Wings and saw me drive her out tonight. Ow!" Tessa flinched as Evangeline's hand twitched while she was dressing a cut, probably from the ring Dan had been wearing.

Evangeline frowned. "I'll talk to one of the Wings's directors tomorrow."

"I don't want to get anyone in trouble," Tessa protested.

"Joseph Tucker needs to hire admins who don't give away information on clients who are hiding from abusive boyfriends," Evangeline snapped, her dark brows drawing low over her eyes. "For these women, mistakes like that can have serious consequences. If it had been anyone else taking Erica to the bus depot tonight, Dan would have gotten to her and hurt her. Again."

Tessa had nothing to say to that. Even Karissa's lively dark eyes were somber as she watched Evangeline attach a bandage to Tessa's cheek.

Evangeline slapped the ice pack over Tessa's face. "There."

"Ow."

"So if you deliberately crashed your car and let Dan beat you up, you've got to have some other injuries," Evangeline said briskly. "Fess up."

"My ribs feel like I'm wearing a steel corset. Probably from the seat belt."

"Let's see." Evangeline lifted Tessa's shirt, but it was Karissa who gasped.

Tessa looked down, but she couldn't see anything around the icepack and her swollen cheek but a mass of red, green, and blue swimming together. "What? What's wrong?"

"N-nothing." Karissa swallowed. "I've never seen your tattoos before."

"I got that one when I was seventeen."

"I didn't know you were so young when you got it. Weren't you still living with your mom?" Evangeline said.

"That's why I had the artist draw it around my torso. Easier to hide it. Later, when I got more tattoos, I kept putting them in places I could cover up, because my sister wouldn't have let me visit my niece if I'd looked like yakuza." She didn't want to alarm Karissa, but like most of the yakuza, she had large, vibrant tattoos all up her back and down her thighs. But the flaming dragon that circled her waist was different from other yakuza tattoos, yet it was similar to her uncle's dragon tattoo, and she liked it the best. She hissed as Evangeline, who had been gently feeling her ribs, touched a sore spot.

"I think it's broken. Why didn't the police insist you go to the hospital?"

"They did, but I told them it looked worse than it felt. I don't have health insurance."

"What do you want me to do?"

"Just bind me up like you did last time. I healed fine."

"Yeah, right." But Evangeline dug out the flexible cloth ACE bandage from the first-aid kit. "That's the reason you're always whining and complaining."

"At least I've never been wrong. If my ribs ache, it means it's going to rain." She gritted her teeth as Evangeline bound her torso.

"I saw two guys with big dragon tattoos at Uncle Jerry's ramen shop the other day," Karissa said. "It was all over their arms and stuff."

Tessa didn't say anything, but if they had large dragon tattoos and were hanging out in a shop owned by Tessa's mafia uncle, they were probably yakuza.

"It was kind of weird," Karissa said. "At first I thought they were accountants or math geeks, because they were talking numbers like in some code. But then they mentioned television and a singing competition and odds. I guessed they were talking about gambling odds and were betting on one of the singing shows on TV."

Betting on a singing show? Even though gambling was Uncle Teruo's bread and butter, it surprised Tessa that the yakuza would take bets on something as unpredictable as that. Unless ... She looked away from Karissa. Unless they were rigging the show. If that were the case, the less Karissa and Tessa knew about it, the better.

Karissa's eyes narrowed. "You've got that look."

"What look?"

"That 'I can't talk about it or I'll have to slice off your pinky' look."

Tessa rolled her eyes. "Yakuza do not slice off other people's fingers."

"Aha! I knew it was about the yakuza."

"It's not. Or if it is, I don't know about it, since I've been going to insane lengths to avoid most of them for a year now."

"Yeah . . . I suppose mafia relatives make family parties rather interesting."

"By the way, Erica said to give you this." Evangeline reached into her cardigan pocket and withdrew an envelope.

As soon as Tessa touched it, she knew it was cash. "I told her not to pay me."

"Erica is almost as stubborn as you. Besides, you need the money."

"You do?" Karissa's brow wrinkled. "I thought your former client, Elizabeth, was referring all her rich friends to you, since she knows the entire world."

"She still is, but the jobs haven't been steady or long-term. Usually just a weekend or two, or even just a one-night event. I'm not penniless, but I'm not making enough to be able to rent an apartment of my own. That's why I still live with my mom."

"Can't Charles get you clients?" Karissa asked.

At Charles's name, Tessa felt like a boot had hit her in the stomach.

Karissa continued without noticing. "He's got to have some clients who need protection from whoever's suing them."

As Karissa was speaking, Evangeline's eyes widened and her mouth pulled down at the corners. She seemed to be trying to signal Karissa to stop talking.

Tessa swallowed against a tight throat. "I haven't talked to Charles in a year either."

Karissa ignored Evangeline's hand, which was not-very-subtly twitching in a slicing motion to get her to shut up, and said, "A whole year? You mean since the last time *I* saw him at that party at your house? I thought he was on retainer with you or something like that."

Heat began to radiate from Tessa's neck and cheeks. "I . . . haven't needed him."

"Isn't he costing you a ton since he's on retainer?"

"No, he said he waived his retainer fee because I saved his mother's life from those Chinese assassins." Saying it that way made it sound like Tessa was talking about a Jet Li action movie. "But I can't see his firm really agreeing to that, so I think Elizabeth got the firm to waive the fee, seeing as how one of their former senior partners had tried to kill her." And now it sounded like a John Grisham novel.

And she was babbling. *Shut it, Lancaster.*

Time to go. "Well, thanks for patching me up." She got gingerly to her feet. "Let me know if you hear of anyone else who needs a bodyguard."

"I still think you should ask Charles—" Karissa started to say.

Evangeline, standing slightly behind the young woman, whipped her hand up and clapped it over Karissa's mouth. She spoke to Tessa over Karissa's shoulder. "And how are you going to get home? Didn't you crash your car?"

Tessa froze. "Oh. Yeah."

"I love you, but I'm not driving you home to San Jose, because it'll take too long. And it's late to be using public transportation. The beds are all filled here, but you could sleep on the couch—"

Karissa yanked Evangeline's hand from her mouth. "You can come home with me. I'm ten minutes away, and I have an extra bedroom because one of the roommates moved out."

Karissa's eyes held a rather predatory gleam that Tessa didn't trust. "Uh ..."

"And we can spend some time chatting. We haven't done that for a while. And you can tell me what's up with you and Charles."

A topic of conversation Tessa would sell her car in order to avoid. Oh, wait. She didn't have a car anymore. "Why are you suddenly asking me about him?"

"Oh, because I saw him yesterday."

"Where?" Tessa asked before she could stop herself.

"At Sophie's Cajun Restaurant. Josh and I went there for lunch, and I saw Charles there with his mom."

What did he say? Did he look like he was doing well? Did he say what he was up to? Tessa swallowed the questions that leaped to her mouth and instead croaked out, "Oh."

"He spent an awful lot of time on his cell phone, so I talked mostly to his mom," Karissa said helpfully. "She invited me over for dinner sometime. She said Sophie's is the best Cajun restaurant she's tried in California, but it doesn't compare to her cooking. She promised me shrimp creole to die for."

"Yeah, it's great."

Tessa realized her mistake as Karissa's expression became curiously suspicious. If that was an expression someone could have. "You've seen Mrs. Britton?" Her voice was deceptively mild.

"I go over to visit her once a month or so." Whenever her son was at work.

The first time Vivian had asked her over, Tessa had been a bit nervous considering her mixed emotions about Vivian's son. But Vivian had just enfolded Tessa in a warm embrace, and everything had been the same as before ... when Tessa hadn't known that Charles had urged the judge to add two years to her prison sentence.

"Uh, you know, I think I'll brave mass transit tonight. Thanks for the offer."

"Oh, don't be silly. Just stay here. I'll head home and leave you in peace." Karissa sighed with disgust as she went to pick up her purse. "I don't know why you won't talk about him ..."

"It's complicated." As in she couldn't understand how she could want to both kiss him and punch his lights out at the same time.

"I used to tell that to my counselor when I was talking about my ex-boyfriend," Karissa said as she headed for the door. "My shrink said it usually wasn't as complicated as I thought."

After Evangeline left for her bed, Tessa observed her nightly ritual of reading a few chapters in her Bible, but the words swam in front of her eyes. Similarly, her prayers that night for her family's health and another bodyguard job seemed to be hitting the ceiling and bouncing back.

As she tried to find a comfortable spot on the lumpy couch, which was covered with musty-smelling blankets, she reflected that Karissa's counselor was right. Her relationship with Charles wasn't complicated.

It all boiled down to the fact that she would never, ever forgive him.

Chapter 3

His brother was going to die right in front of him.

Charles Britton winced as he watched the tall, black-haired fighter swing a roundhouse punch that caught his brother on the jaw. Eddie stumbled back a few paces, looking dazed and almost touching the ropes edging the fighting ring. His opponent followed with a flurry of jabs to Eddie's face and head. But Eddie flinched away from most of the blows and swung an uppercut through his opponent's guard, making the man's head snap back when Eddie's fist glanced against his chin.

"You get him, son!" Charles's mama hollered from where she stood next to him. She punched a fist into the air. "Woot! Woot!"

Had Mama seriously just said *woot woot*? Charles didn't know what was worse, watching his brother getting pummeled in the middle of the fighting ring or standing beside his mother with her teenage vocabulary. Thankfully, no one had heard her, since everyone around them was also shouting.

Eddie's opponent did a strange diving move and grabbed Eddie's waist, driving them both to the mat with an alarming thud. Mama had a pained look on her face, but she wasn't hysterical or panicking, so this must have been a normal thing for a mixed martial arts fight. Which Charles would have known if he'd gone to any of his brother's scrimmage fights earlier this year.

The guilt leeched away as Charles watched Eddie's opponent press his forearm against his brother's throat. It looked like the opponent was having trouble. Eddie had a hand clamped to the base of the other man's head and was tilting it forward and down, and his legs were wrapped around the man's waist.

The man tried to get out of Eddie's grip, planting his foot, trying to get leverage for his body. But then, suddenly, Eddie grabbed the man's wrists and did some twists that pushed the man's head closer to the mat. And then Eddie's legs jumped from the man's waist to encircle his head and one arm.

Charles recognized that choke hold. Eddie had used it to subdue the Chinese assassin at his house last year.

The opponent struggled for a few moments, his arm trapped against his head within the triangle formed by Eddie's locked legs. The fighter's face was screwed up in pain and frustration. Then the fighter's hand tapped against Eddie's leg, and Eddie released him.

It was over. Eddie had won by tap-out submission.

"Glory, hallelujah! He won!" Mama jumped up and down like a teenage girl at a Justin Bieber concert.

Out of the speakers, the fight announcer's voice boomed. "The winner of this fight, at two minutes, twenty-three seconds, in the third round, by triangle choke submission ... Eddie 'The Fighting Britton'!"

"What?" Charles said.

"I know. His name needs work," Mama replied before going back to screaming and jumping.

Charles and Mama squeezed past people and scrambled over chairs to get to the ring as Eddie stepped out of it. He practically fell on Mama in his joy.

"I did it, Mama!"

"I'm so proud of you! And that other boy was so much bigger than you too!"

Charles winced a bit at the backhanded compliment, and Eddie's face also twisted into a grimace, but then his normal good-natured smile shone out. "Thanks, Mama."

"Great job, Eddie!" Charles said as Eddie crushed him in a sweaty hug that made Charles exhale a short, "Ooof."

Suddenly Eddie's voice in Charles's ear shouted, "Tessa!"

The ringing in his hears distracted Charles for a moment as Eddie moved behind him. Then he realized what his brother had said.

Tessa.

Charles whirled around to see Tessa's luminous face above his brother's sweat-streaked, bare shoulder. Charles swayed in dizziness, although maybe it was because he had turned around so quickly. Or maybe it was because of the look in Tessa's amber eyes — part surprise, part longing.

Then she blinked, and her eyes chilled.

"Did you see?" Eddie was asking as he released her. "In the second round, I did that feint you taught me, and he fell for it."

"It was textbook. You were magnificent." Tessa's smile glowed up at Eddie, and Charles felt something slithery uncoil in the pit of his stomach.

He should go. He was expected back at the law firm and had

a mountain of material to go over before court tomorrow morning. But the sight of Tessa made him want to stay, just to hear her voice, see her smile. Even if her smile wasn't for him.

"Tessa." Mama reached for her to give her a hug. "I knew you wouldn't miss Eddie's first official fight."

"I arrived a little late," Tessa said. "I had to borrow my sister, Alicia's, car, and she was late coming home from work."

"Why did you have to borrow her car? Is Gramps okay?"

"Oh ..." Tessa scratched the back of her neck, just under her glossy golden-brown hair. "He was having problems. He's so old, you know. I'm not surprised he was on his last legs."

Something about her tone or face or gestures made Charles think she was lying. Or at least stretching the truth a bit for Mama. What would she be lying about? She was only talking about her car being out of commission ...

He studied her face intently and thought he detected a slight puffiness on her left cheek, and her skin seemed powdery, even under the dim lights from the rafters above. Was she wearing makeup?

"What happened to you?" he asked before he could stop himself.

The look she gave him would have vaporized butter.

Mama said, "Charles, what do you mean?" She turned to Tessa. "Did something happen?"

"I'm fine, Vivian. I don't know what Charles is talking about." Tessa glanced at him, her face hidden from Mama. Her expression clearly said, *Shut up before you worry your mother, you moron.*

Okay, well, maybe he mentally added the "you moron" part.

"Are you coming to my victory party?" Eddie asked Tessa.

Charles didn't think a person could half-look at him, but Tessa managed it. Her smile was a little stiff, but she said, "I wouldn't miss it."

She was going to the party. He hadn't considered that. Then again, he hadn't been sure it would be a victory party or a keep-Eddie-from-wallowing-in-misery-after-his-crushing-defeat night. If Charles stayed for the party, Tessa might eventually mellow enough to talk to him. She might even warm up to him enough to talk about the weather.

No, he had to get back to the firm. Two of the senior partners were there with Rick already, and while they understood he'd had to leave for an hour, they wouldn't appreciate him ditching them for a party.

"Mama, Eddie, I'm afraid I have to get back to work."

Mama's blue eyes had that same expression they'd had when he'd come home from school with a bloody lip and dirt all over his new clothes because he'd been fighting. "Why?"

"We have court in the morning, and my team is still at the firm going over documents. They're expecting me to come back after the fight."

Eddie's eyes faltered, but his smile was friendly enough. "That's okay, I understand. I'm glad you were here."

"I wouldn't have missed it, Eddie." He pulled his brother into another hug.

Tessa's neck was flushed — probably her face, too, but it was covered with makeup. However, she seemed more composed than before as she said good-bye to him.

As Charles turned to leave, he heard Mama say, "Tessa, you should come over for lunch again. I haven't seen you in over a month."

Charles had the strange sensation that his legs were marching him away faster than he intended, even while a heaviness in his gut seemed to weigh him down. He already knew Tessa visited Mama—always when he wasn't home—so why did it upset him now? Why was he acting like this?

He got into his car and slammed the door. Tessa obviously wanted nothing to do with him. Before tonight, she'd avoided talking to him for a year—a whole year!—even though he was on retainer for her.

Maybe she just hadn't needed a lawyer.

Maybe she hadn't been able to get away to see his Mama except during weekdays.

Or maybe she'd never, ever forgive him for what he'd done to her.

Charles drove out of the gym's parking lot and headed north out of Daly City into the heart of San Francisco. It was early evening, but the traffic was still a bit sluggish.

He arrived at Pleiter & Woodhouse and immediately headed to the conference room, where his friend Rick Acker, another partner in the firm, was poring over discoveries and making notes. At the other end of the table, two senior partners in the firm, Jon Yee and Edward Dennis, were fingering through two more boxes full of paper.

"Finally." Rick tossed down his pen and leaned back in his chair. "Did Eddie win?"

Charles nodded. "By triangle choke submission."

"Triangle choke? Maybe I should learn MMA. Then my kids would listen to me." He grinned but then rubbed his forehead with his fingers. The skin around his eyes was tight with pain.

"Another headache?" Charles asked softly.

"I'm fine." Rick dropped his hand and gave his normal slanted grin. "I was worried you might not come back. Like the dog when one of the kids leaves the front door open too long. Whoosh!" He sliced his hand forward.

Charles gave him a level look. "I'm so flattered to be compared to a bolting dog."

"Okay, maybe you're more like Lightning McQueen. Or Miguel Camino. Or—"

"Have you been watching *Cars* again?" Charles demanded.

Rick shrugged. "Hey, I'm just glad the youngest finally outgrew *Sesame Street*."

"Charles, if you're done chitchatting, Rick could use some help sorting through those papers," Jon called from the other end of the table in a droll tone.

Charles guiltily dropped into a chair and pulled a stack to him. "Where'd the associates go?"

"They're going through another twenty boxes of papers in the copy room," Rick said. "We're 'all hands on deck' tonight."

When they finished three hours later, Charles felt as if his eyeballs were going to fall out of their sockets. Tempers had flared, and both Jon and Edward had snapped at Rick and Charles several times as they scrambled to get ready for court the next morning. Charles took it in stride with his usual resilience, but Rick's face seemed to be getting grayer as the night wore on.

When Jon and Edward finally left the office, both tired and frustrated, Rick flicked his pen on the table with a loud clatter. "I wish Jon would just get off my back."

Charles glanced up at him. "Don't take it personally. I seem to recall a hotshot lawyer telling me that when I first started here."

Rick snorted, but it was a dispirited sound. "That hotshot

lawyer didn't have three losses under his belt in three weeks. It's like they've forgotten about all the clients I've brought into this firm, all the settlements ..." He sighed.

Charles clamped down on a pang at the thought that in the past few months, he hadn't been as successful as he needed to be in bringing in high-profile clients either. His highest profile client was actually Tessa, or rather, her San Francisco-mob-boss uncle, who had paid her retainer fee, but since Charles couldn't actually tell the firm where the money came from, it didn't add to his street cred with his peers. "I need more clients," he mused.

"Everyone needs more clients," Rick snapped. "I had a dozen leads, and none of them panned out."

"I had about that many too."

Charles and Rick finished up the last few pages they had left, then finally packed up. "Are you still in that marathon training group?" Rick asked him.

"Yeah, we're on target to be in shape for running the Napa Valley Marathon in the spring." He picked up his briefcase. "I never thought I'd enjoy running like this. I was a terrible athlete in school. But it's been satisfying. And I've met some nice people."

"Any cute girls?" Rick winked.

Charles laughed because Rick expected him to. "I don't have time for girls."

Rick sobered. "You're still too hung up on that yakuza woman."

"She's not yakuza."

"She used to be. Not to mention the fact she's an ex-convict."

"Hello, she's my client. I wouldn't bad-mouth her to you if she paid me."

Rick followed Charles out of the conference room and shut off the lights. "You need a wife, you know."

Charles did a double take. "Did you somehow body-snatch my friend and replace him with my mama?"

"I'm serious, Charles. Now that you're partner, you have to set your sights on senior partnership. They look for two things — success and stability. You have to win your cases, and you have to show you have a stable home life. That usually means a wife and kids."

"I'm only thirty-two."

"I got married when I was eighteen."

"The love of your life was your next-door neighbor. My next-door neighbor was Colonel Morrisey, a die-hard bachelor with twelve pet pigs."

Rick blinked at him. "You're making that up."

"Ask my mother."

"You're not distracting me with your weird Louisiana stories," Rick said. "You need a wife to further your career. And preferably not one who's an ex-convict, ex-mafia woman."

"I'm not about to marry an ex-convict, ex-mafia woman," Charles said. But the words grated against his throat as they came out.

"Look, I could come up with a list of eligible young women. And I promise they'd be pretty, smart, and socially adept."

"Are you sure they'd want to be with me? I may be pretty and smart, but I'm a social clod."

"In reality, you're pretty ugly and only smarter than a chimp, so you're actually perfect."

Charles glared at Rick as they exited the office and then punched the button for the elevator.

"So I'll help you on the female front, but you're on your own for getting new clients," Rick said. "And while you're at it, get me some fresh leads too."

"I'll be sure to pick them off my tree when I get home."

"It's too bad neither of us golfs."

"What is it with golf and wealthy businessmen?" The elevator doors opened, and they both got in. "Why can't wealthy businessmen play some other sport? Then I could meet them while playing beach volleyball or something like that."

"Hey, you said you met some people in your marathon running group. Any candidates?"

"They have a rule that you can't talk business during the runs," Charles said. "Apparently, one time some guy joined the group specifically to hit people up for his roofing business."

"Yeah, I guess even Bill Gates would want to run in peace."

The name jolted Charles as much as if the elevator had slammed to a full stop. "I don't run with Bill Gates, but I do run with Steven Nishimoto."

Rick's mouth dropped open for a full five seconds before he pulled it closed. "And you've done something about this beautiful lead, right?"

"I told you, no business during the run."

"What about afterward, doofus?" The elevator doors opened but Rick stayed where he was, staring incredulously at Charles.

"He leaves right after the run. He's probably pretty busy since the next Sapphire computer is rumored to hit the market next month."

The doors closed with both of them still inside, but the elevator didn't move. Rick shook his head. "I forgot. You probably don't know."

"Don't know what?"

"Just about every lawyer here at Pleiter and Woodhouse has tried to get Steven Nishimoto as a client."

"You're starting to exaggerate like your kids, Rick."

"No, I'm dead serious. I've gone after him. Rodriguez. Jon. Doug. You name anyone here, they've tried. And not just our firm, but I know people from at least three other firms who've tried to get him."

"Well, he's probably happy with his own law firm."

"That's the thing. He's still using some small firm in San Jose. His business has already grown too big. He's going to need a larger firm eventually." Rick backhanded Charles in the shoulder. "Charles, get off your bum! Steven Nishimoto owns the most high-profile computer company in San Francisco. The profits from Neesh are starting to rival Apple. You can run and talk at the same time, right?"

Rick's words made Charles's insides squirm, but not with embarrassment that he hadn't tried to talk shop with Steven. Charles had started training for a marathon as a bucket-list sort of thing, but he'd found that running cleared his head, made him feel more centered after the craziness of work. He knew Steven felt the same way.

He didn't want work to intrude on the one place he could escape it. And it seemed underhanded to take advantage of his new acquaintance when Steven obviously needed the escape too.

But Charles also wanted to consider his future. The senior partners wouldn't be satisfied with a partner who only maintained the status quo. Dozens of other associates would love Charles's position, and he was in competition with other partners too. The firm would get rid of dead weight in a heartbeat.

He'd been working hard to network and meet new potential clients, and if he met Steven anywhere else, he wouldn't have any qualms about getting to know him better. But the running club seemed a different place than a corporate party or a charity auction. These people and this group somehow seemed to require a respect for the haven they had created, a place for people to forget their "real lives" and instead focus on a single goal — the marathon — and their own personal mile markers.

But Charles would gain an incredible amount of respect from the senior partners if he landed the one fish no one else had been able to catch. And because of that, it might be worth pushing the boundaries of the running group. Charles knew how to network without being pushy. He would try to get a handle on Steven, his personality and lifestyle, and develop a relationship they could take outside of the running club.

"You're right," he told Rick. "I've been treating the no-business rule like the Great Wall of China, but it's just a chain-link fence."

"That's the mind-set you should have! Now how about your love life?"

Charles groaned and pushed the door-open button on the elevator so they could exit. "Somehow, getting dating advice from you seems socially claustrophobic."

"What do you mean?"

"You're like a nun."

"A monk, not a nun. And just because I wouldn't allow my oldest daughter to date until she was eighteen doesn't make me unusual; it makes me — "

"A control freak with a key to her chastity belt."

Rick sighed. "That's what I should have gotten for her."

"That only proves my point. You'd pair me up with either *Sound of Music* Maria or *Hand That Rocks the Cradle* psycho-nanny."

Rick gave him a long-suffering look as they walked through the parking garage. "Your movie references are so out of date."

"Yours are all rated G."

"PG–13, thank you very much. The middle daughter is officially a teenager now."

Rick paused at Charles's car, his face drawn and somehow seeming more lined than it had a few minutes ago. "I'm serious about the whole perception of stability in the firm, Charles. How about if I promise to ask Annelissa to help with my list?"

"How about if you promise to ask your wife to make up the list *without* you?"

Rick gave a disgusted sound and looked like his old self for a moment. "Fine, fine. At least you're willing to move on from your pretty little assassin."

"She never killed anyone."

Rick was already walking away, and he raised a hand without turning around. "That's what they all say. Good night."

"'Night."

As Charles laid his briefcase on his passenger seat, he realized it was vibrating. Or rather, his cell phone inside was vibrating. Who'd be calling him now? It was close to midnight.

It wasn't a call. It was a reminder that he'd received a voice mail from Elizabeth St. Amant, his mama's goddaughter and a former client. She'd called a couple hours ago, but it still would have been almost one in the morning in Louisiana. He played the voice-mail message.

"Hello, Charles. It's Elizabeth. I know it's a little late, but I saw your brother, Eddie, online, and when I IM'd him to congratulate him, he mentioned you were at work, so I decided to call. I was up talking to a friend of mine in Los Angeles who might need your help. I know you're terribly busy—well, you're still at work right now, and it's . . . goodness, it's ten o'clock in California. Anyway, I know you're busy, but my friend is very desperate, and I took the liberty of setting up a meeting with you at Lorianne's Cafe tomorrow night at seven o'clock. If you can't make it, just let me know. Sorry to talk your ear off, Charles. Bye!"

Her syrupy accent always seemed like sunlight, and her rambling was typical, but something about her voice mail struck a funny chord in Charles. Not funny as in "ha-ha," but funny as in "Elizabeth St. Amant is up to no good."

She had never left such a long voice mail. She preferred chatting with him in person. And for the several clients she'd sent his way last year after he'd helped her out, she had never set up a meeting for him without talking to him first so he could consult his schedule.

She was trying to avoid talking to him.

Charles stared at his cell phone. He was free tomorrow night as far as he knew, but he considered calling her and demanding to know what was going on. The problem was that Elizabeth would probably take the passive-aggressive way out and simply not answer his call.

Charles had the sinking feeling she was setting him up. But for what?

Chapter 4

Tessa had the sinking feeling that Elizabeth was setting her up. The tension in the air was like walking into an ambush.

Of course, this was Elizabeth St. Amant, so an ambush wasn't entirely out of the question.

Even though she was now several states away, Elizabeth had kept in close contact with Tessa through phone calls and emails. Since Tessa had rescued Elizabeth from several attacks on her life, a bond had formed between them.

Which was how Tessa knew that Elizabeth's mysterious voice mail and this set-up meeting stank like week-old fish.

The black-suited valets at the entrance of the high-end restaurant looked askance at her sister's slightly scratched-up SUV as she handed over the keys. Tessa entered the first-floor "portal," which was just a small elevator foyer that had been decorated with a few potted plants and painted a subtle shimmery oyster color. She rode the elevator up to the second floor, where, a few steps away from the elevator, a mahogany hostess desk sat. A woman with understated makeup looked up from the desk with a polite smile. The black dress she was wearing might have cost more than Tessa's sister's SUV, which Tessa had borrowed for the evening. The woman never even let her gaze flicker to Tessa's bargain-rack blouse and slightly worn stretch-polyester slacks. At least Tessa's clothing looked somewhat upscale, being a matte black. But she hadn't gotten out of the habit of wearing free-moving clothes in case she had to use her mixed martial arts skills to protect a client. Or herself.

"Elizabeth St. Amant set up a meeting for me," Tessa told the woman.

"Yes, your party is already here. Just this way, Miss Lancaster." The woman led Tessa up a flight of stairs to the third floor of the restaurant, which held rooms for private dining parties, and opened the third door on the left of the short corridor.

Charles's startling blue-green eyes met hers.

It seemed melodramatic to say it was like lightning, but Tessa couldn't describe it any other way. The shock jolted through her, and the edges of her vision snowed in for a moment. Then she put her hand out to touch the doorframe, and the floor righted itself under her feet.

Elizabeth, you matchmaking stinker.

Then she realized two other people sat at the dining table, and she recognized the handsome man who rose to his feet with a nervous smile.

George Mynheir. One of the top contenders in the television singing show, *Grab the Mic.*

Whoa. Tessa's sister, mother, and maybe even her teenage niece were going to throw a fit when she told them who her new client was.

Charles had also gotten to his feet. "Tessa, this is George Mynheir—"

"I've seen you on television." Tessa reached out to shake his hand. His clasp was warm and firm, and his smile was natural and open, though his dimples weren't as deep as Charles's. George gazed at her ... appreciatively. It made her stand a little taller. She also couldn't stop herself from glancing at Charles.

He was scowling at them.

"This is my daughter, Hannah." George had a smooth speaking voice, reminding Tessa of how a slip of silk felt under her fingers.

Hannah looked about thirteen years old, a little younger than Tessa's niece, Paisley. She wore long narrow glasses with green sparkles on the outer edges, and from behind them, her father's green eyes looked out. They widened in surprise when Tessa held out her hand, but she tentatively rose to her feet and offered her hand to shake. The narrow bones were delicate but strong. She tossed her long, slightly wavy blonde hair over a bony shoulder as she sat back down.

"Did you need both a lawyer and a bodyguard?" Tessa asked as she sat.

"It's complicated," George said. "That's why Elizabeth wanted me to meet with both of you. It'll save me from having to explain the situation twice."

"Let's order, shall we?" Charles said smoothly. He seemed to be handling this surprise encounter with more calm than she was. No lightning appeared to be jolting through *him* at the sight of her, anyway.

The last time Tessa had been here, she had opted not to taste

45

the unique California fusion cuisine because she'd been on duty guarding Elizabeth, but today she couldn't resist ordering the macadamia-nut-encrusted sea bass.

After they'd ordered, Charles glanced at her. "No turkey sandwich for you today?"

He remembered what she'd eaten last time. The knowledge made her feel as if she'd swallowed a cup of hot tea that radiated in her stomach. "You always raved about this place, so I figured I'd try something that looked good."

Their eyes met briefly, and Tessa had to struggle to shift hers away. She happened to look at Hannah, who regarded her and Charles with a quietly speculative expression.

Charles cleared his throat. "George, why don't you tell us your story?"

George ran his hand through his wavy hair, sending it askew and making him look younger than his thirty-three years. (Tessa happened to know how old he was because Alicia had told her all about George after watching *Grab the Mic* and conducting a few stalkerish Google searches.)

"I grew up in a tough neighborhood in Oakland," he said. "The show is filmed down south, but Hannah and I have been driving back and forth from Los Angeles when we can, because our home is here. That's why we're in so much trouble."

"Dad, you're confusing them." Hannah had a low, sharp voice that contrasted with her father's smooth one. She turned to Charles and Tessa. "It was my fault. Dad's a single parent — my mom died when I was born — so I have to go with him to the studio in LA. When Dad's in rehearsal, I get kind of bored after I finish all my homework."

"You're going to school in LA?" Tessa asked.

"No," George said. "When I got onto the show a couple months ago, I pulled her out of school and began homeschooling her. The online curriculum is better for her anyway, because she can go at her own pace rather than being held back by the pace of her classes. But I'm the oldest contestant, and although a couple others have kids, they're small children. Those contestants tried to rope Hannah into babysitting for them—for free—a few times, but I wanted her to do her homework, so I told her to start saying no."

"But when I'm done with my homework, I don't have much to do. That's why I started wandering around at the studio, and how I found an empty office." She sighed and said, unselfconsciously, "I'm really good with computers, so I got on the computer in the office and hacked into the studio servers."

Charles winced a little.

The teen saw his expression. "I didn't do anything bad. It wasn't like I was trying to hack into the Pentagon."

"Hannah ..." George had a pained look on his face. He turned to Charles. "You have to understand, I came from a tough background, and I didn't have the smarts or the opportunities to do much with my life. When my wife died, I worked hard to get good jobs and make sure my daughter would have everything I didn't. She's great with computers, so I always encouraged her in it, because it'll help her go far."

"So hacking into the server was easy," Hannah said blithely. "I only wanted to play around, nothing serious. I found some embarrassing pictures from some guy's private folder on the server—they were from some office party, I think—and I ..."— she gave an innocent shrug—"I only forwarded it to some of the studio executives. No biggie."

Charles gave a soft half moan. Tessa knew how he felt. Paisley had the same tendency to downplay some of the worst things she did at school.

"That's all I did, I swear," Hannah continued. "Besides, someone came by and saw me through the door window and yelled at me to get off. So I didn't really have time to cover my tracks."

"This happened a few days ago," George said. "We had some free time, so we drove home. Then Hannah got an email."

"What happened was that when I emailed the photos to the studio executives, I used a phantom email address I had set up. But because I was kicked off the computer, I didn't have time to smudge the IP address, which would have made it so no one could trace the account. Then my phantom address got this weird email message from the studio. It had all these numbers and the contestants' names."

"From whom at the studio?" Charles leaned forward.

"I couldn't tell. Whoever it was used a complicated software program to make the sender anonymous. The only reason I knew it was from the studio was because that was the only place I've ever used that phantom email address."

"You said the email contained numbers and names?" Tessa remembered what Karissa had mentioned only a couple days ago, and her own suspicion about the yakuza rigging a singing competition. Was this it? A chill passed through her. The last place she wanted to be was caught between her uncle and yet another illegal enterprise of his.

"She showed it to me," George said. "I could tell immediately it was gambling odds against the contestants of the show. It looked like someone inside the studio might be trying to rig the voting."

"Can they do that?" Tessa asked. "I thought it was the viewers who voted people off the island."

Charles gave her a dry sidelong look. "Wrong show."

"The voting is by phone and online," George said. "But who's to say they're not controlling the vote count somehow?"

"Dad, I keep telling you, it's too hard for them to do that," Hannah said. "It's probably easier for them to create a computer program that sends votes to the system so their favored contestants won't get booted."

"I suppose I should be flattered," George said. "According to the email, I'm not going to get voted off until after the final four."

"But you're really popular," Tessa said.

Charles gave her a sharp look.

She felt heat rising up from her collarbone. "Alicia and my mom watch the show a lot," she explained to Charles with a shrug. She turned to include George as she continued, "They said that everybody likes you best, because you're not some young thing right out of high school like half the contestants, and you're a single parent. Alicia, my sister, says that on the online forums, everyone wants you to win."

George's smile was a perfect mix of embarrassment and hope. He really was quite handsome. She could see why Alicia was so gaga over him.

At that moment, the server arrived with their food.

After the server left, Charles sprinkled pepper on his jumbo shrimp, which were served in a cream-prosecco sauce that smelled richly of garlic. "How did the message even get sent to your phantom email address? Obviously it was meant for someone else."

Hannah looked wide-eyed at her burger, which was almost as big as her head, and cut it in half. "I'm not totally sure, but I think maybe whoever sent the email meant to send it to someone whose email address started with the same letter or two of my phantom address. When I was on that computer, I noticed the system has a pretty robust autocomplete function for the email program, and when I sent those pictures to the studio executives, my phantom address got added to the company-wide address book. I'm guessing the sender typed a few letters of the email address he wanted and expected the autocomplete to pick the recipient he normally sent the gambling odds to. But the autocomplete accidentally selected my phantom address instead."

Charles was nodding. "I've done that once. Sent an email to the wrong person because I typed a few letters and hit return, and the autocomplete selected the wrong address. But you mentioned something about the IP address?"

The girl paled and swallowed. "The phantom address isn't easy to trace, but it's not impossible. Whoever sent the email with the gambling odds can get an IT person to trace the phantom address, and they may be able to figure out where the email went."

Hannah had used one acronym too many for Tessa. IT? IP? She didn't really want to ask, because she had a feeling the answers would only confuse her further. She concentrated on her sea bass, which practically melted in her mouth.

"You didn't bounce it off several servers?" Charles asked.

"I did, but it's not like I'm hacking into the Pentagon. I didn't set up a really difficult backtrace."

George dropped the bite of apple-chutney pork chop that had been on his fork. "Hannah ..." he said again.

That was the second time she'd mentioned it. "Did you try to hack into the Pentagon?" Tessa demanded.

Hannah concentrated on wiping up some chipotle sauce, which had dripped off her burger, with a couple of her french fries. "It was only once, and I made triple-double sure they couldn't find me, and besides, I didn't get far ..."

Charles gave a loud groan. "I really don't want to hear this."

"You and me both," George said.

"Fine. Like I said, the phantom address isn't easy to trace, but it isn't impossible either," Hannah said. "I mean, I wasn't going to do anything really bad with the phantom address, so I didn't try too hard to hide it."

Tessa finally had to ask, "And tracing this address is bad because ...?"

Hannah chewed her lip and glanced nervously at her dad. "Because if the person at the studio who sent the email finds a good hacker, the hacker can figure out the physical address of the person he accidentally sent the gambling odds to. And that address belongs to Dad's house in Oakland."

Tessa exhaled long and deep. "This is not good."

"Ya think?" Hannah said.

From dealing with her niece, Tessa knew that Hannah would appreciate knowing the truth about the situation so she could be on her guard. Hannah was at an age where she would respect Tessa only if Tessa treated her like an adult, but this wasn't going to be easy for Hannah or her father to hear. "If I were rigging the show," Tessa said slowly, "and I knew you knew, in order to prevent either of you from telling anyone, I'd probably try to kidnap Hannah as leverage."

A french fry dropped from Hannah's fingers back onto her plate. "Me?"

George's eyes were serious and unsurprised. "That's what Elizabeth said when I talked to her about this. It's why she recommended I speak to both of you."

"They need you to stay until the semifinal round, right?" Tessa said.

"If she were kidnapped, I'd be lucky if I could sing 'Twinkle Twinkle Little Star,'" George said.

"Hmm, that's true. I didn't think of that," Tessa said. "But I also don't know if this person at the studio would have thought of that either."

"They could rely on threats to keep you in line," Charles said.

"Until I got booted," George said darkly.

Then Tessa knew exactly what would happen to both him and his daughter. It's what she knew her uncle would do.

Charles set down his fork. "You need to go to the police with this. You have the email. Maybe they can trace it to whoever sent it."

"I told you, he used a program to mask the sender," Hannah said.

At the same time, her father said, "No way. No police. Then we'd really be in trouble."

"What do you mean?" Tessa was the last person to want to go to the cops, especially if her uncle might be involved in this, but she was surprised George didn't want the police involved either.

"I've seen several policemen at the studio," George said. "There's a detective who's friends with one of the producers of the show, and they go out for lunch every so often."

"You can't know that that particular person is the one who's involved in this," Charles said.

"But I can't know for sure that he's not, can I? And I'm not about to risk my daughter if there's a chance a crooked cop is involved. When I was growing up, I had a few run-ins with one or two of them." His mouth was a hard line.

Tessa had known one or two herself. They weren't all bad, but if one bad apple got ahold of the right information, things wouldn't end well for George or Hannah.

"I got to know Elizabeth because the construction company I was working for helped build her ex-husband's new house, and one day I saved her from getting seriously injured by some falling debris. Well, you know how she is." George shrugged. "She said to keep in touch, and she really meant it, even though I was just a grunt worker. When I got onto *Grab the Mic*, she called me up to congratulate me, and she's been helping me with the changes we've had to make because of the show. She said that you two could help me find out who's rigging the show and turn them in."

"But we're not investigators," Tessa said. "We don't have as many resources. Besides, you have proof of the rigging from the email, so couldn't you just turn it into the police?"

George shook his head. "The email makes it look like the show is being rigged, but it's not proof. It's just names and numbers."

Charles sighed. "True. There's deniability."

"And while Hannah said the message has to be from the studio because that's the only place she used that phantom email address, we only have her word for that."

"Do you have any idea who sent the email?" Charles asked.

George's face grew set and hard. "It has to be someone who can see the results of the voting, because the email was missing one contestant's name, but the voting results don't come out publicly until the show tomorrow night. I think the missing contestant is the person who's going to be voted off this week."

"Who has access to that data?"

"Besides the producers of the show? I dunno. Some people in the studio's computer department have got to be able to find the results."

"I'm not sure what I can do, but I'll try to find out who might have access to the computer tally," Charles said.

"I have to drive back to LA tomorrow morning," George said to Tessa, "but I don't want to take Hannah with me. I was hoping I could leave her with you." His eyes on her were solemn, trusting.

She nodded. "I'll keep her safe." She expected a sarcastic remark from his teenage daughter, but apparently Tessa's frank warning about the danger Hannah was facing had sunk in, for the girl simply glanced at her father and then down at her half-eaten plate.

Tessa's paranoia kicked in. "Have you talked to anyone about your connection to Elizabeth?"

"Uh ..." George thought for a moment. "No, I don't think so. Not at the studio."

"Some of the people there are such snobs," Hannah said airily. "If they knew he needed Elizabeth St. Amant's financial help just to stay on the show, they'd totally look down on him."

"Make sure no one knows about Elizabeth," Tessa said, "because she's your connection to me. That way, no one will be able to find Hannah when she's with me."

George nodded.

"Let me make arrangements tonight, and I'll pick up Hannah tomorrow morning." Tessa hadn't yet heard from her cousin Itchy about the Suburban his dad had bought, so she'd visit him tonight to make sure she had wheels tomorrow. "Can you give me your address?"

"Sure thing." George wrote it down on a business card and passed it to Tessa. As she reached to take it, his hand settled on top of hers for a brief moment. "Thanks for doing this for me."

"Sure."

Charles abruptly stood, causing his chair to emit a loud scraping noise. "We'd better go."

As Charles paid for their dinner, Tessa realized that neither of them had discussed their fee, but it didn't seem right, since George was nothing like the wealthy socialites Elizabeth typically sent to Tessa for protection. She wavered, not sure what to do and supremely uncomfortable bringing up the subject.

Charles caught her eye and somehow read her mind. He gave a slight shake of his head.

That small gesture put her questions to rest, but then she abruptly turned away. She didn't want Charles to be able to guess what she was thinking. She didn't want Charles to be able to ease her worries. She didn't want to feel this bond with him that seemed to crop up every time she was with him.

She felt the wide chasm between them, but she also felt a pull toward Charles like a rope around her waist, trying to drag her over the edge.

She walked George and Hannah downstairs and waited on the sidewalk for the valet to retrieve his car. Charles stood behind her, a silent presence she couldn't ignore.

Suddenly, a tall man, slender and wearing a dark trench coat, approached them. Something about his gaze made him seem like more than just a pedestrian walking past. He seemed to be trying to give off the impression that he wasn't looking at George and Hannah, but even though he looked around at the passing cars and the buildings opposite, his eyes kept flicking back to them.

A prickling sensation shot up Tessa's back and over her scalp. She moved quickly, trying to thrust herself in front of Hannah, but she lost precious moments when she became entangled in the folds of George's jacket. She managed to plant herself in the man's way in the middle of the sidewalk just as he reached into his pocket and made a menacing gesture toward Hannah and George.

Tessa used the man's forward momentum and misdirected it, swinging him in a circle as if they were dancing, except she flung him into the valet's desk, which stood next to the sidewalk. Although the man was taller than Tessa, he was light and lean enough that she could toss him with ease. The heavy desk rocked into the valet standing behind it, and he yelped and grabbed the edge to keep it from falling on him.

Tessa shoved her forearm under the man's chin to keep him off balance. She felt his pulse beating rapidly against his throat.

And then he gurgled something that sounded a bit like, "Erp."

She paused. That wasn't exactly the sound of an assassin.

His hand was still in his coat pocket, so she grabbed his wrist and yanked his hand out.

He held a pen and a receipt between shaking fingers.

Tessa released him.

"I, uh ... I was hoping Mr. Mynheir would autograph this for me," the man said, his Adam's apple bobbing. "If he doesn't have time, I understand ..."

"Glad to." George stepped forward hastily and helped the man get his balance again.

"Sorry," Tessa mumbled.

"Oh, it's okay," the fan said with more grace than Tessa deserved. "He's got his daughter with him and all that ..."

Behind the man, the valet's wide eyes regarded Tessa. "Whoa," he breathed. "You were, like, way quick when you took him down."

"I didn't take him down," Tessa said, her face as hot as a boiling teapot. She reached into her pocket and shoved her claim ticket at him. "Will you just get my car?"

He grabbed her keys out of the desk and bolted, as if afraid she'd put him in a headlock.

She turned back to George.

"To Neville, you said?" George scribbled on the back of the receipt. "So what do you do?"

"I'm an engineer at a semiconductor company."

It made Tessa think of trains at first, but even though she didn't know what a semiconductor was, she was enough of a Silicon Valley girl to know it had something to do with technology. The engineer probably had a slew of letters after his name that qualified him to do his job.

"You must be really smart," George said with an admiring look. "I never went to college."

"I went to Washington State on scholarship," Neville said, beaming. "First person in my family to go to college."

"Good for you." George seemed to have a gift for pulling out the best in people and making them feel good about themselves, rather than playing the rock-star card and eating up his fans' admiration. "I'm hoping my daughter will be able to go to whichever college she wants." He handed the autographed receipt back to Neville.

"Thanks, Mr. Mynheir."

"Please, call me George." He gave Neville a firm handshake and a smile that seemed to include Neville in George's personal circle of friends.

When Neville left, George turned to Tessa. "Well, now I know you can do your job, that's for sure."

"You're like Nikita," Hannah said in awe. "Or Sarah Connor. Or Annie Walker. Or Alice."

Tessa had no idea who the latter three were but figured it wasn't a bad thing to be compared to bad-guy butt-kicking La Femme Nikita.

And the slightly amused but impressed gleam in Charles's eyes made her feel as sexy as Nikita too. For a moment, she forgot why she was mad at him, forgot how he had hurt her and who he really was under that handsome face.

But then the memories came back, like they always did, along with the pain of losing the one person who'd meant so much to her. And even though it was ridiculous, a part of Tessa couldn't forgive Charles, because he couldn't understand her. She turned coldly away from him as George's car arrived, driven by a valet.

She saw them off with a wave, then checked her watch. How long had it been since she gave her keys to the other valet? She took a step away from Charles as they waited. San Francisco traffic rushed past them. He was silent, and she hoped he would take the hint and keep quiet. She knew she needed to talk to him eventually, but she just didn't want to do it now.

Maybe in a couple years.

No such luck.

"Tessa," he said.

"What?" She didn't turn to look at him.

A pause.

"It's good to see you."

It was good to see him too.

No, it wasn't.

"Nothing has changed, Charles." His name on her lips was like a taste of decadent chocolate.

He spoke so softly she almost didn't hear him. "I've changed."

She heard the rawness of his voice and closed her eyes for a moment. She opened them again as a bus rumbled past them. "I just ..." She swallowed. "I can't forget what you did."

"I'm sorry—"

"It's not a matter of you being sorry. You'll never understand how painful it is for me to know it was your fault I never said good-bye to her."

"I can understand—"

Her gut began to boil, and she swung to face him. "No, you can't. You've always had a loving mother and brother. You don't know what it's like to feel like the only person who cared about you is gone, like you're completely alone in the world."

His eyes were stricken. They wavered, then dropped.

It was an empty victory. She turned away to watch a Volvo switch lanes in front of them. The roiling mass of acid still burbled under her breastbone, and she breathed shallowly through her nose.

She didn't know why she couldn't let it go. Maybe because the pain had formed so much of her life that last year in prison and during the months after she'd been released, when it had seemed her mother was only grudgingly giving her a place to stay. Things were better with Mom now, but the hole still gaped in her heart, the edges raw after learning the truth about Charles last year.

Her sister's car finally arrived, and Tessa climbed in after tipping the valet, who gingerly took her folded bills as if afraid she'd smack him.

As she drove away, she made the mistake of glancing in her rearview mirror at Charles, who was still waiting for his car. He was watching her depart, wearing a granite-hard expression she'd never seen on him before. Resolution framed his flat mouth and glittering eyes.

The sight of him looking like that—hurt and angry and cold—shot a pang of regret through Tessa. Stupid. What else had she been expecting? The less contact with him, the better. Maybe since she didn't use his legal expertise very much, she could explain to her uncle that she didn't need to have Charles on retainer. Then she could let him go, and her uncle would understand. But would Uncle Teruo continue to leave her alone if she did? Right now, having Charles on retainer was the only thing keeping Uncle from nagging her about working for the yakuza again.

She shook away the vision of Charles's face. This was what she'd wanted. To hurt him the way he'd hurt her. To hurt him so much that he'd try to avoid her as frantically as she'd been trying to avoid him.

So why did she feel as if she'd just made a colossal mistake?

Chapter **5**

eorge had been right. The name missing from the email mistakenly sent to Hannah was the name of the contestant who was voted off *Grab the Mic* a few days ago. The problem was that it now made Charles's job a bit tougher.

For one thing, it meant he had to talk to Tessa.

But first, he confirmed his date with Rick's wife's uncle's cousin's dog's former roommate's daughter ... or something convoluted like that. Marcy seemed nice (read: sane) over the phone, which was a relief.

As Charles drove to San Jose to find Tessa, he wondered why he hadn't done this months ago, when it first became obvious Tessa didn't want anything to do with him.

Because Charles was a chump, that's why. A hopeless, thick-headed chump.

Well, he was a chump no more. He'd go on this date and enjoy it. Tessa could wallow in her bitterness and pain and go hitch up with some yakuza captain and have children who won martial arts tournaments. Or grew up to make offers people couldn't refuse.

He had a difficult time finding the hotel Tessa was staying in, but he supposed that was a selling point for her. He walked into the tiny lobby and asked the front desk to ring her room.

"I'm sorry. We don't have a Tessa Lancaster staying with us," the young man said.

Of course. But what name would she use? With Tessa, it could be anything.

Charles pulled out his cell phone and dialed her number, hoping she hadn't ditched it for another burner phone. Keeping up with her phone numbers was a pain, although he understood she did it to protect her clients and to keep from being found.

He probably should have been glad she wasn't so averse to him finding her that she'd neglected to give his mama her new number each month.

On the fourth ring, she answered coolly. "Hi, Charles."

He heard the voice of a radio station personality in the background. Maybe she wasn't at the hotel. "Where are you?"

"Why?"

"I have information I need to discuss with you and some questions to ask Hannah."

She paused for an infinitesimal moment, then said, "We're driving to Almaden Lake Park." She gave him directions.

Of course, this being Tessa, the park *would* be on the opposite end of San Jose. "I'll be there in half an hour."

⚓

The park was a small but rather nice oasis in the midst of the two apartment complexes on either side and the light rail station across the street. The large lake had a tuft of grass in the center.

The tuft was attempting to be an island and was covered with birds sunning themselves. Charles drove down a side street to a small parking lot, then wandered past a boccie ball court and a fenced-in children's playground.

Where were they? Geese and ducks patrolled the green lawns, while a group of older men played checkers on cement tables near a small, covered picnic area. Joggers and bikers whizzed past Charles along the asphalt walkway, heading for the paved trail that followed Calero Creek out of the park.

He finally took out his phone to call her, but she called him just as he was about to hit redial. "Where are you?" he asked, not bothering to say hello.

"We're not in the park. I parked the car along a side street near the last apartment complex."

He turned his steps back toward the parking lot and headed out of the park, crossing the empty street to the row of cars parked alongside the curb.

The large apartment complex rose like a palatial white city that had a street running down its center. The clean lines of the buildings marched next to a neat row of trees alongside the road, each tree trimmed to look almost identical to the one next to it.

Wait a minute. Charles scanned the cars parked on the street. What car was Tessa driving? The SUV she'd driven from the restaurant?

Then she walked out from behind the other side of a gigantic old Suburban, its white paint a bit scratched up and a dent in the rear fender. He got the feeling she'd been watching him for a minute or two from behind the truck as he'd been searching the cars for her.

He joined her, and the passenger door opened, Hannah's legs

swinging out and bumping against the car frame as she turned sideways on the seat, a laptop on her lap. "Nope, can't find a nonsecure wireless network. Are you sure I can't just hack—"

"Absolutely not," Tessa said. "We want a nonsecure network you can ride off of if you're going to be logging on to your home computer."

"What's going on?" Charles asked. "Are you telling me you're using someone's wireless network without telling them? That's illegal."

Tessa gave him a look. "Fine, we won't admit we're doing anything illegal. There, you have deniability."

Charles glared at her. "Why does Hannah need to log on to her home computer in the first place?"

"Because I was brilliant," Hannah said carelessly, a smug look on her face.

Tessa waved her hand in an impatient circle. "Yes, we discussed this and praised your extraordinary mind. Get on with it."

"Before I left home, I set up my wireless webcam in my room," Hannah said. "I hid it on a shelf with a view of my computer. I set it up to start recording if my computer is booted up and to save the video files in a special hidden folder only I can access through a backdoor I set up. So now I'm going to log in remotely and download to my laptop any video that was recorded on my home computer. But Tessa said I needed to find an anonymous wireless network so they can't trace me." She gestured to the apartment complex. "We drove up and down the street but can't find a wireless network that isn't password protected."

"But the neighborhood schools let out a few minutes ago." Tessa glanced at her watch. "Hannah says that some families don't leave their wireless networks on all the time. We're hoping that kids will come home and turn on their family's wireless networks, and more networks might show up soon."

"Is there a bathroom nearby?" Hannah set down her laptop on the floor of the SUV and hopped onto the sidewalk.

"In the park." Tessa held out her hand. "Give me your computer. It's probably better to be safe than sorry and not leave it in the Moose."

"The Moose?" Charles asked.

She tilted her head toward the Suburban. "I thought it was a fitting name."

Yes, Charles thought it fit the vehicle perfectly.

They crossed the street and skirted around the boccie ball courts to the restrooms, which Tessa checked before letting Hannah inside. While waiting for Hannah, Tessa asked him, "What did you need to talk to me about?"

"I hired a private detective, Kurt Proctor, to check into the studio and see who would have access to the voting results. The phone and website votes are tallied in a computer room in the studio complex."

"George mentioned the producers can get in."

Charles nodded. "There are seven producers, and they all have access to the room. So does the head IT manager. But supposedly there's a way for any studio personnel to get into the room."

Tessa frowned. "Anyone? There must be hundreds of studio staff."

"Plus the contestants."

"You're kidding." She ran a hand through her straight hair, which was glinting auburn in the thin October sunlight. He liked it when she wore it down this way instead of in a ponytail.

Pull your head back in the game, Charles. "The studio is leasing the building—they don't own it. The way the building is set up, all the rooms that have a keypad lock can be accessed by the building manager's master key code."

"The manager doesn't just give his master key code out, does he?"

"No, but the janitors have several key codes that are written on the wall in the janitor's closet, alongside the areas each code accesses. The janitors aren't allowed in sensitive areas like the voting room, but Kurt found out that one of those janitor codes is actually the master key code."

Tessa gaped at him. "Do the janitors know? Do any of the other studio staff know?"

"Kurt doesn't think so, although he wasn't about to go around asking people."

Tessa chewed her lip and absentmindedly watched the geese waddle toward the edge of the lake. "Okay, so let me wrap my head around this. The email message with the gambling odds was sent by a crooked studio staff member—let's call him Bob."

Charles had to suppress a smile.

"And apparently Bob used a special software program to mask his identity. Because of that, I would guess that Bob is studio staff who has his—or her—own office computer."

Charles nodded. "That rules out the contestants and any staff who don't have their own offices. But that still leaves at least fifty people."

"The studio has that many offices?"

"It has that many personal computers that are hooked up to the studio network and assigned to staff. I checked with Kurt."

"But I thought the only way that autocomplete mess happened was because Bob was one of the people Hannah sent the embarrassing pictures to, right?"

"No. I'm pretty sure Hannah mentioned something about the company-wide address book. We can ask her again."

"Ask me what?" The teen came up behind them.

"You said when you emailed the embarrassing picture to the studio executives, your phantom email address was added to the company-wide address book, right?"

Hannah chewed the inside of her lip. "Yeah. It was the only way I could send the email to the executives. Otherwise my email would have ended up in their spam folders."

Tessa said, "So Bob could be —"

"Bob?" Hannah asked.

"The crooked studio staff person. We're calling him Bob."

"Oh, okay. Cool."

"So Bob could be any of the fifty staff who has their own computer?" Tessa asked.

Charles and Hannah nodded at the same time like in-sync bobbleheads. Hannah clarified, "There's the company-wide address book and also Bob's personal address book, a contact list Bob set up on his company's email program. The autocomplete function would suggest addresses from either address book. The person Bob was trying to email could have been in Bob's personal address book, but the autocomplete function pulled the phantom email from the company address book instead."

Tessa sighed. "I was hoping we could narrow it down to Bob being one of the executives you sent the pictures to."

"Nope, it isn't that simple," Hannah said. "See, what I did was —"

Tessa waved her hands in the air. "No, I don't want to know. My head is spinning with the information you've already told me."

Hannah sighed and rolled her eyes as if to say, *I'm working with Neanderthals.*

Tessa ignored her with what looked like a supreme effort. "Let's see if there are any new wireless networks available now." She led the way back to the Suburban.

Charles asked Hannah, "Can we limit the suspect pool to just the people who have studio computers, or could studio staff who aren't assigned a computer, say a janitor, send that email from any studio computer?"

Hannah looked thoughtful. "Ye-e-es," she said slowly. "It would mean whoever sent the email has to be somewhat computer literate. Even if some hacker wrote that identity-scrubbing program for them, they'd still have to hook up an external drive and run the program before they sent the email. But yeah, it's possible that someone who doesn't have a studio computer could have sent the email."

Tessa made a disgusted noise. "So we're back to square one. It could be anyone who accidentally sent that email to Hannah."

"Not anyone," Charles said. "There are the obvious suspects — the seven producers and the IT manager. But if Bob isn't one of those people, then he has to be someone who found the master key code in the janitor's closet. And he has to be someone proficient enough with computers to be able to send emails using a program that hides his identity."

Hannah's face was pensive. "That actually narrows it down a lot. Like I told you before, a lot of people at the studio are snobs — and not just the contestants. There aren't many who even know where the janitor's closet is, much less look inside. They treat the janitors like slaves."

"How many janitors are there?" They had reached the SUV, and Tessa unlocked the door before handing the laptop to Hannah.

"Three for the entire building, which isn't enough. The place is huge and people are pigs. Dad used to be a janitor." Hannah opened the laptop. "Hey, I got a new network. And it's not password protected. Hang on. The signal's weak. Let me get closer." She started walking up the street that bisected the apartment complex, her eyes solely on the laptop screen. She stumbled a little when she veered into a front lawn but kept walking as if she hadn't even noticed.

Tessa shadowed her footsteps, but when Hannah abruptly pivoted to head back, she nearly crashed into her. Hannah put a protective arm around her computer. "Hey, watch the laptop."

"I'm watching you."

"D'ya see anyone?" Hannah flung an arm out at the quiet facades of the buildings. "Unless you think there's an assassin hiding behind the bougainvillea." She pointed to a squat bush with a few pink flowers.

Tessa put up her hands. "Fine. I'll give you space."

Charles walked beside Tessa as she stayed a few feet behind Hannah, who walked down the street and then turned to stroll along the sidewalk, searching for the source of the signal. The girl was muttering to no one in particular.

"What are you going to do now?" Tessa asked him.

"After she checks her computer, I'll see if Hannah can give me a few names of people who might have discovered the master key code and would have been able to send the email message.

We have to find out who's behind this, or George and Hannah will be on the run for the rest of their lives."

Tessa's face closed up. Charles hesitated, then asked, "What's wrong?"

She blinked as she came out of her own thoughts. At first he didn't think she'd answer, but then she said, "I don't know if this is a good idea. For me to be protecting them."

"Why? What do you mean?"

"My uncle likes to gamble."

It was the closest she'd ever come to saying what her mafia uncle did. "You think he might be involved in this?"

"No, I'm not saying that," she said quickly. "But I don't want to get caught in the middle, just in case."

He frowned at her. "You can't mean that. You can't abandon them."

"I wouldn't be abandoning them." She looked at Charles, her eyes troubled and unusually vulnerable. "I'd recommend a different bodyguard is all."

Not working with Tessa would be best for Charles; he knew this. But her giving the job to someone else seemed wrong. "Elizabeth entrusted you with this."

"I think Elizabeth would understand. She knows how sticky my family situation is." Her eyes flickered back to Hannah, then her entire body stiffened. In a flash she darted forward.

A short, scruffy man had appeared out of nowhere and was talking to Hannah.

Charles ran after Tessa. Had he distracted her from watching over the girl? Regardless, if he knew Tessa, she'd only blame herself for not being vigilant.

Tessa was tall enough to look the scruffy man in the eye. "Can I help you?" Her voice was deceptively silky.

"No," the man said insolently. "Just chatting with this pretty lady." He smiled at Hannah.

The teen, who'd seemed mildly bored with the conversation before, flashed him a faintly disgusted look.

"You leave her alone," Tessa growled.

The man only raised a bushy eyebrow and looked her up and down.

Tessa's jaw tightened.

Charles couldn't quite blame the man for not taking her seriously. Tessa didn't look like much of a threat these days. Rather than the black leather she used to wear, she had on comfortable clothes that any soccer mom or yoga instructor would don for an errand to the post office. And she stowed significantly fewer weapons on her person these days—exactly zero, because of her parole. Before she'd been arrested, she could have armed a small country.

She glared at the man now, putting her body between him and Hannah, and for a moment, her stance and expression made Charles recall a fleeting memory.

His mama, standing up to his daddy, wearing the same expression, her body in the same taut curve. Charles had been on the floor behind her, his lip bleeding.

Then Daddy had slapped Mama, and Charles's memory went black.

Unlike Daddy, this man had a more indolent look, as if the effort to push Tessa away was too much for him. But Tessa was as protective as his mama had been, and Charles couldn't help but be drawn to her. Her fierceness was what he'd want in the mother of his own children.

He almost laughed. Like that was going to happen.

"Look, lady—" the man started.

"It's Desiree," Tessa said loudly.

Charles got the hint as he caught up to them. "Desiree, honey, leave the man alone."

"I'm only watching out for my niece," Tessa said.

The man scratched his round face, shadowed by a two-day-old beard. "I only asked the girl about her computer."

"That's all he said, Aunt D-Desiree," Hannah said.

Rather, that's all he had the time to say before Tessa the Avenging Fury descended to chop off his head.

Tessa grasped Hannah's arm and inadvertently knocked the laptop half-closed. "You know you're not supposed to talk to strangers." She led the girl away, Charles following.

"Where did he come from?" Tessa asked in a low voice.

"He walked out from between two parked cars," Hannah said.

Tessa turned around to look, and Charles did too. The man was still standing on the sidewalk, fingering his car keys, looking at them. He turned his attention back to the keys in his hand a little too quickly.

"How'd he find us?" Tessa exhaled sharply. Then she looked at Charles. "When and where did you meet your private investigator?"

Uh-oh. "At a coffee shop near the law offices. Yesterday."

"And the PI had been checking into the studio in Los Angeles. Someone could have noticed him snooping and followed him all the way back up to San Francisco. They could have seen him meet with you and followed you back to your law firm.

Then they would have waited and followed you home."

Ice water flowed down Charles's spine. Mama was still living with him.

"And then they could have followed you here today," Tessa continued.

"Isn't that kind of far-fetched?" Hannah was still fiddling with her computer with one hand while holding it with the other, and she didn't look up at Tessa.

"How else did he find us here?"

Charles looked back at the man. He seemed to be taking a long time getting into his blue Kia to drive away. "What if he's really just some innocent guy interested in Hannah's computer? Or maybe he's a pervert who was trying to pick her up. Either way, it doesn't necessarily mean he was hired by Bob to get to Hannah."

Hannah suddenly gasped. "I have a video file on my computer in Oakland."

Tessa grasped her by the arm and pulled her toward the Suburban. "Get inside."

"But the wireless signal's too weak."

"I'll drive us closer to the signal." Tessa pushed Hannah into the passenger seat of the Moose and slammed the door.

Charles scrambled into the wide backseat. The vehicle was built like a tank. Which might be a good thing, since Tessa had to protect her clients. She fired up the engine, which roared like a tank too.

For a moment, Charles worried that the stranger would be able to see what car Tessa drove. But then he realized that if the stranger had indeed followed him, the man would have seen Charles approach the Suburban and seen Tessa and Hannah exit from it.

Tessa pulled into the street and headed toward the man, who was still sitting in his blue car.

He pulled out in front of her and took off down the road.

"Good," she muttered. She slowed as she reached the slot where he'd parked. "Tell me when."

"Stop," Hannah said, and the Suburban jerked to a halt.

"Maybe less lead in that foot, Danica Patrick?" Charles said.

Tessa gave him a dirty look in her rearview mirror.

"The video recorded yesterday morning," Hannah said. "It's almost done downloading."

Tessa put the Moose in park and leaned over to look at the computer screen. Charles scooted forward on the slick vinyl backseat to be able to see the video. Behind them, a car pulled out from a parking space and resignedly passed around them. The driver didn't even toot the horn, since the small street was empty.

The video started. The first few frames were grainy and had lines through the picture, but then it cleared up to show a small white bedroom with posters on the walls and an extremely messy bed in the far corner. Clothes littered the floor and were piled on top of a dresser whose drawers were half-opened.

In the center of the picture was a clear shot of someone sitting in front of Hannah's desk, staring at her computer monitor. The video cam had been placed a bit above the monitor, so they got a glimpse of a balding spot on the top of the man's head. He squinted at the computer, scratching his round face.

It was the scruffy man who had stopped Hannah about her computer. The man who had just driven off in the blue Kia.

Tessa had been right.

Chapter **6**

Tessa was completely out of her depth as she watched Hannah's uncontrollable shaking. Charles had his arm around the girl and was saying soothing things. Tessa even found herself starting to calm down just hearing him say, "It's all right, darlin'," in that comforting Southern drawl of his.

This was a side of him she hadn't seen before. She was used to Charles as The Attorney—smart, logical, sharp-witted. Had he always had this softer side and she just hadn't seen it, or had he changed over the past year?

Did it matter?

Suddenly her phone rang, and she was almost relieved. It was her mom. "Hi, Mom."

"Where are you right now?" The edges of her voice were raw and slightly frazzled.

"San Jose."

A short sharp sigh. "Well, it can't be helped. I can't keep it here."

"Keep what? Where? Are you at work?"

"Of course I'm at work," she snapped. "And your niece's cell phone has been going off practically every minute."

"Why do you have Paisley's cell phone?"

"Because Alicia dropped it off, why else?" she retorted, as if Tessa had asked something idiotic.

But Mom, a hostess at Oyasumi, a Japanese restaurant in Palo Alto, didn't go into work until late morning, whereas Tessa's sister usually dropped her daughter off at school in San Jose early in the morning, before driving to her job in Menlo Park. "Mom, still not getting it."

"Paisley left her cell phone in the car when Alicia dropped her off this morning, but Alicia didn't notice until she was almost at work. So she dropped it off at the restaurant—Nez always gets here early to do the books—and left a message for me, asking me to drive home during my afternoon break to give it to Paisley after she got home from school. You know how Paisley is when she doesn't have her phone. Alicia didn't want her daughter calling her all afternoon to nag her about the phone."

"Would Paisley really do that? Alicia gets home around eight—"

"Of course Paisley would do that. Anyway, I haven't had time to take it home this afternoon because we've been so busy, and the phone is in my locker, which is next to Nez's office, and Paisley's friends have been texting her constantly, so her phone beeps every single minute. And Paisley has already called the restaurant from the home phone three times . . ."

Now Tessa could understand why Mom sounded unglued. "You can't turn off the phone?"

"Do *you* know how to turn off Paisley's phone?"

Good point. It had a gazillion buttons partially obscured by the dozens of pink sparkles Paisley had placed all over it. "Sure, I'll pick it up. I'll be there in about forty-five minutes."

"No, you will drive fast and be here in thirty minutes so Nez doesn't blow a gasket and I don't either!" And her mom disconnected the call.

Tessa exhaled slowly and stared at her phone, expecting it to self-destruct in her hand, her mom had been so flaming mad. But instead, it beeped with another incoming call—from her mom's house. She could guess who that was. "Hi, Paisley."

"Hey, Aunt Tessa. Are you free right now?"

"Whyyyyy?"

"Well, I left my phone in the car, and Mom said it's at Grandma's workplace, and I was expecting my friend to call to tell me how it went when she asked this boy to the Winter Ball, and I've been on pins and needles all day—"

"Wasn't your friend at school with you?"

"Well, yeah, but I don't have every single class with her or anything like that. Anyway, I was wondering if you could pick it up and bring it to me."

Tessa wasn't about to drive north to Palo Alto and then south again to San Jose, all for the sake of a teenager's cell phone and some gossip about a friend and the Winter Ball. At least, not without some incentive. "What will you do for me if I do?" she asked coyly.

Paisley made a disgusted noise amazingly similar to the one her grandmother had made a few minutes earlier. "Aunt Tessa, honestly, you're not yakuza anymore, so I don't understand why you can't get rid of this extortion habit."

Tessa just waited.

Finally Paisley said, "Fine, fine. I'll bake you chocolate chip cookies, okay?"

"You can't use the oven until I get there."

Another disgusted noise. "I don't understand why Mom still won't let me use the stove without an adult in the house. I think it's completely stupid. I mean, I'm fourteen years old. I'm a teenager, not a kid, and —"

"You know, I don't have to drop your phone off right this moment —"

"Okay, okay. I'll wait till you get here."

Tessa eyed Hannah's pale face. She didn't know a problem a freshly baked chocolate chip cookie wouldn't fix. "Can I bring a couple friends over?"

Her niece's voice turned coy. "Are any of them male and cute?"

"Paisley!"

"That means yes."

Tessa couldn't help but glance at Charles and felt a blush flame under her collar. "I hope you don't say things like that to your mother."

"Are you kidding? She'd kill me."

"We'll be by in about an hour." She hung up and turned to Hannah and Charles. "Are you up for a road trip?"

"I have to get back to work," Charles said. He got out of the car after giving Hannah one last pat on the shoulder.

"Are we going back to the hotel?" Hannah asked.

"No, we're going to Palo Alto, then to my house."

They arrived in Palo Alto in a little under forty minutes despite the traffic, since Tessa had a lead foot. Mom looked up from the hostess desk at the front of the restaurant as Tessa and Hannah walked in. "Finally," she said in the exact same tone Tessa would expect from Paisley. Mom led them to the back of the restaurant, past tables and a few private dining rooms, to the door marked "Employees Only." Tessa appreciatively breathed in a lungful of the scent of deep-fried shrimp and sweet teriyaki sauce as they passed tables of diners.

She caught sight of two men at a table in the far corner, almost hidden in shadow, and recognized one of them as one of her uncle's *kobun*. It reminded her of what Karissa had said about the television singing competition.

Tessa sidled closer to her Mom. "Mom, have you heard anything about Uncle Teruo and a television singing show?"

Mom stopped dead in her tracks, and Tessa almost ran her over. She turned to her daughter with a gimlet stare, while Tessa teetered, trying not to fall on her face.

Mom frowned at her. "What did you hear about a television show?"

"I, uh, heard Uncle might be ... interested in a singing competition."

"And why does it interest you?" Her gaze was sharp, but then her eyes flickered to Hannah and narrowed. Hannah was usually briefly shown on *Grab the Mic*. Did Mom recognize her?

"Mom, this is Hannah Mynheir. Her dad is George Mynheir."

Mom's face suddenly transformed, and she beamed at Hannah. "I love your father's singing."

"She and her dad are my new clients," Tessa said. "That's why I'm interested."

Mom sobered, her mouth forming a small O. She hesitated, then leaned in closer to Tessa, though Tessa could barely hear her mom over the noise from the restaurant. "Do you really want to get involved in this?"

The question, phrased the way it was, in a cautious tone

different from her mom's normal voice, caused Tessa to turn to stone.

Was her uncle involved in *Grab the Mic* after all? Tessa had managed to stay out of his business for an entire year. She didn't want to meddle with the yakuza's plans again, upset him, and force him to make difficult choices. And she knew that even though she was his niece, he would always be forced to choose his business over his family.

Mom stood there for a long moment, just looking at Tessa, her face grave. "Think about it," she said, then turned and continued to the back of the restaurant. Tessa followed, feeling both numb and apprehensive at the same time.

The employee area in the back was a rather small room with high-school-type lockers and a counter with a sink and a microwave. On the right side was a door marked "Manager" that was half-open. Tessa peeked in and saw the balding head of the manager, Nez, as he bent over papers on his desk and occasionally squinted at something on his computer screen. The bones of his right forearm sat at an odd angle. This is how they'd healed after a Filipino gang member had come for him after Nez's daughter had dumped the young man and hidden at Nez's house. After injuring Nez, the gang member had beaten up the girl. Nez had always been like an uncle to Tessa, so when she'd found out about the incident, she'd gone to rearrange the Filipino man's face.

She shook away the memory. She wasn't that person anymore. But she still had a close relationship with Nez.

He saw Tessa and gave a grunt and a wave. "Keeping out of trouble?" he growled.

"Of course not."

He frowned at her and then went back to his papers. Without looking up, he said, "You better be here to take away that phone."

"No. I thought I'd turn up the volume and hide it in the junkyard you call an office."

He looked up from his papers to glare at her. She gave him a cheeky grin, then he returned to his work.

Mom had gone to her locker and now thrust the cell phone at Tessa, which gave an ear-splitting trill at exactly that moment.

Tessa jerked away. "Is she deaf or something?"

"It's been doing this all day," Mom said sourly.

At the same time, Nez shouted, "It's been doing that all day!"

Mom shooed them out of the restaurant like they had the Ebola virus.

As they were heading out of the restaurant parking lot, Tessa caught sight of an old blue Honda sedan pulling out of a parking spot. The sight of it made her fingers clench the steering wheel. She thought that earlier she might have seen the same car pull into the parking lot as they were walking from her truck into the restaurant.

That short, scruffy man had followed Charles from his workplace to the park, so Tessa had kept an eye out for a tail on the way to the restaurant, but she hadn't seen anything suspicious at the time. But that didn't mean they hadn't been followed.

She signaled right, then jerked the Moose left directly in front of an oncoming pickup truck that blared its horn at her.

She didn't immediately head toward her house. Instead, she went north toward San Francisco. She didn't see the blue Honda behind her, and though she kept her eye out in case a team of cars was following her, she didn't see anything suspicious. She also stopped at a gas station but didn't find a tracking device planted on the Suburban frame when she looked, so she finally headed toward her mom's house.

They arrived in her mom's quiet neighborhood in San Jose, the street lined with trees and small forty- to fifty-year-old homes. The neighbor, Mrs. Fleming, was weeding the flowers lining her walkway, and Tessa waved as she drove past.

She felt a twinge of apprehension in her gut as she opened the front door. She remembered being the awkward girl being introduced to her sister's friends, and she was kind of throwing Hannah and Paisley together like throwing two cats into the same house and hoping for the best.

"Paisley?" She entered the foyer, listening for where her niece could be in the house. Kitchen. Naturally. Probably got a head start on the cookies. Footsteps approached the foyer.

Tessa tried to smile, although it felt a bit strained. Hannah hung back behind her. "Paisley, this is—"

"Gosh, Aunt Tessa, were you in San Francisco or something? It took you so long to get here. Do you have my phone?"

Tessa passed it over. "I—"

"I've been waiting for you so that I could turn on the oven. My PMS is soooooo bad, and I totally needed a chocolate chip cookie all day at school like you wouldn't believe, and there weren't any in the cafeteria, and I was so bummed—oh, hi," she said to Hannah, then turned and headed back to the kitchen.

Tessa felt a bit like she'd been caught in a dust devil, but at least the cats hadn't started fighting.

They entered the kitchen just as Paisley turned on the oven. "Did you check to make sure there wasn't anything inside?" Tessa asked.

Paisley paused, turned red, then opened the oven to take out the large wok that Tessa's mom kept stored in there. Tessa could hear Alicia's voice in her head, *And that's why I want an adult at home when Paisley uses the oven.*

Paisley handed two spoons to Hannah. "Want to help me?"

Hannah froze for a brief moment, then took the spoons and watched as Paisley scooped cookie dough into little balls on the cookie tray. She tentatively scooped out her own ball, and then suddenly the two of them were giggling and chatting.

Tessa headed to her bedroom at the back of the house. While they were here, she might as well check her email.

She flopped onto her bed and reached for her laptop, a gift from Elizabeth St. Amant to her favorite bodyguard. Before getting it last year—a few months after Elizabeth moved back to Shreveport—Tessa had been using Mom's computer and Charles's computer whenever she had been at his house. It was nice having her own now. She fired up her email program—not that she really had that much email. Most days she opened all the spam just to feel like somebody wanted to chat with her.

There was a new spam email. Subject line: From dad.

Ha-ha, good one. Tessa had to open it just to see. It was probably selling pharmaceuticals to enhance the production of belly-button lint.

Dear Tamazon…

The room suddenly shrank. Yet it also expanded. Tessa had that weird out-of-body experience she'd usually only felt if she'd been up playing Bejeweled Blitz for too long and her brain was fritzing.

The only one who had ever called her Tamazon was her father. When they'd played together, she always pretended to be one of the mythical Amazons, and "Tess the Amazon" had been slurred into Tamazon by her childish tongue.

I know you're probably surprised to hear from me after all these years. I've wanted to reach out to you, but it's been out of my power. I've watched you grow into a beautiful, confident woman.

Suuuuuure . . . If he had really been watching her, he'd know she got out of prison sixteen months ago. Yup, a beautiful and confident ex-convict.

I'm proud of you for the sacrifices you've made for the family — for Alicia, for your mom, for your uncle. No one else would go to jail for Fred, but you did.

Something inside her grew colder than subzero. No one except Fred, Ichiro, and Uncle Teruo knew about that. Only Itchy had been with her when she'd found Fred with the knife. Only Itchy had been with her when she'd cleaned up Fred and the knife, planting the knife in the dumpster. And she'd been completely alone when she was arrested.

How would he know this?

I have things I need to tell you that are vital for you to hear. I don't know if you'll understand why, but my time is short, and I can't risk not telling you. I've come to realize that you are the one thing in my life I don't want to miss.

What in the world did that mean? What was up with all this *Fringe/X-Files* vague mysteriousness that never failed to drive her nuts?

Below is a post office box I'm using. I will only have it for a week, so please write to me right away. This email address will be deleted as soon as I send this message.

I love you, little girl,
Dad

Her emotions were like *shabu-shabu*, a mix of a dozen different meats and vegetables combining to create a unique broth. Her feelings were unique, all right. She couldn't decide if her anger was frustrated-anger or disgusted-anger or contemptuous-anger or hysterical-anger.

But definitely anger. That he would dare write her now. That he would dare try to show his affection in words and phrases. That he would dare hint at something more important that had kept him away for so long.

He was twenty years too late.

Dear Tamazon ...

The girl who'd played with that man was dead. She'd died the day he left without a word or note.

But more than likely this wasn't her father, so she didn't want to get sucked into it at all.

She clicked Delete.

If her father did have a good reason for walking out on them, he could make the effort to find a way to talk to her face-to-face, not through a post office box and an email address that self-destructed in fifteen seconds. She didn't intend to go out of her way to make it easy for him.

Besides, the email was just a hoax ... right?

Chapter **7**

A few days later, Charles hadn't even taken his keys out of his front door lock before Mama announced, "I want to see Tessa."

He looked up to where she stood in the front foyer, handbag already on her arm.

"Am I late?" He glanced at his watch. Maybe distraction would work.

"No, you're on time. Did you make reservations at the restaurant?"

"Yes, for six thirty, so we'd better hurry."

"No, you're going to call and change the reservation. I want to see Tessa first." She stood firm, as if trying to keep him from entering his own house.

"Why do you need to see Tessa? You saw her last week."

"It was almost two weeks ago. She didn't have her clients yet." A faint flush rose to Mama's cheeks.

Charles finally saw where this was going. "Mama, she's protecting them."

Mama waved his protest away like she would a fly. "They're probably bored silly and want a visitor."

"Mama ..." But he knew he was fighting a losing battle. It was always a losing battle when it came to Mama, it seemed. "So you'd rather be introduced to a *Grab the Mic* contestant who might not even make it to the next round than have dinner with your loving son?"

Mama gave him a warm smile. "You are a loving son. And yes."

He sighed, then stepped aside so she could sweep past him out the door.

His cell phone rang as he drove Mama to the hotel Tessa and her clients were holed up in. He had his Bluetooth headset on, so he couldn't see who it was. He answered anyway. "Hello?"

"It's Rick. I know you're out to dinner with your mom, but I need to look at the Anderson deposition notes and I can't find them."

"They're supposed to be on my desk."

"I looked there. I don't know if maybe your admin put them away somewhere before she left tonight or what. I don't need them right away, but can you come by the office after your dinner to look for them? I'll still be here."

"Sure, no problem."

"Thanks." Rick hung up.

"Mama, do you mind if we swing by the office for a few minutes after dinner? It's close to the restaurant where we're eating."

"No, I don't mind. Tessa really does care about you, you know."

Her conversational volleys always left his mind spinning. "What?"

"Tessa really does care about you. She might not show it, but you can't really blame her, considering what you did."

He fought the urge to defend himself, because he really had no defense. He had been young and full of legal fervor, and he had unwittingly caused Tessa intense personal pain because he had thought he knew best what to do about the niece of the San Francisco Japanese mafia boss.

"She needs time," Mama continued, "but she does love you—"

"I hope not, because I don't love her."

She gave him the same stern, disappointed look she always gave him when he tried to convince her it was Eddie who'd fed his peas to the dog.

"I'm dating some other women now," he added.

"Like who?" she challenged him.

"Rick set me up with a woman named Kayla. We're going out tomorrow night."

"Is she the only one?"

"I went out just a few days ago."

Her eyes narrowed. "What was her name?"

"Uh …" What had her name been? He could picture her face—long, narrow, eyes a bit close together. Toothy grin. Horsey laugh.

"I see she really made an impression on you."

"She was only the first one. You can't bat a thousand."

"What? You took her to batting practice?" Mama's eyebrows nearly met her silver hair. "What kind of son did I raise?"

"A loving son who's taking you to dinner."

Mama rolled her eyes.

"A loving son who's taking you to meet George Mynheir."

She gave him a sidelong look as if to say, *You are only marginally forgiven.*

"How did you find out about George, anyway?" Distraction

instead of defense. He eased his foot off the gas as the stoplight turned yellow.

"From Teruo."

Charles's foot jerked on the accelerator, and the car jumped forward. He slammed on the brakes in time to keep them from leaping into the intersection.

"Charles, really—"

"Teruo Ota?" he demanded. "Since when do you chat with yakuza bosses?"

"Since they come over to the house for lunch." She gave him a *duh* look.

"Teruo Ota stopped by for lunch?"

"What can I say? He loves my cooking."

Considering her fondness for twelve kinds of chili peppers, the man must have an iron stomach.

"Since when have you two been friends?"

"Oh, well, I met him last year, you know."

Charles wasn't about to forget the day he'd walked into his home after work, depressed because he expected to be fired any day, to find Teruo Ota at his kitchen table with documents that not only saved his job but also got him promoted to partner. "Mama, I know you haven't been keeping in touch with him all year."

"Oh, well, I happened to see him at a Japanese restaurant a week ago, and he stopped by to say hello." She preened. "He remembered my delicious cannoli."

Well, all right. Mama's cannoli were pretty good. But it still didn't explain why Teruo Ota was suddenly so chummy with Charles's Southern belle mama. "And how did he invite himself over for lunch?"

"Don't be silly. I invited him over to have cannoli again."

"And he said yes?"

"Of course he said yes. He's not rude."

"No. He's just a mafia boss."

"Really, Charles, he's quite nice. It's not as if I'm interested in dating him."

The light turned green, and Charles stepped on the accelerator to avoid thinking about his mama being friends with Teruo Ota.

Charles was almost relieved when they arrived at the hotel and knocked on the door to the suite Tessa had booked. She and Hannah slept in one bedroom, while George slept in the other, which made Charles feel a bit more comfortable with the close quarters.

When Tessa opened the door, she immediately ignored Charles and smiled at Mama. "Vivian, this is a nice surprise."

"You can't really expect me to stay away when I find out your new client is George Mynheir." Mama was as perky as a teenager.

Charles couldn't help but frown as George appeared behind Tessa. "Hello," he said, his hand stretched out to Mama and a smile on his face. "Nice to meet you."

"Vivian Britton," Mama gushed, clasping his hand in both of hers. "I just love your singing."

"Why, thank you."

Charles struggled not to gag. The man was flirting with his mama, for goodness' sake.

He was about to enter the hotel suite after Mama, but Tessa stood in his way and hissed, "Why did you show up here? Don't you remember that scruffy guy in the blue Kia who followed you to us a few days ago? You might have just led him here."

He was speechless for a moment, because he realized she was right. "I'm sorry. Really."

She sighed. "It's not that big a deal. I have to move them often anyway, just to be safe. I'll move them again tomorrow morning." She stepped aside so he could enter the room.

Mama was talking to George. "Would you sing something for me?"

Charles groaned. She was shameless. "Mama, I'm sure—"

"Oh, I'd be honored." George led the way to the suite's living area. Hannah was sitting in a chair doing something on her laptop, although she looked up and waved at Charles. She responded politely when her father introduced her to Mama.

George picked up a guitar from where it rested against an overstuffed armchair. He gestured to the sofa. "Have a seat."

Mama plopped herself down. Tessa sidled along the far wall, but George said, "You too, Tessa. I can't sing to only two lovely ladies when there's a third one in the room."

Hannah rolled her eyes and said, "Daaaaaaaaad . . ."

Tessa, the Xena Warrior Princess herself, actually blushed. But she didn't immediately sit down.

"Come on." George flashed his dimples at her.

"Hurry up, Tessa." Mama patted the cushion next to her. "I want to hear George sing."

Tessa sat.

Charles slouched over to a tall chair next to a bistro table that stood against the far wall. All George had to do was flash that pretty smile and women obeyed. It was pathetic.

George strummed his guitar and fiddled a little with the tuning knobs, all the while giving Tessa highly inappropriate looks with his green eyes. Then he launched into "Invisible Man" by 98 Degrees.

Charles felt like an invisible man himself as George serenaded the two women. Tessa had fairy-dust sparkles in her eyes as she stared at him, and Mama was absolutely transfixed. Charles had to admit George had a great voice, smooth yet passionate and powerful. But Charles got more and more irritated as the song went on — far too long, in his opinion — and George seemed to be trying to seduce Tessa right there in front of all of them.

They all clapped when he finished, even Hannah, who must have heard him sing hundreds of times.

"Oh, how romantic," Mama gushed.

Charles needed to stop this nonsense right now. "Tessa, I need to speak to you." His voice came out sounding louder than he intended, with a peeved edge that made him regret opening his mouth at all.

The look she gave him was unreadable, as if someone could be both pleased and annoyed at the same time. But that was ridiculous, right?

Despite her inscrutable look, she got up from the couch to come sit on the other tall chair at the bistro table while Mama chatted comfortably with George, talking about the other contestants as if they were her good friends.

Tessa stared at him, eyebrows raised, for a good minute before she said, "What did you need to talk to me about?"

He suddenly realized he didn't have anything to tell her. At least not about the investigation. If he said something about her creamy skin or glossy hair, she'd probably pop him one in the nose.

"I, uh ..." What had he done this week? Oh, right, the scruffy man who'd been in the video of Hannah's room and who'd approached her at the park. "I asked some people I know about finding out the name of the man who approached Hannah near Almaden Lake Park, but no one could find anything. One of them also mentioned that he might be from out of state."

She nodded. "Some of the good private investigators work in one state but have their information in another. What are you going to do next?"

Next? He had no clue. After all, he didn't think like a criminal.

But he did think like an officer of the court. And if he followed that direction, he knew which resources he'd pull from. "I'd like to talk to an FBI contact about this guy."

She immediately stiffened and leaned away from him. "No. Absolutely not."

He mentally kicked himself for being ten kinds of moron. It had been federal agents who questioned her after arresting her for murdering Laura Starling. Still ... "I understand you wouldn't want them involved, but it might help us find who's after George and Hannah."

She chewed on her bottom lip.

It made Charles want to lean over and kiss her.

Instead, he grabbed the edge of the bistro table until his nails scraped some of the enamel off the wood.

Kayla. He had to remember Kayla. He had a date with Kayla tomorrow night. Nice, safe, non-mafia Kayla.

Tessa finally stopped chewing that delectable bottom lip. "Tell you what. Give me a few days. I'll see if I can find something out through my, er ... contacts." Meaning, the heavily illegal kind. "Then we can talk about this again."

"So you're not waffling about whether you should be doing this or not?" Bad choice of words. Why couldn't he just put a muzzle over his mouth?

Tessa, being Tessa, gave him a sour look, but otherwise didn't react to his gaffe. It was kind of nice that even though he was eating shoe leather twenty times a conversation with her, she wasn't like other women and didn't fall into a hissy fit every time he said something rather stupid, which, admittedly, he did at an alarmingly high rate when around her.

"I think we were followed from Palo Alto the other day," she said.

He leaned forward. "That same guy in the Kia?"

"No, it was a Honda. But I'm not entirely sure it was tailing me. I immediately pulled an aggressive left turn so the driver couldn't follow me, and then when I looked for a tail, I didn't see one."

"I know you can take care of yourself and your clients, but just continue to be careful, okay?" Especially now, in her yoga pants and stretchy top, she seemed fragile rather than the tough street rat she had been eight years ago. "Anything else suspicious?"

She blinked a few times before answering him. "Uh ... sort of. I got an email from my father."

He drew a breath but didn't know what to say. "Who? I thought for a minute you said your father."

Her eyes were serious and steady on him now. "I did."

"But I thought Wayne Lancaster was dead." Then again, in the documents Charles had seen, it was assumed Wayne was dead, since his brother-in-law was the San Francisco Japanese mafia boss and Wayne had disappeared rather suddenly when Tessa was ten. It didn't take a math genius to add two and two together.

"I thought he was dead, too, and at first, I thought the email was spam or something. And while the majority of it was myste-rious hocus-pocus language, he called me Tamazon." Her voice cracked. She cleared her throat. "That's a pet name he had for me and the only other people who know about it are Mom and Alicia."

"Would they tell anyone?"

"Mom may have told Uncle Teruo, but he wouldn't say any-thing to anyone about it. Alicia might have told her ex-husband, Duane, back before they started having marriage problems, but I don't really think she would have mentioned it to him at all. I don't think Alicia would even remember the name."

She shook her head and changed the subject. "The fact that we may have been followed by the blue Honda is too coinciden-tal with the man who followed you to the park and broke into Hannah's room. Since there seems to be a clear threat against Hannah, I asked my mom if Uncle Teruo might be interested in the TV show." She paused.

Charles was dying to know, but he felt the need to say to her, "You don't have to tell me. I understand."

She shook her head again. "Mom didn't say anything explicit. The thing is, if the yakuza are involved in this, I'm the best one to protect George and Hannah. I just …" — she sighed — "I don't want to get involved with yakuza business again like we did last year."

Even though everything had ended with the best outcome, the memory of the dread and worry he'd felt those few days when Tessa was pulling through the surgery after being shot, when he thought his entire career was about to be flushed down the toilet, still slugged him in the gut. "But if you don't help them, who will?"

She didn't answer, but just looked down at the tabletop.

"And if you did find some other bodyguard but something happened to Hannah, would you be able to live with yourself?"

She stilled at his words, then looked up at him with surprise. And maybe a little admiration. "You're right. You're absolutely right."

She held his eyes in a steady gaze, and Charles's breath caught. But this time, he blinked and looked away. He couldn't get involved with her. It wouldn't be good for his career. And she didn't like him for obvious reasons. No need to rehash any of that.

He checked his watch. "Mama," he called to her, "are you ready to go to dinner?"

"My goodness, yes. I'm famished." She stood and shook George's hand. "It was wonderful talking to you."

"The pleasure was all mine, Mrs. Britton."

"Oh, call me Vivian," she tittered.

Oh, land's sake. His mama was laying on Southern charm as thick as butter on a biscuit. Despite that, Charles managed to get her out of the hotel room without having to knock George in the space between those rock-star dimples.

He took Mama to dinner at Lorianne's Cafe, which served the kind of weird — er, exotic fusion — food Mama loved, like oysters with mango or chicken with cilantro-dill-oregano-five-spice pesto. Lorianne's also served regular food, so dinner wasn't as much of a strain on his stomach lining as it would have been if he took her to her favorite Mexican-Japanese fusion restaurant in Daly City. (Their wasabi-and-smoked-tomato salsa was absolute "killer," as Mama put it. Charles and Eddie agreed, although not in the same way Mama meant it.)

"So what did you talk about with George?" he asked after they had ordered. He'd chosen a safe garlic-roasted chicken, while Mama had been ecstatic over the evening special — squid parmesan.

"Oh, just his background. He apparently grew up in a very bad neighborhood. He's done everything he can to give his daughter everything he never had."

"After our first meeting, he mentioned he didn't go to college."

"No, he's had lots of jobs, sometimes taking three of them at a time."

That was a tough life. Charles felt guilty for being jealous of him.

"He married very young, right out of high school, and became a father a year later."

"How old is he?"

"Thirty-three."

"And he's the oldest contestant?"

"Yes, but the most eligible bachelor." Mama winked at him.

"Mama, since I'm not on the lookout for a boyfriend …"

"Anyway, his wife died because of complications during childbirth, so poor Hannah never knew her. George has worked very hard to raise his daughter, and he does everything he can for her."

He had seemed like a doting father. He had that in his favor. Charles's own daddy had only caused grief and pain.

"What new cooking classes are you taking?" Charles asked Mama, and she waxed poetic about the new techniques she was learning and the people she'd met in her classes.

It was as they got into Charles's car that he remembered he

had to stop off at work. "Mama, I have to go to the firm for a few minutes."

"Oh, that's fine. I'd like to see your new office."

"You saw it last year when I got it."

"But then it was all bare and ugly and impersonal. I want to see what you've done to make it more homey." She beamed at him.

The smile Charles returned felt a bit sickly. He actually hadn't done anything to make his office homier, and he had a feeling it would send Mama into a Pottery Barn shopping spree.

He called Rick on his cell phone as they drove to the office. "Are you still at work?" he asked.

Rick's voice was thready and strained. "Yes. I had a bunch of papers to go through before the deposition tomorrow morning, and some idiot associate reorganized them, probably thinking that putting them in the Dewey decimal system would make it easier to find information."

"Careful, your acerbic tone is going to melt my phone."

"It'll melt some associate's behind tomorrow, that's for sure," Rick snapped. "Are you on your way here?"

"Just pulling into the parking garage."

"Well, hurry up." And he hung up the phone.

Mama's wide-eyed look as she entered his law firm always made him swell with pride. She'd sacrificed so much to help him get here, and he wanted to make her proud. He wanted to be able to make sure she would be in luxury the rest of her days because of what she had to endure at Daddy's hands for so many years. He not only owed it to her, he wanted her to have it. He wanted to give her the world.

Rick was in his office surrounded by cardboard boxes of

documents. More were piled on top of his desk. His bloodshot eyes glared at Charles above a tall stack of paper sitting in front of him. "Finally."

"Sorry, the teleporters were out of order. Mama, I think you met Rick Acker before. On good days, he's my friend."

Rick nodded at Mama with more politeness than Charles had seen him accord even to his clients. "Hello, Mrs. Britton."

"Good to see you again, Rick." Charles noted she didn't ask him to call her Vivian.

Better get her away from Rick ASAP. "What did you need again?"

"Anderson deposition."

"That's right. I'll get it for you." Charles headed toward his own office, Mama trailing him.

Even though he was in his office several hours a day, he'd never noticed the mess before—papers and folders on the small circular table in the far corner; more piled on the chairs arranged around it; papers on his desk and in the two clients' chairs opposite. He hastily swept the papers off the clients' chairs and deposited them on top of some other folders that sat on the corner of his desk. "Have a seat, Mama."

"Charles Durand Britton, I'm ashamed of you." Mama settled into the chair like an affronted queen, perching on the edge with her back ramrod straight. Her voice was sharper than a knife. "I declare, I did not raise a pig, but you work in a sty dirtier than your uncle Earl's farm."

"Uh ... sorry, Mama. I've been busy with several cases at once." He knew why Rick couldn't find the deposition—it was buried under the files Rodriguez had given to him earlier today, which Charles had tossed onto his desk to disappear among the rest of his paperwork in this sea of wood pulp.

"Let me give this to Rick, Mama, and then we can go." He caught her eyeing some of the piles on his desk. "Mama, do *not* clean up."

She harrumphed and settled back in the chair.

Charles headed to Rick's office and found him with his head bent, his eyes squeezed shut, and his fingers massaging his forehead. "Headache again?" Charles asked.

Rick immediately raised his head and scowled at Charles. "I'm fine."

"You should go home."

"I'm too far behind. Last week I took off work for my daughter's volleyball game and my son's baseball game, and both went longer than expected. Extra rallies and innings." A ghost of a smile passed across his drawn face. "They're both so good at their sports. I wouldn't have missed it for the world. But now I'm paying for it."

At moments like these, Charles remembered that beneath his barracuda exterior, Rick had a slavish devotion to his family. Last year he'd taken off an entire week of work and arranged for childcare so he could surprise his wife with a trip to Italy for her birthday. And he hated Italian food.

"Here's the Anderson deposition." Charles held out the files to him.

But Rick just stared at his desk, his eyes doing a strange jerking motion—left, right, up, down. His shoulders were tight, his neck muscles spasming.

And then suddenly he slumped in his chair, his head hitting his desk.

Thankfully, a pile of papers cushioned his fall, rather than the hard wood surface of the desk or his keyboard, but his forehead still crashed into the papers hard.

"Rick!" Charles circled the desk and righted Rick in his chair. Rick's eyes were closed, but Charles felt the man's shoulder muscles twitching beneath his fingers. His jaw was tightly closed, but saliva began to run out of the sides of his mouth.

"Mama!" Charles roared, hoping his mama would hear him all the way down the hall. Rick's door and Charles's office door were both open, so maybe . . .

He wasn't sure what to do. Should he lay Rick out on the floor?

Charles swung the chair around and put his arms under Rick's arms, pulling him to the ground with a heave and a grunt. Charles laid Rick's head gently on the carpet, then turned it to the side so his saliva would drip to the ground rather than choke him.

"What is — oh, good gracious!" Mama hurried to his side.

"Mama, stay with him while I call 9-1-1." He dialed from Rick's desk phone and got the operator immediately. He gave the operator the building's address and the firm's suite number and then switched lines so he could call the building's security guards on the ground floor to tell them about the EMTs who would arrive in a few minutes.

"Don't you worry, Mr. Britton," said Frank, one of the guards. "I'll come up with them and let them into the offices."

Rick's seizure stopped before the EMTs got there, but he didn't regain consciousness. He just lay on the floor, deathly still. Mama stroked his head gently as she sat beside him. "I'm sorry for every rude thing I ever thought about you," she said.

"I don't think he would have minded if you'd said them out loud," Charles said.

"I'm certain he would have just laughed. And that would have made me even more ornery." Her breath caught. "He's been such a good friend to you. I should have remembered that when he annoyed me."

"He's not gone yet, Mama." Charles's throat was tight.

"I know, I know. If the good Lord lets me, I'll be much nicer to him in the future."

Charles doubted Rick even noticed his mama wasn't being nice to him. Rick's thick skin and sharp tongue were what made him a successful attorney.

The EMTs got there within minutes, and Charles stepped aside as they gathered around Rick's still form. He answered their questions as best as he could.

"We're taking him to Good Samaritan," one of them said to Charles. "Do you know his family?"

"Yes. I'll call his wife." Charles's gut tightened. He didn't want to be the one to tell Annelissa, but he had to.

He and Mama headed out of the office with the EMTs, and while they were on their way to the hospital, Charles called Annelissa Acker.

"Hi, Charles. Are you with Rick at the office?" She sounded sleepy, as if he'd woken her up. With four kids still at home, she'd probably been busy all day shuffling them to their various activities.

"Annelissa . . ." A frog stuck in Charles's throat and croaked.

"Charles, what is it?" Her voice was sharper now.

"Rick collapsed at work."

"Is he —?"

"He's unconscious but still breathing. The EMTs are taking him to Good Samaritan Hospital."

"Oh, my goodness ..." She began to hyperventilate on the phone.

"Annelissa, stay calm. He's in good hands. I'm on my way there."

There was a pause, then her voice sounded businesslike and focused. "Let me call my mother to take care of the kids, and I'll meet you there." She hung up the phone with a snap. Just like her husband, she was efficient in her actions and calm in the midst of stress. Charles knew why Rick loved her so much.

They arrived at the hospital, and Charles wasn't sure what to do. He gave his mama a clueless look, and she said, "Let's see if we can check him in. Annelissa will be here soon, so we might as well see if we can get the paperwork started for her."

Mama was polite and patient with the harried nurses, although the skin around her mouth was white and strained. Charles remembered that she'd been at hospitals several times when he was young, sometimes for him or Eddie, sometimes for herself.

He cursed his daddy. He didn't feel the burning anger he used to only a year ago, but it still flickered there, muted only by hours of counseling with his pastor.

Annelissa burst through the doors to the ER, her eyes wide and red, her mouth pulled into a tight line. Charles held her in a tight embrace. "Mama started the paperwork. They only need a little more info. We can't see him just yet, though."

"What happened?" She was breathing quickly and shallowly, so Charles made her sit down on the hard plastic chair next to Mama.

"He was fine one minute — he had another headache — and then he suddenly had a seizure." It had happened so fast. Charles had been quipping with Rick as usual, talking about Rick's workload, and then it had all changed in the blink of an eye. What had been the last thing Charles had said to Rick? "Go home"? "You're working too hard"? No, it had been more work. "Here's the Anderson deposition." More things for Rick to catch up on.

Annelissa was weeping silently, Mama's arm around her. "I kept telling him to slow down," she said, her voice thick. "I told him I didn't care if he never made senior partner. He's been working so hard lately."

And suddenly Charles had a vision of Tessa there, weeping for him, saying, "He's been working so hard lately."

He had to close his eyes and turn his head. It would never be Tessa there.

"He'll be fine," Mama said soothingly. "We called the ambulance right away."

"I spoke to him only a couple hours ago," Annelissa said. "How could this happen so fast?"

Charles sat next to her and automatically put his arm around her, but his mind was whirling. "I don't know," he said numbly. "I don't know."

Chapter **8**

I don't like this," Tessa said to George as she drove the Suburban to the departures terminal of the San Francisco airport.

"We get it," Hannah said from the backseat. "You don't need to say it a million times."

"It would help if your father would actually listen to his bodyguard," Tessa said. "At first we thought the threat was just to you, but now we're not so sure. I don't like him going down to LA without us, even if the studio did send a guard. He's only there to protect your dad from the crowds, not from potential killers."

"I'll be fine." George searched the sidewalk, which was milling with people dragging suitcases behind them. "There he is."

The bodyguard hired by the studio was easy to spot. He was extremely large and looked very intimidating as he stood on the sidewalk waiting for them.

"Whoa," Hannah said. "He's got shoulders like the Incredible Hulk."

He did look quite Hulk-y, with a wide upper body and thick corded neck that reminded Tessa of MMA fighter Brock Lesnar.

"I guess you'll be safe with him." She pulled the Suburban up in front of him.

"Mr. Mynheir, I'm Brody," the man said as George got out of the front seat.

George shook his hand. "Nice to meet you."

"I have our tickets, so if you'll follow me?"

George turned to his daughter, who had climbed out of the backseat of the Moose, and gave her a gigantic hug. "Listen to what Tessa tells you."

"Unlike your father," Tessa added.

"I'll be fine. I have a bodyguard from the studio," George said. "Besides, you need to follow up on those leads and find the man who followed Charles and talked to Hannah. You can't do it if you and Hannah come with me to Los Angeles for the show this week. I'd be a bad father if I didn't ask you to try to figure out who's after my daughter."

"You're a great father, Dad," Hannah said. "Even if you do stick me with this super-paranoid bodyguard."

Tessa watched them hug each other again, and a fist clenched around her heart. Her father used to hug her like that, but he hadn't loved her enough to stay out of trouble. He'd left either because it was too dangerous or because he just wasn't happy with their family anymore, or he'd been killed. Whatever his reasons, he hadn't loved his family enough to make good choices. And Tessa hated him for it.

She hadn't even thought of him much until that email. Now suddenly she couldn't stop this burning in her lungs when she thought of him. Maybe it was because George loved Hannah so much, and it made her both miss and hate her own father.

With one last kiss to Hannah's cheek, George left them to

head to Los Angeles for the next episode of *Grab the Mic*. Tessa didn't like it, but George was right—Hannah was in more danger than he was, and Tessa needed to be here in the Bay Area to try to figure out who that scruffy man was. But she intended to do that as fast as she could so she could move Hannah down to LA.

They climbed back into the Moose as soon as George was out of sight, Hannah sliding into the passenger seat. "Are we going to our new hotel now?"

"Nope." Tessa fired up the engine and pulled away from the curb, noting the cars around them. "We're going to see Itchy."

"What?"

"My cousin Ichiro. He, er ... has connections."

"Oh, is Ichiro a yakuza?" Hannah asked nonchalantly.

Tessa's hands jerked on the steering wheel, and she had to yank it back to the right to keep from ramming the car next to her. "What are you talking about?"

"Oh, please." Hannah rolled her eyes. "As soon as Dad hired you, I checked you out on the Internet. I liked your old look better, but black leather is so out of fashion right now."

"Does your father know about me?"

"Of course."

And he apparently didn't have an objection.

Hannah continued, "But when I told him, he already knew because Elizabeth St. Amant had told him."

Of course.

"Hey." Hannah suddenly sat up straighter in her seat. "Are the yakuza behind the gambling and the show being rigged?"

She was too smart for her own good. "I don't know."

"So then why would Ichiro know anything?"

"Even if it's not the yakuza behind the gambling, Itchy will still have contacts I can talk to about who may have hired that guy."

Tessa drove to the Excelsior District of San Francisco. Not the hippest place to live, but Itchy lived in his grandmother's old house, and even if he sold it, he hadn't yet saved enough to move to a condo in a new, cooler, more expensive neighborhood in San Francisco. Tessa doubted he'd ever move, since most of the money he earned working for Uncle Teruo went to his car, his clothes, his car, his home theater, his car, his liquor cabinet, and his car.

She pulled up in front of his house and saw his new BMW in the narrow carport that ran alongside the building. Most of the houses here had only a one-car driveway, or the house had been remodeled, taking over the driveway space completely, which forced the residents to park along the street. Finding parking for Tessa's massive SUV was like trying to shove a large person into a girdle.

With Hannah on the sidewalk spotting her, Tessa managed to squeeze in between a Lexus and a Honda without accidentally bumping into either car. Then they climbed the stairs to the front door of the house and knocked.

No answer.

Tessa promptly went back to the sidewalk and knocked on the sidewalk-level window to the basement. "Itchy!" she called.

Still no answer, but Tessa bent closer and heard faint video-game sounds from behind the closed, curtained window.

"Itchy, I know you're in there!"

"Don't you ever call before you come?" he called out peevishly.

"It would help if you picked up your phone."

"I was busy."

"With what? Extra-sexy zombies you had to obliterate to save the planet?"

She heard him clump up the stairs, so she led Hannah back up the staircase just as he swung open the wooden front door. "I was up late last night, and I was unwinding," he said with a sniff.

"I'll let you go back to unwinding in a minute." Tessa entered his house and closed the door behind Hannah, gagging a little on the smell of stale pizza coming from the open pizza boxes that were sitting on the coffee table in Itchy's living room. Dust lay thick on his couch, on the lamp and side table next to it, and on the shelves packed with Blu-ray DVDs next to the massive flat-screen HDTV mounted on the far wall. The television had, naturally, been meticulously wiped clean of dust.

"I don't want to hear it," Itchy said quickly. "Mom already came by last week to complain."

"I'm surprised she didn't clean."

"She left when I suggested it." Itchy gave a toothy grin, then eyed Hannah warily. "Who's that?"

"My client's daughter."

Itchy's deceptively sleepy eyes were bloodshot, and Tessa suspected his evening activities—probably all illegal—had kept him out until the early morning hours, and he probably hadn't even gotten any sleep yet. He was barefoot—which she couldn't understand considering the nasty things smeared on the dingy carpet—so she towered over him more than usual.

"What do you need?" he asked.

He must have been about to head to bed. Hopefully he

wouldn't stiff her on the information she needed. "Who would I talk to about hiring a ..." She glanced at Hannah, who was looking in disgust at the open Chinese take-out boxes on the windowsill. Best not to use the words *hit man*. " ... an investigator who wasn't from California?"

"No connection?"

To the yakuza, he meant. "Yeah."

He scratched his head, which had started to wilt despite the enormous amount of gel that usually kept it in fashionable spikes. "I'd go to Nez."

"Seriously?" What would a restaurant manager know about out-of-state hit men?

"He has, er ... family in Seattle."

Ah. Tessa hadn't known that. The Japanese mafia didn't often interact with groups in other American cities, but it wasn't unheard of. "Do people always go to Nez when they need someone from out of town?"

"Usually." Itchy gave a wide yawn.

Tessa turned away at the atrocious smell of his breath. "Faugh. Itchy, buy a toothbrush."

"Hey, I didn't ask you to visit me before I did my nightly toilette."

"I'm impressed you even know the word *toilette*."

"I have sophisticated girlfriends."

Hannah was now peering at the underside of her shoe, and her face indicated she was three seconds away from losing her breakfast.

"Thanks, Itchy." Tessa turned to go.

"This doesn't have anything to do with that game show, does it?"

She paused and turned back to him. "What game show?"

He raised his short, square hands up. "Nothing, nothing."

She approached, glaring down at his stocky form. "Spill, Itchy, before I start cleaning your floors with your head."

He rolled his eyes. "Can't you come up with better insults? I've heard that one before."

"How about this one?" Hannah held up her phone. "Spill before I unleash a virus onto your DVR with my phone."

His eyes narrowed as they stared at her. "You can't do that."

Hannah waggled her phone. "I don't even have to plug it in."

"You'll miss *The Bachelorette* and *Rock of Love's Motel of Passion*." Tessa crossed her arms and waited.

Itchy looked pained. "You really know how to cut out a person's vital organs."

"Just hurry up and tell her so we can leave. I think I saw a rat." Hannah stalked toward the front door.

Itchy lowered his voice. "Rumor has it that 'people we both know' are betting on a reality or competition TV show."

"How about rigging the results?"

Itchy shrugged nonchalantly. "I wouldn't put it past them."

Tessa shook her head. "Itchy, this isn't anything I don't already know. Why did you think I was talking about a TV show?"

"I heard there were investigators being hired to look into the show contestants. No. Investigators. Not hit men," he said when she opened her mouth.

But the person after Hannah hadn't wanted to investigate her, had he? It had seemed more menacing than that. An investigator would certainly check out her computer, but would he follow Charles and approach Hannah face-to-face?

"Hear anything else?" she asked him.

"No, I swear."

"Can we go now?" Hannah said from the door. "Before we die from the lethally toxic black mold on the baseboards?"

His baseboards did have some rather blackish mold. "You might want to get that checked out, Itchy."

He pondered the mold. "Maybe I'll ask Mom to clean it."

"Itchy!"

"Okay, okay, I'll . . ."

"Find a home inspector," Tessa finished for him.

He looked like someone had shot his PS3. "Find a home inspector," he said glumly. "Aw, man. That means I have to clean up."

"For that, you might be able to bribe your mom."

"With what?"

"Buy her an iPad." Tessa followed Hannah out the front door. Being out in the relatively fresh San Francisco air was a relief after being in the horrific stench of Itchy's house.

"Your cousin has serious hygiene issues." Hannah climbed into the Moose as soon as Tessa unlocked the door.

"Itchy has serious issues in general." Tessa got in and started the engine.

She took the long way to Palo Alto, along I-280, which had rolling foothills cascading on either side. It had rained recently, so the hills were dark green instead of the golden brown they'd been all summer. Tessa and Hannah opened the windows and fired the heater full blast so they could enjoy the crisp fall air without freezing their fingers and toes off.

They pulled into the parking lot of Oyasumi right at the

height of lunch time. Great. Nez would be working in the kitchen, and Tessa would have to find a way to talk to him while he battled orders of *tonkatsu donburi* and *tempura udon*.

Actually, the thought of a fried pork cutlet over rice with Japanese gravy made her stomach rumble. Or maybe she wanted fat ramen noodles in fragrant broth with fried shrimp. "Hungry?" she asked Hannah.

"Japanese food?" Hannah made a face. "Do we have to?"

"What Japanese food have you ever eaten?"

"Raw fish, and I am not doing that again."

"How about some country-style Japanese home cooking? Sound better than raw fish?"

"Next you're going to tell me there's a Japanese version of biscuits and gravy."

"Wait and see."

They entered the restaurant and squirmed through the crowd of people in the foyer to reach the hostess desk. Mom wasn't at the desk, but another woman, Kakiko, was.

To say that Tessa was not Kakiko's favorite person was an understatement.

The woman's heavily mascaraed eyelashes met and clung together when she blinked at Tessa. With pinched lips, she said, "I'm sorry. We have no tables available for another *thirty years*."

Tessa was torn between clenching her jaw and rolling her eyes, so she did both. "Table for two, please," she said through clenched teeth. If they could just get seated—and she was certain Kakiko wouldn't give them one of her tables—then Tessa could flag down Nez when he made his rounds of the dining room. Or if necessary, she'd hunt him down in the kitchen, but

Nez being in arm's reach of cleavers wasn't her first choice for asking him about his "family" in Seattle.

"You're kidding, right?" Kakiko asked.

"Do I look like I'm kidding?"

Kakiko leaned forward and hissed in Japanese, "Why do you have to come here and make trouble?"

While Tessa understood Japanese, her pronunciation sounded like she had *mochi* sticky rice in her mouth, so she answered in English. "I don't make trouble."

"You got tossed out of here a year ago."

"I got tossed out by my sea-urchin-brained cousin who insulted my mother. Who still works here, in case you haven't noticed."

"And how does that relate to you showing up at lunchtime and demanding a table?"

"I'm not demanding anything. I'm asking you to put us down on the list like any other customer." Why was it that no matter how differently she phrased her words, people still assumed she was expecting yakuza privileges all the time? She wasn't asking for an immediate table at lunchtime and hadn't exactly drawn a switchblade and held it to Kakiko's saggy throat.

"You're just trying to get me in trouble," Kakiko said, still in Japanese. "If I just put you on the list, your mother will tell Nez or her brother I didn't treat you politely."

"Oh, for goodness' sake. My mom would be the first to tell you to make me wait for my own table."

Tessa wanted to just tell Kakiko to put her name down on the list and stop arguing, but she had a feeling Kakiko would take that as a threat. And Tessa supposed this was just payback for the times before she'd been arrested when she'd come in here, all swagger and insolence, and demanded preferential treatment from the overworked staff. Except now that it was widely known she was no longer working for her uncle, people felt safer in treating her as they'd always wanted to treat her—like the jerk she had been, not the new creation in Christ she was now.

Suddenly Hannah pushed her way forward. "Where's your bathroom? I reeeeeeally have to go." She bounced a bit on her toes for emphasis.

Kakiko's eyes flickered to Tessa. "She can show you," she said in English. Then to the customer standing behind them, she asked in a sugary voice, "Welcome to Oyasumi. How can I help you?"

But it was Hannah and not Tessa who led the way into the restaurant, and Hannah seemed to be searching for someone rather than making her way toward the restrooms at the back of the building. "Gosh, that lady has it in for you," she said to Tessa.

"How did you understand what she was saying?"

"I didn't, but it was pretty obvious. What'd you do, knock off her brother or something?"

Actually, now that she thought about it, she had beaten up Kakiko's second cousin once after he tried to cheat Uncle Teruo out of a large sum of money. Was that the reason Kakiko was so antagonistic?

"There she is." Hannah made a beeline toward Tessa's mom, who had just delivered an order of drinks to a table of Japanese businessmen. Mom was in her element, gently flirting with the men while maintaining a professional distance, being accommodating and attentive without being clingy or annoying. Then she turned and saw Tessa, and her expression went from strawberry candy to pickled plum.

She struggled to keep her face neutral as she approached them. "What do you want?"

"Hi, Mrs. Lancaster." Hannah almost shoved Tessa to keep her behind her as she stepped forward. "Do you remember me?"

Mom's demeanor suddenly became all smiles. "You're Hannah Mynheir, right? How nice to see you again."

"I told Dad all about this restaurant, and he said we should try it out, and if I liked it, I could take him here when he gets back from Los Angeles," Hannah lied blithely.

Tessa was surprised to feel a niggle of unease at the lie. Was she, who'd lied almost with every breath to the people she'd strong-armed, finally growing a conscience? Was this what her Bible meant when it said "Christ in me"? It was such a strange feeling.

But nice.

"But that lady at the front was really mean." Hannah put on a tragic face. "I think she doesn't like Tessa much."

Tessa expected Mom to say something sarcastic like, "I wonder why," but instead she huffed and put her hand on her hip. "Kakiko is just jealous because I always get pay raises and promotions before she does. It's because I give good customer service while she scowls at all the businessmen. I don't know why she thinks insulting my family will magically get her a raise, but there you have it."

"I thought she was still mad because I once beat up Toby Kawazaki," Tessa said.

"You did?" Mom's penciled eyebrows rose toward her jet-black-colored hairline. "I'm surprised she's not your BFF for life. She hates her second cousin."

Well, there went that idea.

"She gave your sister, Alicia, the same treatment when she

came in a few months ago to try to have a quick lunch," Mom said. "Alicia was livid because she was with her coworkers."

Oooh, Alicia livid was like the leviathan stark-raving mad. Tessa almost wished she'd been around to see that.

"Anyway, do you think you could get us a table? I'm starving." Hannah had that plaintive look only a teenager can pull off and still look cute.

"Oh, certainly. One of mine just opened up. Let me get a busboy."

She sat them at a small table still littered with the previous customers' empty plates and cups. Mom snapped her fingers at a pock-faced twentysomething guy slouching near the door to the kitchen. He slouched to their table and then slouched away with the dirty dishes. Mom herself grabbed a wet towel and wiped down the table.

One of the hostesses came by with two diners who had been waiting in the foyer, saw the table was occupied, and stood there blinking for a moment. "Oh … come with me." She turned back toward the hostess desk. "There must have been a mistake on the seating chart. I'll get you seated right away."

Mom gave them menus. "What would you like to drink?"

"Tea for me," Tessa said.

"Can I get a cosmo?" Hannah asked with a pixie smile.

Mom gave a tinkling laugh that would have been right at home in a ballroom. "Oh, you're just adorable. Ginger ale it is." She bustled away before Hannah realized exactly what she'd said.

At Hannah's dumbfounded expression, Tessa shrugged. "Remember whose mother she is."

Hannah mimicked her shrug. "You're right."

As they looked at the menu, Tessa said, "You better hope you like Japanese food."

Hannah frowned at her. "Why?"

"Because after you told my mom that corker, you *have* to bring your dad here to eat when he's back up in Northern California."

Hannah gave a long-suffering sigh. "Can't I just—"

"No."

"But even—"

"Absolutely not."

"Fine." There was copious eye rolling before Hannah scanned her menu. "What should I eat?"

"Do you like pork chops?"

"Yeah."

"*Tonkatsu donburi* is a fried pork chop on top of rice with an egg-based gravy that's kind of like a mild teriyaki sauce."

Hannah had a thoughtful look as she considered it. "Yeah, that might be okay."

"There's also shrimp *tempura*, which is deep-fried shrimp."

She shook her head. "I was never much into shrimp."

Hannah asked questions about some other things on the menu but eventually decided on the *tonkatsu donburi* while Tessa had her shrimp *tempura udon*.

After they ordered, Tessa scanned the room. Nez usually made his rounds of the dining room once an hour to ask diners how they were doing. Then he'd go back to supervising the chefs in the kitchen. She hadn't seen him yet, and it had already been thirty minutes since they'd arrived.

"Are you sure this Nez guy will talk to you?" Hannah said. "He didn't seem to like you much last time we were here."

"He's always that way. He's afraid that if he's nice, the world will come to an end."

At that moment, Nez emerged from the door to the kitchen. He approached a few tables, asking customers how they were doing, and he went to speak to a few waitresses and hostesses if the diners requested something. Then he looked up and saw Tessa at her table, staring at him.

Before Tessa could wave him over, he paled, took a sharp breath, then turned and scurried back to the kitchen.

"Oh no, you don't." Tessa leaped to her feet. "Come on, Hannah."

"But there's your mom with our food." Hannah pointed to Tessa's mom, who was headed their way with two plates.

"It'll still be here when we get back." Tessa hauled the teen up by the arm. As they dashed past Mom, Tessa said to her, "We'll be right back, Mom."

She entered the kitchen and was immediately engulfed in a warm, sticky cloud that smelled like teriyaki sauce. Voices in English and Japanese called to each other across the room, echoing against the steel counters, stoves, and ovens.

Luckily, Tessa's height allowed her to peer over the heads of the shorter cooking staff to see Nez's balding pate weaving his way back toward the freezers, darting here and there like the mouse he was named after.

Despite her desire to grab hold of Nez, Tessa kept a firm grip on Hannah's wrist as they dove into the sea of white-uniformed cooking staff. They skirted the fryer and the hot oil it was splattering into the walkway and avoided the wildly chopping knives at the prep table as peppers and celery and carrot pieces went flying like a tabletop fountain. They ducked under a couple of

staff members who were carrying two large platters of food—
probably for a large party in one of the private dining rooms—
and narrowly avoided getting scalded when a cook bumped into
another staff member who was carrying a hot tureen of miso soup.

"Nez!" Tessa pitched her voice just under a roar so Nez
couldn't say he didn't hear her.

He started, glanced back at her, then ducked behind a rolling rack holding trays on shelves.

Two doors were behind the rack—the walk-in refrigerator
and the walk-in freezer. Tessa knew he could be in either one.

"Hannah, go into the fridge." Tessa pointed to the left door.
"And make sure you slam the door really hard."

"What are you going to do?"

"Catch a mouse."

Hannah gave the door a shuddering slam that reverberated
through the small alcove, and Tessa waited outside the freezer.

As soon as the sound began to die away, the freezer door
opened and Nez emerged.

"Gah!" he squealed when he saw Tessa waiting for him.

"I might think you're trying to avoid me, Nez."

"How'd you know I was in there?"

"I didn't. I had a fifty-fifty chance. If you had been in the
fridge, you or Hannah would have come bolting out, and I'd still
have gotten you."

He frowned at her and crossed his arms just as Hannah
emerged from the fridge. "What do you want?" he asked gruffly.
"I'm busy."

"Obviously. Checking the freezer for rotten food?"

"None of your business. I have to get back to work." He tried
to move past her, but Tessa planted herself firmly in his path.

No, she wasn't her uncle's enforcer anymore, but she still knew how to stand intimidatingly.

Nez knew her well enough to know she wouldn't actually do anything, but he still stopped, which was what she wanted him to do. "Look—"

"I know you can't say anything," Tessa said. "I'm not here to get you in trouble."

"That's what they all say," he muttered.

"Did anyone ask you to hire an investigator from out of town?" Tessa fished in her pocket and took out the printed photo of the scruffy man, but Nez swatted her hand away.

"Don't show me anything," he snapped. "Are you trying to get me in trouble? All I give them is a name, and they do the rest—making contact, arranging the contract."

"Anyone recently?"

His gaze was as sharp as a bamboo skewer. "Are you really dumb enough to think I'd tell you?"

"Nez," Tessa said quietly. "I need to know if I might be involved in my uncle's business, or if it's just some other chump."

He sighed and looked away.

"Nez, the last thing I want to do is get in the middle of something. I did once, and we only got out by the skin of our teeth."

Nez shook his head. "Not your uncle."

She loosed a long, slow breath. "Good."

"But it's still yakuza."

Her breath turned to putty in her throat. It took her a moment to clear it. "One of his *kobun*?"

"I don't know who. It was all through phone calls, but the man mentioned a television show about singing." Nez's gaze flickered to Hannah. "I recognized her as soon as I saw her."

"How'd you know it was one of Uncle's men?"

Nez's eyes were wary, but he met her gaze. "Everyone calls me Nez or Nezuyabu. Only your uncle ever calls me Nezumi. It was my nickname when he and I were growing up. Only his family—you and your mom—and his captains would know he refers to me as Nezumi."

"And the man who phoned you called you Nezumi."

He nodded, and his hand reached out to grasp Tessa's forearm. "Don't get involved in this, Tessa. If this man is going against your uncle, you want to be as far away from this as you possibly can."

Chapter 9

You couldn't at least get a hotel with wireless Internet?" Hannah complained as Tessa unlocked the door to their new room.

"Logging on to wireless Internet kind of defeats the purpose of being under the radar."

"It's not like we're going into the wilderness to live off the land."

"Keep up your smart mouth, and I will take you to a cabin in the mountains. I know exactly which snakes you can eat without being poisoned."

Hannah turned a little green as she dropped her backpack on her bed, a bouncy little thing with a stained orange-soda-colored bedspread. "Let me guess. You tried out for *Survivor*."

"Twelve times before I went to prison. I could have won." Tessa was about to drop her overnight bag on the avocado-green vinyl chair in the corner of the room, but noticed a dark brown, crusty stain on the seat. Instead, she laid the bag on the other bed in the room. She went to close the mustard-yellow canvas drapes but peered out the window as she did so, noting the cars in the hotel parking lot. Two of them had weeds growing out of their flat tires, and the third was a flashy red Mustang she would have definitely noticed on the road if it had been within fifty feet of her car.

"Can't we go somewhere I can get online?" Hannah whined.

"You're not posting your location on Facebook, are you?"

"Of course not. But all my friends think I'm a total loser because I haven't answered any of their posts."

"Hmm, let's weigh those two options." Tessa held up both hands, palms up. "Explain to friends later that you went dark because you hacked into the studio server, or die from an assassin who wants to keep you from talking about the fact the show is rigged. Tough choice."

"You don't have to put it quite like that."

"Oh yes I do, if you're going to insist that you'll lose all your friends if you don't get onto Facebook."

"How about if I log on to my computer in Oakland?" Hannah's eyes brightened. "They already know that computer's IP address, so it's not like it'll give away my location."

"You really think they're not going to hire someone to try to figure it out if you log on again?"

"They weren't smart enough to notice my webcam was videotaping that guy who was checking out my computer. Besides, what if someone else has checked out my computer since then? The webcam is still set up to record."

"Absolutely not."

Hannah pouted and flopped onto the bed. A cloud of dust shot up from the bedspread, sending them both into coughing fits.

"This place is awful!" Hannah wailed. "I would totally leave a bad review on Yelp if I hadn't lost my password ..." She suddenly froze. Turned deathly pale. "Oh, my gosh. I totally forgot ..."

Twitchy tendrils of panic started to jitter in Tessa's arms and legs. "Forgot what?"

"My computer at home has all the information about this laptop." Hannah pointed to the laptop on the bed. "I bought it online a few months ago. My desktop has this computer's IP address, my passwords, everything."

For someone as smart as Hannah, that seemed pretty stupid. "So anyone can log on to your computer and find that info?"

"No, no. Sensitive stuff like that is hidden in a special folder tucked away in the utilities with a bogus extension and—" Hannah broke off with an annoyed twist to her mouth as she stared at Tessa. "I completely lost you."

"Like a hiker on Mount Everest." And Tessa had thought she'd been doing a good job hiding her utter confusion.

"Okay, well, here's the fourth-grade version. The information is hidden, so no one except an experienced hacker would even be able to look for it, and it would still take time to crack the passwords. But I think I should log on to my computer through my back door and get that info off the hard drive."

Tessa regarded her with narrowed eyes. "You just want to log on to your computer and jump on the Internet."

"No. I just want to get out of this asbestos-clogged hotel room from the 1960s and smell me some nice clean Starbucks instead."

Tessa eventually gave in after Hannah spent a half hour explaining how no one could track back to her laptop, drawing numerous pages of diagrams that looked like maps to the Holy Grail for all Tessa could tell. But she didn't give in to the

Starbucks plea, and instead they drove to a quiet residential neighborhood so Hannah could scan for an unsecured wireless network.

"Got one."

Tessa nudged the Moose to the curb in front of a blue house with dark blue trim and lots of cobwebby juniper bushes in the front yard. And not the fake cobwebs from Halloween, either. Hopefully the spiders wouldn't crawl into the SUV. Tessa wasn't afraid of spiders, but spider bites were completely unnecessarily painful and annoying.

"Okay, I'm in my Oakland computer," Hannah said. "Hey, there's another video."

"Same guy or someone else?"

"I don't know yet. Let me downlo—" Her laptop screen suddenly began flashing as thousands of numbers scrolled past. "Whoa." She started typing like crazy. "This is awesome."

It didn't look very awesome to Tessa. In fact it looked like someone was trying to hack into her computer. "What's happening?"

"Someone's trying to hack into my computer."

"What? That's not awesome. That's terrible." Tessa started the Moose's engine with a vicious crank. "We're getting out of here."

"No, wait. This is actually a good thing."

"How is it a good thing that someone is invading your computer and discovering your location?"

Hannah gave a frustrated sigh. "I told you. No one can find my location."

Tessa thrust a hand toward the laptop screen doing the electric light show. "That looks like they found you to me."

"No, they set up ... hang on."

Tessa wanted to snap, "Don't tell me to hang on!" but held on to her temper. Just barely.

Suddenly the screen went black. "Aw, bummer," Hannah said.

"Please tell me you didn't just announce to every illegal gambler in the state of California that you're here in Blossom Valley, San Jose, with the email evidence that could get you killed."

Hannah gave her a sidelong look that spoke volumes about her low opinion of Tessa's IQ. "Someone set up a computer that would try to hack into my laptop as soon as I tried to log into my Oakland computer."

"So far none of this has any of that awesomeness you were talking about a few minutes ago."

"It was just a program, not a person, so I was able to hold off the attack pretty easily. But what I could also do was hack into that other computer myself." Hannah did a preening raise-the-roof motion with her hands and shoulders. "I am so brilliant I surprise myself."

"Your ego is taking away my airspace," Tessa said drily.

"Be ready to be amazed." Hannah hit a few keys on her keyboard, and the most horrible-looking spreadsheet appeared on her screen.

"Yaaaah! What's that?" Tessa shuddered at the mass of numbers.

"I think it's an accounting spreadsheet. Whoever set up the hack hadn't fully erased it from the hard drive of the computer that was trying to break into my laptop."

"The computer that *broke into your laptop*."

Hannah waved a negligent hand. "It didn't get anything important."

"Define 'anything important.'"

"I made sure it only got my iTunes song list."

"Oh." Okay, that wasn't anything important. "It didn't steal back the email evidence you had, did it?"

"Oh no. I put that on a flash drive ages ago. And I overrode the storage on my computer so no one could recover it too. That is why I am a genius. Up top." She raised her hand to Tessa.

Tessa stared at her.

"Oh, come on. High five."

"You just took five years off my life." Ignoring Hannah's raised hand, Tessa gunned the engine. "You ought to be spanked."

～ ❧ ～

"Hey buddy, how're you doing?" Charles entered Rick's hospital room and immediately saw that Rick was not in his right mind at all.

For one thing, he was watching an entertainment television show, *Entertainment Bay Area*. Charles knew Rick detested entertainment TV and would rather skim the comics section of the newspaper.

However, Annelissa was sitting next to him, and Rick had often lamented her secret crush on the show's anchor.

Somehow, the memory didn't seem funny just now.

Rick's eyes were barely at half-mast, and he breathed very slowly.

"Is he okay?" Charles asked.

"When he finally regained consciousness, he had terrible headaches," Annelissa said. "The doctors had to put him on morphine for the pain." She hesitated, then said, "Charles, sit down."

He sat, and his stomach dropped to his feet too. "What is it?"

"The scans came back. Rick has a brain tumor."

Disbelief. Charles couldn't speak for almost a minute. "No, that can't be right. He's only forty-one."

"That's why they're hopeful." She paused. "But it's inoperable, and it's very aggressive. Fast growing."

The words were horrible. Hollow and horrible.

"They're going to start chemo as soon as possible," she said. "They want to do something to relieve his headaches first."

He looked at his friend. "Should I ... talk to him?"

Annelissa nodded sadly, although her eyes were bright. "I think he'd like that."

"Oh, I almost forgot." Charles passed her the small bouquet of flowers Mama had insisted he buy, even though he told her that Rick detested flowers.

But now he was glad, because Annelissa gave a delighted smile. "Oh, gerbera daisies. I love these."

"Sorry, Annelissa, my taste isn't that good. My mama picked them out."

"Well, tell her thanks from me. Rick wouldn't have even cared for these, but I feel bad that I had to give some lilies your coworkers brought to the nurses because they made my allergies act up."

Charles winced. "Sorry to hear that." He took a deep breath and turned to Rick. What to talk about? What would Rick want to talk about?

That was easy. Work.

"Hey, so I finally had to talk to Fisher Daley today. I know you joked that he was like a human computer, but I never believed you until today. I needed to hire him to look over some accounting spreadsheets one of my clients found. And for the amount of money that forensic accountant charges the firm, Daley better do a stellar job."

Daley's expenses technically came out of what Teruo Ota paid for Tessa's retainer fee, which made Charles a little uncomfortable after what she'd told him about one of Teruo's captains being involved in the gambling without telling Teruo. But if they found solid evidence of who was behind the betting on the television show, Tessa said she'd feel more comfortable talking to her uncle about it. Until then, she didn't want to say anything to him because it could make things uncomfortable for everyone involved, including her.

Charles faltered. What else could he say to Rick? His eyes wandered to the television, and he was surprised to see Hannah at the San Francisco airport.

"Do you see that?" Charles pointed to the television screen. "That's one of my clients."

"Hannah Mynheir?" Annelissa asked.

"Yeah. And her dad."

"What do they . . ." Annelissa cut herself off with a chagrined look. "My bad, I know you can't talk about this. Rick would meow whenever I did that, because curiosity killed the cat." She tried to smile, but it was strained.

"Uh . . . that's Hannah's bodyguard."

"The man in the leather jacket?" A tall, lanky man with a goatee stood a few feet away from Hannah. He turned and helped a young girl out of the car he was standing next to.

"No, the woman." The cameraman had tried to get a shot of Hannah's bodyguard, but all they could see was Tessa's back.

However, the backpack slung over her shoulder had caused her shirt to ride up, and the audience could see a glimpse of a colorful dragon tattoo marching across her lower back.

Great. Charles hoped no one would see the tattoo and automatically think yakuza, and then put two and two together. Then again, no one could see her face, and even then, since Tessa was only half Japanese, she didn't look very Asian. At least not Asian enough to scream "Japanese mafia."

"She's such a little thing." Annelissa nodded toward Tessa's slight figure as she ushered Hannah into the airport.

The entertainment reporter was saying, "A lot of security for George Mynheir's thirteen-year-old daughter, Hannah. Several weeks ago, there were rumors that a group of fans snuck into the studio and hid in the stage props, intending to jump out during the live performance. Studio security found them only minutes before *Grab the Mic* went live. Fans fought back, and contestant Jannelle Wilder got clipped in the jaw by a flying fist." The video flipped to a photo of Jannelle singing at the performance that night, one side of her face obviously slightly swollen despite the makeup. "With that kind of violence happening, it's no wonder George has hired a bodyguard for his daughter. George, the oldest contestant on *Grab the Mic*, is currently the unexpected fan favorite after being the clear underdog in the first rounds."

Charles turned to Rick. "When George comes back to the Bay Area — assuming he isn't voted off this week — I'll bring him here and introduce you, just because I know it'll annoy you."

Rick didn't respond, but Annelissa gave a small smile.

Charles suddenly realized that while it was possible, in his drug-induced haze, that Rick couldn't hear him, Charles could at least try to amuse Annelissa and keep her hopes up. It had to have been a difficult week, finding out about the brain tumor. Entertaining Rick's stressed wife was the least Charles could do.

"I'm still faithfully going through that list of women you gave to me," he said to Rick with a dramatic sigh. "I'm tempted to say you gave me that list as a practical joke."

Annelissa gave a real smile now. "He asked me for help on that list of potential dates."

"He promised me that they were all, quote, 'excellent candidates.'" Charles made quotation gestures with his hands and lifted his eyebrows ironically.

"How many dates have you had?"

"Two. The first one was Marcy, an office manager for an investment firm. All she talked about was stocks and investors I didn't know, and she laughed like a horse every thirty seconds, no matter what she'd said."

Annelissa winced.

"Yes, it was that bad," Charles said. "What was worse, she didn't even laugh when I told something genuinely funny. My Yoda-and-ice-cream joke got barely a grimace from her."

Annelissa rolled her eyes. "Your Yoda-and-ice-cream joke only gets giggles from my youngest, and that's because he's nine."

"So maybe our senses of humor aren't on the same wavelength. My next date was Kayla."

"And how did that go?"

"Kayla was ... okay."

Annelissa gave a wary look. "Define 'okay.' Was she pretty?"

"Gorgeous. Long blonde hair—real blonde, by the way. Big blue eyes. Sweet face. And she was a complete terrorist."

Annelissa burst into laughter, which she stifled with her hand. "What makes you say that?"

"Oh, she wasn't a Muslim extremist or anything sinister like that. But she insisted that city funds are being illegally shunted to road repair when they should be going to saving the magic mushroom wildland."

Annelissa's eyes widened, and she had absolutely nothing to say in response.

"That was my reaction too," Charles said. "Kayla went on to talk about her pet project. By day she's a tax preparer, and by night she's the Mushroom Miss."

Annelissa looked like she wasn't sure whether to laugh or cry.

"Her words, not mine," Charles said. "She's forming a coalition of like-minded citizens called the Citizens for Stability, Not Tyranny."

Annelissa's eyebrows furrowed. "I don't see what that has to do with magic mushrooms."

Charles threw his hands out. "Neither did I, but I wasn't about to argue. I was trying to get the waiter to give me the check. However, before we parted ways, I pointed out that her coalition could have the acronym C-SNoT. And then I ran for it."

Annelissa snorted with laughter. When she caught her breath, she said, "You're making that up."

"I testify that I am telling the truth, the whole truth, and nothing but the truth, so help me God."

At that moment, a nurse knocked on the door. "Mrs. Acker, I'm here to prep your husband for his next scan."

Charles stood. "I'll leave. I have to get to my marathon running club anyway."

"That sounds fun. Rick told me about it." Annelissa reached out to hug him. "Thanks for stopping by."

His throat was a bit tight as he said, "I'll be by again tomorrow."

As he drove to the community center where his running group met, Charles couldn't stop the trembling that seemed to start near his heart and eventually overtook his arms and hands.

Cancer. How could a word be so frightening?

And seeing Rick that way ... Charles had been joking with him only a week ago. Rick was healthy. He worked out at the gym regularly—he was more consistent than Charles had been before he joined his running group. It was as if ... as if God had struck him down.

That was ridiculous. God didn't strike people down. And why would he take Rick this way? Sure, Rick was a firm atheist, but he was a good father, a kind man. A good friend.

And Charles had never had time to tell him that. Or to tell him about Christ. He had always meant to, waiting for a good moment that never came. Even if Rick just scoffed at him, Charles knew it wouldn't affect their friendship. So why hadn't he ever said anything?

No, Rick was going to be okay. He had to be. The doctors were hopeful.

Charles parked and headed to the track, unzipping his warm-up jacket and slipping off his track pants over his running shoes. The air was brisk despite the fact it was noon, and the sun shone feebly through a few scattered clouds.

The group gathered at the far end of the track, some people stretching quickly. Jeff, the group leader, insisted stretching could increase injury, so those who chose to ignore him tried to do it before he arrived. Others were doing slow warm-up jogs.

Charles tossed his pants on a bench next to several other jackets and pants and prepared to do a series of warm-up exercises he'd recently read about in a running magazine. Then he spotted Steven Nishimoto.

The tall half-Asian man had the regal bearing of a prince and the lean, muscular physique of a man half his age. His shaved head bobbed up and down as he did some crunches on the grass.

Charles made his way over to do his pre-run exercises near Steven. The two men nodded, and then each continued preparing for the run.

Now that he was here, Charles wasn't sure what to say. If he were in the courtroom, he would know exactly what he needed to say to sway the jury. If he were with a client, he would know how to give sensible advice. If he were with his mama, he'd probably just keep his mouth shut and let her talk.

But how did he somehow start chitchat with this man, who was not only powerful but was also twenty years older than Charles? What did they have in common? And talking about work was out.

Well, it was a running group, wasn't it?

"What time are you aiming for in the marathon?" Charles asked him.

Steven looked up at him, not in a "Don't talk to me before I've had my coffee" way, but more in an "I need to think on that a bit" way. Finally he answered, "Well, that's a bit complicated."

"How so?"

"When I ran my best marathon time, I was forty-one, and I ran it in two hours, forty-seven minutes."

Whoa. Charles tried to keep his face neutral rather than freaking out. The man was a running machine.

"But when I ran my last marathon, I'd just come off of knee surgery, and I was forty-seven. I ran it in three hours, fifty-eight minutes. Since then I've been too busy and have stopped running."

"After running marathons? You didn't miss it?"

"Not really, if you can believe it." Steven rose to his feet. "But now that I'm about to turn fifty-five, I decided to start running again. So honestly, I don't know how long it's going to take me. I just want to run at least one more marathon in my lifetime, even if I have to crawl over the finish line."

Charles nodded, although privately he didn't want to finish quite that badly. He was okay being taken to the finish line by ambulance rather than on bloody feet.

"How about you?" Steven asked.

"I was never athletic," Charles admitted. His jaw clenched in automatic reaction to the memory of his daddy's scornful words every time he tried some school sport. "But my friend Rick ..." His throat tightened, and he needed to swallow. "Rick noticed I was getting pudgy around the middle and challenged me to do something I never thought I could do. I figured running a marathon was one of those things you think might be nice to do, but you never get off your butt to actually do it. So I joined Jeff's running group." He shrugged. "I'll be happy just to finish, I guess."

Steven suddenly smiled, and laugh lines crinkled around his hazel eyes. "You know, that's a great attitude to have. Our society says men have to achieve specific things to feel we measure up, but we're the ones who choose to try to attain those standards."

Charles hadn't realized Steven had such a philosophical bent. He only knew him from press interviews and product unveilings, the CEO appealing to a new technologically minded generation.

"Personal satisfaction is unique to each person," Steven said. "I think I forget that."

"So now what's your time goal?" Charles said.

Steven laughed. "I think I'll just try to finish without injury. I've had at least one injury for every marathon I've run."

"How many is that?"

At that moment, Jeff came sprinting across the field, his baseball cap on his nearly bald head and a bright smile on his face. "Sorry I'm late. Ready to go?" He led the group into a slow warm-up jog.

Steven fell into step next to Charles. "Eighteen," he answered. "Eighteen marathons."

"When did you start running?"

They chatted about running when they could during the session, which was a short run with some speed-work exercises. Steven had a wealth of information that Charles soaked up, things he hadn't gleaned from the couple of running books he'd read.

They were stretching on the grass at the end of the session when Steven said, "You mentioned your friend Rick got you to start running. Does he run too?"

The memory of Rick's face, lax and drugged up only a short hour or two ago, made it difficult for Charles to answer quickly. Finally he said, "No, Rick just goes to the gym."

There was an awkward silence between them, and Charles felt a strange urge to tell this stranger about the short fifteen minutes he'd spent at the hospital before driving here. "Rick's in the hospital now. He collapsed a week ago. The doctors found out he has a brain tumor."

Steven's expression was one of genuine concern, which encouraged Charles to continue. "It happened in a flash. One minute he had a headache, the next he was seizing. I saw him at the hospital before I came here today. It made me want to run — not just to shake off my worry for him, but because I know he'd want me to do this. Before it's too late." He couldn't go on.

Steven put a firm, fatherly hand on Charles's shoulder. A brief squeeze, then release. No words needed.

"I'll see you next week." Charles was pleased that his voice sounded close to normal.

"What's your name again?" Steven held out his hand.

Charles shook it. "Charles Britton."

"Steven Nishimoto."

As if anyone in Silicon Valley wouldn't know who he was. Charles flashed a smile. "I know." Then he scooped up his warm-up jacket and track pants and headed toward his car.

He was pleased about how he'd ended the conversation. Not cloying or clingy. But what had possessed him to share about Rick? He wanted Steven to think of him as suave and cool like the Bachelor, not weepy and emotional like the Bachelorette.

But he'd made contact. Hopefully if Charles could keep from spilling his guts to Steven, it would grow into a friendship outside of the running group.

Guilt dug into his stomach like a sharp stick. Today he had genuinely liked the man for who he was, not for his money, his company's innovative technology products, or the glamour of basking in his fame. Charles didn't want to have an agenda when he made friends.

But he had to. He had to make something of himself.

Before it was too late.

Chapter 10

She would rather have been gutting squid.

Tessa slouched lower in her chair as one of the *Grab the Mic* contestants practiced her song on the big stage. She kept missing the high note, and the screech had started climbing up Tessa's back like a centipede. With claws.

She was so bored.

She glanced around at the other contestants' families who sat near them in the seats of the studio audience. The padded theater seats were comfortable, sure, but not comfortable enough for her to take a nap—not that she could relax her vigilance, anyway. High above, the domed ceiling, painted an inky black, winked with colored lights that cast rainbow spotlights over the audience—if there had been an audience.

George had already sung a rather slow but passionate rendition of "Stronger" by Mandisa, and he'd completely blown the competition away. In fact, he so intimidated his fellow contestants that the poor eighteen-year-old boy who rehearsed after him stumbled through the first few bars of his song and had to start over.

And now they were just sitting through all the other rehearsals. Tessa gave a long, gusty sigh.

"Gosh, you're just hanging on every note," Hannah remarked drily.

The contestant on stage flubbed another high note, and Tessa winced as she felt it grate along her vertebrae. "I have as much musical appreciation as an earthworm."

"How about when Dad sang to you and Charles's mom? Dad makes some girls totally freak out, and he's old enough to be Justin Bieber's father."

Tessa thought back to that evening. She'd been flustered to see Charles unexpectedly, annoyed that he'd shown up when he knew he'd already been followed once, and reluctantly amused to notice that he seemed jealous of George's charm. And George hadn't even been flirting with Tessa; he'd been flirting with Vivian, who'd lapped it up.

But the song? At one point, listening to the lyrics, she had felt a fleeting desire for it to be Charles singing to her with the passion of a man who loves a woman who hasn't yet noticed he's there. Tessa wanted to be the woman to notice him and bask in his love and tenderness. (According to Vivian, Charles couldn't hold a tune to save his life, so naturally Charles would have to serenade her with George's voice.)

And then Charles had acted like such a dweeb, and that had pretty much killed it for her. "Your dad sings really well, but since I'm not attracted to him, it was just entertaining," Tessa said honestly.

Hannah nodded sagely, looking twenty years older for a moment. "That's why I liked you from the moment we met."

Tessa thought back to that first dinner. It hadn't seemed like Hannah cared for Tessa very much at all.

"A lot of the other women Dad works with fall under this weird rock-star charm, you know? They're all like, 'Aaahhh.'" Hannah faked a swoon worthy of Scarlett O'Hara. "And they get all googly-eyed and stuff. And I'm like, 'Dude, you didn't even give him a second look before he sang to you.' Sometimes they get like that when he just smiles. I mean, he's not even that good looking. But you see him as just a client, and I appreciate that you're not being nice to me just to get close to him." She sighed heavily, as if relieved to get that off her chest.

Tessa nudged her with her elbow. "I could go after your dad, but the thought of having you as a stepdaughter sends me into hysterics."

Hannah giggled. "Trust me, if I have any say in it, Dad's second wife has to at least know what an IP address is."

"Hey, speaking of computers, why don't you show me around the studio? I'd like to see the office where you did the dastardly deed."

"Okay." Hannah jumped to her feet just as another high note pierced the air, spearing Tessa's eardrums. They hastened out of the dim auditorium, squeezing past family members who were watching the rehearsals.

"How long do rehearsals go?" she asked Hannah as they walked up the stairs that cut between two sections of seats.

"It could go for hours. Most of the parents take their little kids to McDonald's a block away because it has a playground, so I'd be left here with the grown-ups."

They pushed open the heavy double doors and emerged from the dark auditorium into a brightly lit hallway with smooth white floors and cream-colored walls that were adorned with plaques, awards, and portraits of wealthy-looking old men. In one direction was the studio entrance and reception area, but Hannah led Tessa the other way, then immediately through a door on the right, which led to a stairwell.

They hoofed it up four flights of stairs. Twice someone entered the stairwell below them, but when Tessa leaned over the metal railing to peer down, both times the person exited the stairwell on one of the floors below.

She and Hannah emerged into a hallway, this one carpeted in beige. It had vanilla-colored walls hung with pastel landscapes. Several doors lined the left side of the hallway, and many had windows so people could see inside.

However, only one door was along the right side of the hallway, approximately halfway down. It didn't have a window, and there was a monstrous keypad alongside the door.

"That's the room where the computers tally the results?" Tessa guessed.

"Yup. You need the right ten-digit key code to enter. One of the admins told me that if you enter the wrong key code three times, it sounds an alarm in the security office downstairs."

"And you call me paranoid."

"You *are* paranoid. I can't believe you thought that old lady in the security line at the airport was trying to pickpocket me."

"You didn't see her. Her hand was inching toward you. Just because she looks old and fragile doesn't mean she isn't an accomplished pickpocket."

They headed to the end of the hallway, where they walked through a set of double doors that led into a second hallway, which led straight ahead before branching to the left. Hannah turned left and then tried the second office door on the right. It was locked.

"This is it?" Tessa peered through the window in the door and saw an austere office with a small plant and a single picture frame on the desk next to a computer monitor, keyboard, and mouse. The shelves were neatly stacked with papers and three-ring binders that sat with their spines flush with the edge of the shelves. Each binder had been labeled with bold, squarish printing that Tessa couldn't read from this distance.

"Man, not even a paper clip on the floor," she said.

"Yeah, and the chair was uncomfortable too," Hannah said.

Suddenly the double doors behind them that led into the previous hallway opened, and a young girl came around the corner, looking lost.

She was about ten or eleven, slim-boned with a halo of flyaway brown curls on her head. She looked Asian and had small eyes and a round face. Her skin was deeply tanned.

Tessa froze.

She had seen this girl at the San Francisco airport. She had been eyeing a tall lanky man with a goatee, but then he helped this girl out of a taxi parked at the curb. Tessa had assumed it was his daughter. Or was she mistaken?

Maybe it was one of the contestant's daughters? But hadn't Hannah said she was the oldest, and all the other children here were much younger than she was?

The girl smiled as she skipped up to them. "Do you want to play with me?"

Tessa's instincts were screaming in her head. She grabbed Hannah and shoved her behind her.

The girl's eyes hardened, and she paused mid-skip.

This gave Tessa the opportunity to get a better look at the girl. Though the haircut was childish and she wore a pink princess top, pink stretch pants, and white-and-pink sneakers, her face was older. She was actually probably in her twenties, but the costume effectively hid her age.

And the switchblade she pulled out was definitely not a princess wand.

Tessa realized that in shoving Hannah behind her and taking up a fighting stance, she'd given herself away. The woman was a professional and recognized Tessa's actions as those of another professional, not Hannah's aunt or cousin. The woman would also realize that if she wanted Hannah, she'd have to go through Tessa first.

The woman leaped forward and attacked.

Tessa dodged and parried, but she had to be careful because she didn't have a weapon. She was quick, but this woman was quicker and lighter on her feet. Also, Tessa wasn't used to fighting opponents who were less than four feet tall, and it took her precious moments to get used to the height difference.

Tessa managed a sharp jab into the woman's chin, but she didn't withdraw fast enough, and the blade slashed her forearm. Tessa lashed out with an elbow that collided with the woman's temple, and the woman staggered back.

Suddenly a stapler flew past Tessa's shoulder, and the woman had to whip out a hand to deflect it from her head. The stapler was followed by a pen cup and a volley of pencils.

Hannah had found an open office nearby and was grabbing whatever was on the desk and throwing it at the tiny assassin. Tessa used Hannah's distraction to rush back toward the office, dragging Hannah, who had run out of ammunition, with her.

Tessa picked up a padded chair and used it to stop the knife the assassin had thrown from stabbing her in the shoulder. The knife sank into the seat and lodged there.

Tessa slammed one of the aluminum legs of the chair into the woman's forehead. The attacker stumbled backward.

Tessa pressed her advantage, swinging the chair like a battering ram while continuing to use it as a shield. She followed this with a few kicks to the side of the woman's knee and thigh. The kicks apparently startled the attacker, because her knee buckled slightly with the first blow, and her thigh tightened with the second.

Tessa kept backing her up until they had reached the bend of the hallway, where the double doors led into another hallway. "Go!" she shouted to Hannah, and then dropped into a sweeping leg kick to knock the woman off her feet. She lost control of the chair, which listed sideways, and a sharp kick of the woman's foot sent it flying just out of reach.

Tessa flew on top of the woman, catching her in a grappling stance and grabbing hold of her arm. She struggled to get her into an armbar, but the woman scrambled and twisted like a cat, scratching at Tessa's face and neck, raining sharp blows on Tessa's head with her little fists.

Then, suddenly, an ear-splitting alarm resounded down the hallway.

The woman froze, then twisted out of Tessa's grip. She was on her feet in a millisecond and sprinted down the hallway.

Tessa let her go. She turned to look for Hannah.

The teen ran through the double doors toward her, red lights flashing on the walls of the hallway behind her.

"How did you sound the alarm?" Tessa shouted.

"I entered random numbers in the keypad of that superse-cret room to activate the alarm."

Smart girl.

"I didn't know it would be so loud." Hannah covered her ears with her hands.

The security guards came charging toward them a few min-utes later, and mercifully the alarm shut off a minute after that, but Tessa's ears were still ringing.

First they had to make it clear that they had not been trying to break into the computer room. Tessa explained about the tiny woman who had attacked them with a switchblade.

"Are you sure it was a switchblade?" asked a dubious guard. He eyed the stapler and pencils on the floor where Hannah had thrown them. "Are you sure it wasn't a letter opener?"

Since she couldn't exactly confess that she was quite profi-cient with a switchblade and would never mistake a letter opener for one, Tessa pointed to the discarded chair, which still had the blade stuck in the cushioned seat.

"Do you know why she'd do that?" the guard asked.

Tessa glanced at Hannah quickly, then shrugged. "We really don't know. We wonder if maybe we interrupted her when she was trying to get into an office. Or the computer room."

Which really wasn't true, but she could imagine how well it would have sounded if she'd said something like, "Actually, someone here at the studio is rigging the results, and since my young partner in crime here hacked into the system, she was accidentally sent evidence of it."

The guards might not have believed her story if Tessa hadn't had the deep slice in her forearm, clearly an injury she couldn't have done to herself very easily.

They finally allowed Tessa to go find a first-aid kit when she pointed out she was bleeding all over the nice beige carpet.

"Gosh, I thought they were going to try to have you arrested," Hannah said. "I don't know why they kept ignoring me when I told them to check their video feed to see the woman enter and leave the building."

"They'll have to, since they have the switchblade." Tessa grimaced as she applied an alcohol swab to the cut. One of the guards had grudgingly shown her to a staff break room, where a first-aid kit was under the sink. "You'll have to apply the gauze and tape," she told Hannah.

"She wasn't wearing gloves, was she?"

"No. But that doesn't mean her fingerprints are in the system. Besides, it'll take weeks before they even scan her prints and compare it with the database."

"What do you mean? On TV, *CSI* does it in, like, seconds."

Tessa gave her a dry look. "Really? You get your information from *CSI*? They speed things up on TV, because they only have an hour. Fictional license."

"I wish I'd thought to take a picture of her with my phone." Hannah smoothed a piece of sterile gauze over Tessa's forearm.

"Wait a minute. We already have a picture of her."

"Stop moving or the tape will go on crooked." Hannah applied the adhesive tape to the gauze. "There. How do we have a picture?"

"That video clip of you at the San Francisco airport. The one we watched in the hotel after we arrived in LA. I saw that woman at the airport, on the curb with a tall man."

"I bet that clip is up on YouTube."

They used Tessa's phone and the studio wireless network to view the YouTube video. "Yup, there she is," Tessa said.

She and Hannah looked at each other. Now what?

Tessa was the adult here; she needed to come up with an answer.

She could show the photo of the couple to Nez. He might know who they were. He would probably blow a gasket when she forced him to tell her about them, and she wouldn't put it past him to spit in her miso soup the next time she ate at Oyasumi, but he would tell her.

The thing was, the man who'd been with the tiny assassin didn't look like the typical character the yakuza worked with or that an assassin would pair up with. He looked more like an accountant or a hacker.

"Let's call Charles." Tessa dialed him up and put it on speakerphone so Hannah wouldn't feel excluded.

"Charles Britton," he answered.

"It's Tessa. We were just attacked."

"What? In LA?"

"At the studio. By a very small assassin who I thought was a ten-year-old girl at first. Unfortunately, ten-year-olds don't play with switchblades."

"Are you all right?"

"I'm fine," Tessa said.

At the same time, Hannah said, "She has this wicked cut that'll turn into a cool scar."

Charles's voice rose. "You got cut?"

"It's minor."

"You should see if you need stitches—"

149

"I don't. Refocus here, Counselor."

In the brief pause, she could almost see his gaze narrowing as he glared at his phone. "Fine, I'm refocusing."

"I saw the woman and her companion at the San Francisco airport."

"SFO? You mean they followed you from NorCal?"

"I think so. They waited until we were alone at the studio, and then she followed us and attacked us."

"You mentioned a companion?"

"That's the thing. I remembered seeing her when we were on the curb about to head into the airport. She had a tall, lanky man with her, and I assumed he was her father. Now that I know he wasn't, I need to figure out who he is too."

"Hey, *Entertainment Bay Area* got video footage of you and Hannah entering the terminal. The man and woman might be in the picture."

"That's what we were thinking. The clip is up on YouTube, but it's a bit grainy."

"We don't need YouTube. I'll get the TV show to give us a copy of the video."

"They'll do that? Just because you ask nicely?"

"No, they'll do that because I'll threaten to sue them if they don't."

"What would you sue them for?"

"It doesn't matter. They'll turn the video over faster than a flapjack on a griddle." His Southern accent was getting stronger as he got more excited.

"I'm going to ask my, er, contacts to see if I can find out who the two of them are," Tessa said.

"She's going to ask criminals," Hannah interjected.

"Be quiet, brat," Tessa said to her without rancor. To Charles, she said, "I have a feeling it'll be hard to figure out who the guy is. He doesn't look like anyone who'd work with my, er, friends."

"He hasn't been in jail enough." Hannah sported a wide grin.

Tessa promptly put her in a one-armed headlock—a sisterly headlock, not a guillotine choke.

Her "Hey!" came out muffled as she struggled to escape.

Meanwhile, Tessa told Charles, "I'll call you if I find something."

"Same here. You said it's up on YouTube?"

"Yup." She disconnected the call just as Hannah wriggled free. "Not bad. My niece took almost a minute to get out."

Hannah glared at her. "Thank goodness you're not *my* aunt if your idea of love and good fun is to put me in a headlock."

"No, my idea of love and good fun is to teach you mixed martial arts. Nothing like a takedown to bond women together."

Hannah gave her a look like, *You are so crazy, even the loony bin won't take you.*

"Let's call Nez."

Hannah took a gigantic step away from her.

"What?" Tessa said.

"In case you decide to pull some judo move and flip me over your shoulder."

"If you cease and desist the smart-mouth answers, no bodily harm will result," Tessa said primly. She dialed Nez.

He picked up after two rings. "You're using up my cell minutes," he complained.

"That's kind of impossible, since I called your office phone."

A pause. "I'm busy."

"You're only annoyed because you're watching *Real Housewives of Fiji*."

His voice suddenly perked up. "There's a *Real Housewives of Fiji*?"

A genius idea hit her. "Yeah, of course there is."

"You're kidding me."

"I'm not kidding. You didn't know about it? There's a clip on YouTube. Here, I'll text you the link."

"I don't have internet on my cell phone."

"Type the link into your computer, Nez."

"Oh. Right."

Tessa sent him the link to the YouTube video of the lanky man and the assassin at SFO.

She waited for him to watch the video, listening to the sound in the background on his phone. Then his sharp yelp. "What are you doing? Trying to get me killed?"

"You're only watching a clip from *Entertainment Bay Area*."

The panic in his voice relaxed marginally. "Oh. This is from TV?"

"Yes, your brilliant little, er, cousin got herself on an entertainment show."

"She's not my cousin. She's Thai," he said sourly. "Who's the guy with her?"

Rats. "I was hoping you could tell me."

"She usually works alone."

"So she's not your, er, cousin?"

"Oh, for goodness' sake," Hannah burst out. "Just say the word *assassin*."

Nez's voice grew annoyed. "The kid's still with you?"

"Bringing joy to my life. So, your cousin?"

"She has worked with our friends before, but she likes to work with lots of people."

Freelance contractor, then. Could be yakuza; could be not yakuza. "The guy doesn't look even a little familiar?"

"Nah. He looks like an accountant."

"Maybe she's his bodyguard?"

"Nah. She doesn't do that kind of stuff. If she's with him, he's her partner somehow."

"Has she worked with people before like this?"

"Only if her employer hires them."

So whoever hired her hired the accountant, too, and she was working with him because she was paid to. "Anything else you can tell me?"

"I'm already in trouble for what I gave to you. Leave me alone." And he hung up his phone.

Yup, Nez was definitely going to spit in her soup the next time she ate at his restaurant.

She supposed she should call Charles. Not that she had learned a great deal in the two minutes since she'd disconnected with him, but there was nothing else she could do right now about finding out who these people were. If she were in San Francisco, she could hit up some old contacts in the less-savory neighborhoods, but since she was babysitting an obnoxious teenager in LA, her reach was limited to a very cranky Nez.

She dialed Charles, who answered immediately. "I was just about to call you." He had a smug tinge to his voice.

"You got the video footage from the TV show already? I didn't think you were *that* good."

"I'll get it," he said irritably. "That's not why I called. I found out who the man is."

Tessa's mouth dropped open. It took her a few tries before she got her jaw working and she could close it. "In two minutes?"

His smug tone grew triumphant. "I actually found out something before you did."

"I, uh, discovered the woman is used to working alone," Tessa said defensively. "And she's Thai."

"And . . . ?"

"And what?"

"What do we call her — Daisy?"

Tessa's mouth felt like she'd bitten into a lemon. "She's too dangerous and mysterious to have a name." Nez probably knew twelve of her names, and none of them would be the truth. But she'd still forgotten to ask him.

"Yeah. Dangerous and mysterious Daisy-which-isn't-her-name. The man, on the other hand, is — "

"He's a hacker, right?" Hannah appeared at Tessa's side and looked down at the phone. "He has the pale, pasty look of a man who eats too many Cheetos and Red Bulls in the dark of his basement."

Tessa gave her a sidelong look. "Seriously? That's such a stereotype."

"It's a stereotype because it's true." Hannah nodded sagely.

"The man is Vernon Mead," Charles said. "He's a private investigator."

Hannah sniffed. "I was still right about the Cheetos and the Red Bull."

"How'd you find that out?" Tessa demanded.

"I sent the video link to the private investigator I'd hired earlier. I was going to ask him to find out who the couple was, but Kurt knew Vernon right away. It's a small business world."

"So Vernon owns his own business?"

"Actually, no. He works for a larger agency, Crossman's Investigations. I've never heard of them, but Kurt said they've been doing well for themselves, although they're still not well known."

"They're based, where? Los Angeles?"

"Right here in the Bay Area. Marin, actually."

"I have to stay in LA for another day or two, until the next show, so I can't get up to San Francisco to talk to Crossman's until then."

"You don't have to talk to them," Charles said.

"I don't? Are you going to do it?"

"Nope." Charles gave a rather evil laugh. "Now we sue them."

Chapter 11

Being inside the studio of *Grab the Mic* was not as cool as Charles had thought it would be. For one thing, the team of attorneys from Rendell, Lerman & Hunter staring him down from the other side of the conference table dampened the experience somewhat.

For another, George was as flushed as a menopausal woman and even more emotional. "You're trying to kill Hannah!" He stood and leaned over the table, his body as tight as a bowstring, fists at his sides, as he accused six of the seven producers of *Grab the Mic* who sat across from him.

Producer Holmes Taggart, his pale face calm and impassive, reached out a placating hand to George. "We aren't trying to kill your daughter—" he began, but his attorney cut him off.

"There is no connection between that woman and the private investigator we hired, Vernon Mead." The attorney, Paul Harris, sat back with a satisfied smirk.

"What are you—" George burst out, but Charles laid a firm hand on his shoulder.

"Let me handle this," he said quietly.

George faced him with angry eyes that were also tinged with fear. Charles nodded to him, and George sat.

The one thing he'd definitely discovered was that the producers of the show had hired the investigator Vernon Mead, the lanky guy with the goatee who'd been with the assassin at the airport.

Which meant it was one of the producers who was involved in all this.

"Why don't you try to explain why you felt the need to hire an investigator in the first place."

Seeming to ignore the acid in Charles's tone, Paul said smoothly, "We hired investigators to look into all the semifinal contestants for *Grab the Mic*."

"Nice try. I've already looked through Crossman's files — they were more than willing to give us clients' names, by the way — and there's nothing about investigating any of the other contestants."

Now Paul just looked bored. "We hired different investigators for each of the contestants." He widened his eyes at Charles in a silent *duh*.

Charles had to draw a breath before continuing. Paul was baiting him but also deliberately holding back his answers to force Charles into ferreting out the information. "And the reason you hired Vernon Mead to investigate my client? And supposedly those other investigators for the other contestants?"

"I don't understand what the big deal is, considering Vernon Mead has yet to be in the same city as your client."

"Vernon Mead, whom you hired, was videotaped with the same woman who attacked my client's daughter. You need to look up the definition of 'person of interest.'"

The problem was, Paul was right. Vernon Mead hadn't done anything to Hannah or George—yet. The scruffy man who had been videotaped on Hannah's computer in Oakland and who had accosted her near the park—he was a different story. However, Charles hadn't found any evidence that the scruffy man was also an investigator with Crossman's. Even a perusal of all the photos of their staff hadn't yielded the scruffy man's round face.

Paul shrugged almost negligently. "That video clip shows Vernon helping a young girl out of a taxi. That's it. There's no evidence they entered the terminal together, no evidence that Vernon even arrived in Los Angeles."

"According to Crossman's Investigations, he was issued a plane ticket."

"Which he did not use," Paul said.

"He could have arrived at the studio with the same woman he met at the San Francisco airport and who attacked my clients," Charles said.

Paul gave him a nasty little smile. "He didn't."

"I'm assuming by your answer that you looked at the studio security videos?"

"Of course."

"So you personally pored over all the video from the time that Vernon was to have arrived in Los Angeles, up until the building was cleared after the attack?"

"That's what associates are for." He gave Charles a poor-overworked-understaffed-lawyer look.

Charles's jaw muscles tightened. "You'll forgive me for wanting to see those videos myself."

"We'll get them to you right away," he said with mock helpfulness.

For a fleeting moment, Charles wondered if the video had been digitally tampered with. Charles knew he wouldn't see those videos before Christ returned. "You avoided my question. Why did you hire private investigators?"

"That is company business, not yours," Paul said dismissively.

"Hannah can make that airport video go viral," Tessa said from the far end of the conference table.

She hadn't said much since the attorneys arrived, preferring to remain in the background, next to Hannah, posing as a babysitter. She was leaning back in her chair. Her casual posture reminded him of her tough earlier years when she had been the most dangerous woman on the streets of San Francisco. What was ironic was that none of the other men in the room knew that.

"Go ahead," Paul mocked her. "It's already got a million hits. What are a few million more?"

"I was thinking of sending a nice story to *The Star* gossip magazine." Tessa idly studied her nails. "Here's the headline— 'Why have the producers of *Grab the Mic* hired this man to stalk thirteen-year-old Hannah Mynheir?'"

"That's libel," Paul said in disgust.

"No, it isn't," Charles said. "We have evidence you hired him to 'investigate' George and Hannah."

"And really, how is following her around not stalking?" Tessa said.

Paul's face turned an ugly burgundy. "Muzzle your poodle," he snapped at Charles.

Tessa only smiled, but her eyes became glittering black blades ready to hurl straight at the attorney and all his fellow partners alongside him.

"How dare you spread such ugly lies?" burst out one of the producers, Wilson Weiss.

From where she sat next to Tessa, Hannah feigned a confused expression. "I don't understand, Mr. Weiss. When you wanted me to tell the reporters how much I wanted my dad to get married again, and I said it wasn't true, you said people don't care if it's not true."

Wilson looked thunderous.

"You mean it's not true?" Tessa asked in a conversational tone. "My sister is going to be so disappointed."

Charles sat back and simply stared at the attorney. Paul stared right back, possibly aware that it was (mostly) just a bluff. But would he really take the chance?

Paul's eyes slid to Tessa. She was the unknown factor. Charles hadn't bothered to introduce her, and her name wasn't on any type of documentation connected to George and Hannah, so the producers and attorneys had no idea she was Hannah's bodyguard and not just a babysitter.

Which made Charles feel a bit easier. They were probably searching all the nanny employment agencies in California for information on her.

Paul gave a long-suffering sigh, feigning reluctance. "Fine, we'll tell you." He'd probably been intending to tell them all along but had wanted to see what cards they'd lay on the table before he did so.

Charles was annoyed, but he didn't mind too much. Tessa was like a pair of aces still in his hand.

"We hired investigators to look into the backgrounds of all the contestants," Paul said.

Hannah snorted. "What else would they look into? Our favorite brand of jeans?"

"Hannah," George said quietly, although Charles noticed he hadn't been all that quick to admonish his daughter.

Paul cleared his throat. "The semifinalists are gaining more and more media attention as the show continues and their numbers dwindle. We wanted to make sure none of them had skeletons in their closets, so to speak, that could come out later and cause embarrassment to the show."

"And what were you going to do if you found something?"

"Nothing," Paul said quickly. "The producers and their marketing executives simply want to be prepared in case some dirty little secret came out about a contestant."

Charles's instincts told him this was a blatant lie. The producers would probably find a way to leak the unsavory tidbit and tank the contestant's popularity, getting him or her voted off the show. Or perhaps they had a way to rig the voting. However, no one could prove any of it.

"We're done here." Paul stood, and his fellow attorneys and the producers also rose. He gave Charles a smug look. "And next time, children and girlfriends aren't invited."

The crowd of people left, but Charles kept George, Hannah, and Tessa back in the conference room a moment longer before they exited the law offices, so they could avoid the producers on the walk to their cars in the parking garage.

Once there, they climbed into Charles's rental car and George asked, "Now what?"

"Now the attorneys will probably stall getting me any information," Charles said.

"Doesn't that look suspicious?" Tessa asked.

"Sure, they could do it because they have something to hide. Or they could do it just to be jerks."

"Paul seemed pretty jerkish," Hannah said from the backseat.

As Charles drove out of the parking garage, Tessa said, "The evidence you got from Crossman's Investigations proves that the producers hired Vernon. He was clearly with that assassin woman. What I don't understand is why they'd hire an assassin at this point in the competition. According to the email Hannah got, George is supposed to make it to the final four before being cut. If something happens to Hannah, he'd withdraw. And even if he didn't, how would he be able to perform well enough to make it that far? No one would believe it if he kept messing up but wasn't voted off the show."

"You are really not boosting my self-esteem here," George said drily from the backseat.

"Oh, lighten up, Dad," Hannah said blithely. "You're not the one with a mini-assassin after you."

"Whoever is behind the gambling is voting on more than just George," Charles said. "They might have decided to cut their losses."

Silence descended in the car. Charles could talk about it impassively, but the lives of a man and his daughter were at stake. The producers—or perhaps only one or two of them—needed George and Hannah out of the way, but they were moving cautiously, trying to hide any connection to foul play.

Charles said, "That video clip from *Entertainment Bay Area* put a wrench in their plans and obviously worried them. Otherwise, they wouldn't have pulled in that team of attorney linebackers today."

"What do you mean?" Tessa asked. She wasn't looking at him, but was instead scanning the cars around them, alert to a tail.

"Rendell, Lerman, and Hunter is a top-notch — read, expensive — firm. The studio itself wouldn't have them on retainer, but one of the producers might."

"What do we do now?"

"You protect George and Hannah at the show tonight. I'll keep investigating."

"I wish I could help you. If we were in San Francisco rather than Los Angeles right now ..."

"Just do your job and protect your clients. Leave the investigating to me for now. You can look into things when you're back in San Francisco in a few days." He hesitated, then added in a lower voice, "If the producer who hired the assassin — our friend Bob — speaks to his assassin sometime soon, he'll know you're not just a babysitter or a girlfriend. He's shown himself to be cautious. He'll look into you too."

"He has to figure out who I am first. He can't find out from your records, can he?"

"I started keeping all your files in a safe," Charles admitted.

She gave a half-smile and looked at him, almost with pleasure. "Thanks."

"No problem," he said gruffly. "It's my job."

She abruptly went back to scanning the cars around them.

Hannah began to giggle in the backseat.

"What, baby?" George asked her.

"Just what that man said." She lowered her voice to mimic him. " 'Children and girlfriends aren't invited.' I wonder which of you he thought was dating Tessa."

"Hopefully it was me," George said. "Guys everywhere would be jealous."

Tessa laughed a fun, flirty laugh that said she was pleased.

Charles gritted his teeth. He was going to sever his attraction. He didn't care if she dated the entire 49ers football team. He didn't care that George was handsomer, more talented, and had an effortless charm.

He had to remember what his goals were. He had to remember that flash of memory from the conference room, when her relaxed posture reminded him of the old Tessa, the yakuza enforcer. She would never escape her past or her family. He couldn't be involved with her.

He needed to go down Rick's list of candidates again.

The thought of the list was like a splash of cold water over his head. Charles was such an idiot.

The list had only one woman on it who was connected with a law firm. She was a legal secretary. Who worked for Rendell, Lerman & Hunter.

She'd been far down the list because she lived in LA, but now . . .

Now might be an excellent time to ask her out on a date. For more reasons than one.

Chapter **12**

"Do I *have* to get my hair cut?" Hannah whined as she, George, and Tessa entered the San Francisco motel, the Snuggle Up.

George frowned as he took in the dim interior. "Do we *have* to do this in a seedy motel?"

Meeting them right inside the entrance, Tessa's friend Evangeline complained, "Do you *have* to do this in *my* seedy motel?"

Tessa glared at all three of them. "Yes, yes, and yes. What are you, the three bears?"

"If that's true, then one of us should be 'just right,'" Hannah muttered, her hands grabbing her long blonde hair as if the stylist would have to wrest it off her head.

Tessa addressed the Mutinous One first. "Look, Hannah. I want to keep you safe, and Erica is a hairstylist who owes me a favor. She can make you look completely different, plus she can get you a wig. If that assassin attacks again, you can whip off the new wig and head toward a crowd. The assassin will have a harder time finding you if you have a completely different haircut under the wig. It'll give you a chance to escape."

"I don't want to escape. I want you to break the assassin's arm." Hannah pouted. "And I don't want to get my hair cut."

"Baby, it's for your safety," George told her. "I agree with Tessa about that. What I don't like is that we have to get her hair done in a seedy motel."

"Because ten-year-old assassins tend to stand out when they enter seedy motels," Tessa shot back at him.

"So pick another motel," Evangeline snapped. "I just got this job. I don't want to get in trouble because you left a mess in the room from the dye job."

"I promise we'll clean up," Tessa reassured her. "Besides, the Snuggle Up has an hourly rate, so the rooms are probably none too clean to begin with. It was the only place I could think of on such short notice. Erica is leaving tomorrow to move up to her mom's place in Sacramento, so the only time she can do Hannah's hair is this afternoon." She folded her hands in a pleading gesture. "Pleeeeeeeeeease, Evangeline. You can see both the front and back entrances from your spot at the bar, so you can warn us if the assassin walks in. I really need to do this to protect my clients. Hannah's only thirteen." She gestured toward the teen, who refused to look cute and pathetic and instead looked cranky.

Evangeline raised her brown eyes toward the ceiling. "Fine. Just please hurry. If my boss finds out I let you use a room for free . . ."

"I won't even mention your name," Tessa promised. "Is Erica here yet?"

"Yes, she arrived a few minutes ago. She's already upstairs." Evangeline led them through the motel bar, where the counter ran along the right wall, lined by four barstools. On the left side of the room were some ancient arcade games and a few scattered and heavily scarred tables, a couple sporting poorly repaired legs.

They walked down a short hallway toward the back of the building before turning abruptly onto a narrow flight of stairs that led up to the second floor. Evangeline opened the door of a small room that smelled of mold and BO. There was barely room for the king-sized bed that sported a stained and faded purple velour coverlet, which clung to the mattress and showed how it sagged deeply in the middle. It was flanked by two battered end tables, and there was a mismatched, short chest of drawers against the wall beneath a cracked mirror. A narrow, warped wooden door led to the bathroom.

Erica was setting up her equipment and looked up, smiling, as Tessa, Hannah, and George entered.

Tessa gave her a hug. "It's so great to see you. I'm so glad you called me when you came back to San Francisco."

"I wanted to be able to tell you this in person." Erica held Tessa at arm's length. "Thank you for saving us when Dan was after us."

"It was nothing."

"It wasn't nothing. You sacrificed your car to do it and got beat up."

"You did?" Hannah's eyes were huge. "Who beat you up?"

"I let him beat me up," Tessa quickly said. "And it was Erica's ex-boyfriend. She was on her way to the bus depot to get away from him."

"So isn't it dangerous for you to be back here?" Hannah asked Erica.

"While Dan was out on bail, he did me the favor of robbing

a bank," Erica answered. "Now that Dan is in prison for several years, my mom and I will pack up her Sacramento house, sell it, and start a new life somewhere else."

Tessa introduced everyone, but Hannah became pouty again when Erica asked, "So how do you want your hair done?"

"I don't want it done at all."

Erica cocked her head to one side. "What a shame. You would totally look like Emma Watson if I gave you her pixie cut."

Hannah's expression went from gloomy to full wattage, as if someone turned on a light. "Really? I love her haircut."

"Did you bring the wigs too?" Tessa asked.

Erica rummaged in a bag sitting on the end table next to the bed and held out three of them. "I think this brown one is closest to her natural hair," she said, holding a wig with bangs and shoulder-length mahogany waves. "You said you want the wig to look like Hannah's hair had been dyed and cut, right?"

Tessa nodded. "If it just looks like it's been dyed and cut, the assassin wouldn't expect her to be wearing a wig. If Hannah takes off the wig, her new haircut will throw the assassin off even more."

Erica shuddered. "You say that word like you're talking about a plumber."

"It's not my fault I've dealt with more assassins than plumbers in my life."

"Can you make my hair red?" Hannah was obviously adjusting to the concept of the glamorous remaking of herself.

"That might be too eye-catching," Erica said tactfully. "How about strawberry blonde?"

"Is Emily with your mom?" Tessa asked Erica as Hannah sat on a chair. George leaned against the chest of drawers in the far corner, and Erica busied herself with her shears.

"Yeah. Mom came to the city two days ago — right after I called her about Dan being in prison — and she's been helping me pack up my apartment."

"Everything turned out okay with your inheritance, I'm assuming?"

"Finally." Erica's mouth twisted into a grimace. "When I came back to San Francisco, I had to deal with that lawyer, Joseph Tucker, again, and his secretary spoke to me."

"The one who mistakenly gave Dan Wings' address?" Tessa couldn't stop a flare in her gut. She really should be more forgiving. The woman just made a mistake. Everyone makes mistakes. Tessa had made some massive ones, and Jesus had forgiven her.

Erica's eyes had narrowed as she began brushing Hannah's hair, preparing to put it in a ponytail so she could cut the locks off. She yanked a bit hard, and Hannah winced.

"Yes. Mrs. Quilly. I was ready to forgive her for her mistake, but she told me it was only a tiny mistake, and she didn't understand why it was such a big deal. It was like she only wanted to justify herself, not admit she'd done anything wrong."

"But she did do something really wrong. It almost got you hurt that night Dan came after us."

"That's what I told her. I said that if you hadn't been with me, Dan would have certainly beat me up worse than he beat her up, and he would have done all he could to force me to give him my inheritance money." With one fell swoop, Erica sliced off Hannah's long hair just above the rubber band of the ponytail. She handed the hair to the girl, who began to wail.

Raising her voice a bit above the wailing, Erica said, "It's okay, honey. Think Emma Watson."

The magical name of the pretty actress stopped Hannah's

crying, although she continued to look mournfully at the pony-tail in her lap.

Erica continued talking to Tessa. "Mrs. Quilly didn't listen to me at all. She even implied it was my fault for getting the inheritance, which was why Dan was after me and why he sought her out to beat her up."

Tessa's mouth dropped open. She had to tell herself to close it. "I would've thought she'd regret what she'd done, if only because it thrust her onto Dan's radar. I'm sure she was afraid for her life when they beat her up and kidnapped her."

"I feel sorry for her," Erica said. "She was severely hurt for her mistake. But I also feel sorry for her, because now she seems just full of bitterness and anger about it. She blames me and you for what happened."

"I don't understand." Tessa felt as if she were floundering in only three feet of water.

"I don't either, but I should warn you that she said some rather nasty things about you. She vowed to 'get back' at you for what you did to her." Erica had been brushing and studying Hannah's shortened hair, but now she picked up her shears again. "To his credit, her boss seemed really embarrassed by her."

At the reemergence of the shears, Hannah's eyes grew wide. Tessa, fearing more wailing was in store, hastily said, "I'll leave you to it," and exited the hotel room, heading back downstairs to the bar.

She sank down onto an empty stool at the end of the bar, where she could keep an eye on the front and back doors.

Evangeline appeared in front of her, her bartender's apron in place. "Before you ask, no, I didn't see either the ten-year-old assassin or the tall, lanky guy from the video you sent to me. No one has entered the place since you got here."

"That ten-year-old assassin gave me this." Tessa held up her forearm. She'd removed the gauze so it could heal, but the cut was still long, red, and painful.

Evangeline's dark eyebrows rose toward her cascading bangs. "She actually got a shot at you? I haven't seen that in a long time. Not since those prison fights you got into."

"She works a switchblade better than anyone I've seen," Tessa said. "At least in prison, they only had shanks."

"You remember that Frenchwoman who tried to make a garrote with her hair? That surprised you."

"I still have the scar." Tessa lifted her chin and fingered the faint line the garrote had created before it had snapped.

"I forgot why she came after you." Evangeline placed a highball glass filled with club soda with lime in front of Tessa.

"My uncle asked me to beat up some French banker, who hired the Frenchwoman to come after me when he found out I was in prison."

It was comforting, somehow, to talk to her old cellmate this way. Everyone else questioned her calm attitude about her previous crimes and the matter-of-fact way she described the violence she'd endured in prison. But not Evangeline, because she understood not only Tessa's old life but also the new life in Christ she'd helped Tessa discover four years ago.

"I don't see you much at Wings these days," Evangeline said. "Our volunteer shifts don't overlap much anymore."

"Mina's annoyed with me." Tessa sipped her club soda. "When I started getting more bodyguard jobs, I had to cancel some of my shifts at the last moment, and she hates rescheduling. But she's also happy I've got a real job now, and she doesn't have to field calls from hiring managers asking her about my references."

Suddenly Tessa's new prepaid cell phone rang. She recognized the number as Vivian's. "Hi, Vivian."

"Is this Tessa? I can never be sure, since you're always changing cell phones."

"Sorry. I have to do that when I've got a new client or if I have to protect a long-term client, like now. Did you get the money from Elizabeth?"

"Yes, I have the cash. I feel a bit nervous having so much in my purse."

"I'm at the Snuggle Up motel right now. How soon can you get here?"

When Tessa hung up, Evangeline eyed her sourly. "So not only are you scheduling hair appointments, you're having clandestine meetings to exchange money. In *my* place of employment."

Tessa swung her arms wide to encompass the other patrons in the room — of which there were zero. "Do you see any ten-year-old assassins here? That's why."

"You've already brought in George Mynheir from *Grab the Mic* and his thirteen-year-old daughter, and now you're meeting your lawyer's Southern belle mother." Evangeline shook her head. "Patrons are going to think the motel bar has turned into Jamba Juice."

"It's only two thirty. Your, er, lunch crowd is gone, and your evening drinkers aren't here yet. We'll be gone before your stellar reputation suffers."

Forty minutes later, Vivian entered the motel timidly, her blue eyes taking in the beer-stained walls and scratched floor, her nose wrinkling at the smell of body odor and stale alcohol that never seemed to lessen despite the ceiling fans going full speed on the stripped ceiling. She scurried over to Tessa, trying to avoid eye contact with the man at the bar who had arrived a few minutes earlier and was on his second whiskey.

She sat down just as Evangeline walked up. "What can I get for you?"

"Oh ... nothing ..."

"Evangeline, do you have the ingredients for a virgin strawberry daiquiri?" Tessa asked.

"What in the world is that?" Vivian asked.

"I think you'll like it."

One sip of the fruity, icy drink had Vivian sucking up the rest. "Oh, my. Oh, my. This is better than a Slurpee."

"I had to make it worth your while to meet me at a seedy motel bar in the middle of the afternoon. After all, who knows what your friends will say if they find out?"

Vivian snorted. "They'd probably just ask what I ordered."

Which made sense, considering most of Vivian's friends were people she met at the cooking classes she loved to take.

Very obviously looking around first, Vivian slipped the envelope of cash into Tessa's lap, in full view of anyone who would have been sitting in the room behind them. Tessa stifled her sigh and slipped the envelope into her pocket. "Thanks, Vivian."

"I don't know why you need to go lease a house," she said between sips of her daiquiri. "You should just stay with Charles. He has that lovely panic room."

"Vivian, I can't keep bringing clients to my lawyer's house, endangering him and his mother."

"Oh, pooh. Everything that happened last year with Elizabeth was exciting."

"I don't recall being shot all that exciting."

"Oh, well, that was unfortunate."

Unfortunate?

"But it was so nice having you there." Vivian beamed at Tessa. "And you haven't brought any of your other clients to Charles's house, just Elizabeth. I'm sure George would love being there with Charles's wide-screen TV. I'm sure we could hook up a microphone to Charles's stereo system somehow ..."

The thought of jury-rigging Charles's Bose sound system made Tessa giggle, if only at the thought of the look of horror on Charles's face. But then the normal buzzing, needling feeling she usually felt around Charles these days came back over her, and her smile faded.

"Thank you, but no, Vivian. I've leased a house for George and Hannah to stay at." A small cabin in the Santa Cruz Mountains, just off of Highway 17, very hard to find. Easy to defend with a laid-back landlord who didn't blink an eye when Tessa had suggested paying in cash.

Since Elizabeth St. Amant was paying Tessa's fee for George, she had tentatively asked for some cash for more secure housing, and Elizabeth had agreed without any questions. But getting the cash to Tessa without anyone noticing ("anyone" meaning the investigators who might be trying to find out who Tessa was) had required Vivian to be the innocuous go-between for her goddaughter and Tessa.

Vivian slurped up the last of her daiquiri. "Have you kept up with your knitting?"

Tessa thought back to the jumble of yarn she'd shoved under her bed. "Oh. Yes. When I have time."

"Well, when you want to learn more techniques, just let me

know. In fact, you should come by for dinner, and we can knit together."

"Sure, maybe after George and Hannah are safe."

"No, bring them along."

"Vivian, I'm not going to bring two people who have an assassin after them into your home to have dinner with you."

"Oh, for goodness' sake, we can eat in the panic room if you want. How's tomorrow night?"

Tessa eyed her narrowly. "What's happening tomorrow night?"

"Oh. Nothing." Vivian's soft cheeks were colored by two twin spots. Had Evangeline put alcohol in that daiquiri after all?

They sat in an awkward silence for a few moments as Tessa tried to figure out how to subtly taste the dregs of Vivian's drink to see if there was alcohol in it.

Finally Vivian burst out, "Charles has a date tomorrow night."

Forget the alcohol. Vivian had the heightened color of conspiracy.

"Vivian, you have to stop matchmaking me and Charles." Although the thought of him on a date did make it hard for Tessa to breathe due to the feeling of a barbell suddenly pressing against her breastbone.

"But you two were made for each other."

"Obviously not, since we're not together."

"But he's so sorry for what he did."

"I don't care if he's sorry!" That came out a bit louder than Tessa intended. She modulated her voice. "I have absolutely no interest in him."

"Now, don't lie to me. You obviously feel strongly about him."

"Yes, I feel strongly that I'd like to punch his lights out."

Vivian sighed, and her gaze somehow made Tessa feel a bit ashamed, like she'd come home from school with her dress torn.

"Darlin'," Vivian said in that drawl that felt like a mohair shawl around Tessa's shoulders, "you have every right to be angry. But if you keep feeding that fire, it's only going to burn you."

It did feel a bit like a fire, like crackling coals in the depths of her belly. But the heat kept the pain at bay. "Vivian, he hurt me, and he didn't even know me. What does that say about him?"

"It says that he was a very different man back then."

"How do I know that?"

"You of all people should know how a person can change."

"Sure, a person can change. But I have no way of knowing if Charles *has* changed. He almost didn't tell me he was at my trial — I had to force it out of him. And then he didn't have the guts to tell me what he did. My uncle had to tell me."

"Don't you think those are the actions of a man ashamed of what he did?"

"If he was ashamed, he would have told me. If he felt guilty, he would have told me. But he doesn't even think that what he did was so awful. He has no concept that what he did was wrong."

"He knows you miss your aunt."

Tessa shook her head, and then shook it again. "I don't *just* miss my aunt. She loved me more than my mother. She loved me more than my uncle. She loved me more than any other person in the world, even before I became a Christian. She was the only one who cared if I was happy. When you lose someone like that, when you're not allowed to say good-bye when she's alive, when you're not allowed to say good-bye when she's gone, it leaves a crater in your heart like a bomb went off. There is nothing that can fill that."

Vivian looked stunned. After a moment, she said, "I'm not defending him, but he was only a young clerk at the time, just out of law school, and he was objectively doing his job—"

"No, he wasn't objective at all. He convinced the judge to add two years to the maximum sentence, and he had absolutely no proof I committed any murders. He did what he did because he wanted to."

"He's different now," Vivian said weakly. "Back then he thought his duty was to right any and all wrongs because of all the injustices he saw growing up. He had such a hard time escaping the shadow of his daddy." Vivian's two broken fingers, resting on the surface of the bar, shook. They were mirror images of the two broken fingers on Charles's hand that he'd gotten last year when he was tortured, refusing to give up his mama's location.

Yes, he had strong qualities. But Tessa was just so hurt. "I understand about his childhood," Tessa said. "But it doesn't erase what he did. To me, it felt as if he wanted to dole out the pain he received. And I can't forgive him for doing that to me."

But in treating him like she was, wasn't she trying to dole out the pain she'd received? How was she any different from him?

At that moment, a darling pixie in a cap of damp red-blonde waves stepped out of the stairwell down the hall and danced toward them, followed by George and Erica. "What do you think?" Hannah asked. "Oh, hi, Mrs. Britton."

"You look adorable!" gushed Vivian.

Tessa furtively glanced back toward the windows at the front of the motel, making sure Hannah wasn't visible. She wasn't—

she stood at an angle where the corner of the bar hid her—but in looking around, Tessa noticed that the man who'd arrived just before Vivian seemed to be nervous. He nursed his third whiskey, but his eyes slid to them every so often. His hand rubbed his neck—no, his hand rubbed his throat.

Tessa waited to get a better look. When his hand dropped to reach for some peanuts from the dish on the bar, she thought she saw a short, thin, reddish line on his throat, as if a blade had been pressed against his neck but hadn't broken the skin.

Was she being paranoid again? Better safe than sorry.

Vivian had risen and stood in front of Hannah, so the girl was mostly screened from the whiskey man at the bar, but Tessa now stood and ushered them back a few steps so they'd be completely out of his range of vision. "Looks great. Try it with the wig on."

"Let me blow-dry it first," Erica said.

Tessa glanced back at the man. Had he seen Hannah's new hairstyle? It had only been a scant second or two that she'd been unshielded by Vivian's body.

George was all grins. He tweaked a wet lock of hair. "You look so much older, baby."

"Then don't call me *baby*, Dad," she said with a pert smile. But her pride shone out of her eyes.

As it did more often lately, George's affection for Hannah made Tessa remember her own father. And when she thought about him, and about the email she'd received, she felt barbed wire wrapping round and round her heart.

Why had he left? Hadn't he loved her enough? Why had he chosen to miss those years with her, when she was about to turn from a child into a woman? What kind of choices had he made that forced whatever had happened to him?

And more importantly, had it really been him who sent her the email?

Tessa wondered if she still had that email in her trash folder, or if she didn't, if Hannah could find it again and maybe trace where it had come from. She was almost expecting it to be some practical joke from one of her yakuza cousins who had somehow found out about her father's pet name for her.

But what if it wasn't? What if her father was alive and the email was true?

She squeezed her eyes shut. She didn't want to accept that. It was just too painful for her.

"Such a good father," Vivian murmured to Tessa as she watched George embrace Hannah.

"Uh ... yeah," Tessa answered.

Vivian suddenly turned and eyed her sharply. "Now that's interesting."

"What are you talking about?"

"A year ago you were as cool as a cucumber. Could talk about fathers—and your father—with hardly any emotion. Now you're awkward. What happened?"

The woman was too observant. "Nothing."

"Have you been thinking about your father lately?"

"Uh ..." Tessa was so tempted to lie. But she wasn't that person anymore. "A little. Because of George."

Erica was ushering Hannah back up to the room so she could blow-dry her hair.

Tessa said, "Vivian, I'll be right back. I'm going to the bathroom."

Tessa went to the public bathroom, which was next to the back door, but didn't turn on the light. She shut the door and crept toward the tiny window, which looked out at the small, littered parking lot behind the motel.

It was actually a parking lot for three buildings — the motel, the pawn shop next to it, and the Chinese restaurant on the other side — so it was filled with several cars. The day was cloudy and a little dark. One car had left its headlights on.

She saw the Moose and Vivian's gold Lexus sedan. She saw six of the seven cars that had been in the lot when she arrived — one had left. She saw three new cars, including the one with its headlights on.

As she stood and watched, standing just out of the patch of grey light coming in through the window, she thought she saw movement in one of the cars.

It could be a dog that had been left in the car or maybe a pair of teens necking. Or a female assassin waiting for them to approach the Suburban.

Once she'd had money for equipment, Tessa had bought a Jack Bauer–type monocular small enough to slip into her pocket. She honestly hadn't had opportunity to use it much, since most of her other jobs had been straightforward protection details. But now she put it up to her eye and peered at the silver SUV where she'd seen that brief flash of movement.

She couldn't see anything. Maybe it *had* been a dog.

But did she really want to take that chance? Especially since Vivian was with them?

Better safe than sorry. Although Tessa would be sorry when she told Hannah what they had to do. It might actually be possible to be whined to death.

She exited the bathroom, then gently took Vivian's arm and

steered her upstairs to the room Erica, Hannah, and George were in.

Erica turned off the hairdryer as they entered. Tessa spoke quickly. "We have to go."

"Now?" Hannah touched her hair, which was only half-dry.

"I think someone is outside."

George's face grew tense, and he drew closer to Hannah. After thinking so recently about her father, it made something tighten briefly in Tessa's chest, but she quickly shook it off. "We have to leave the cars."

"All of us?" Vivian asked.

Erica said, "My mom dropped me off and said she'd come by to pick me up when I needed her to."

"Call her now," Tessa said. "I'll make sure you get in her car safely, and then we'll leave."

Erica did and found out her mom was shopping only a couple blocks away. Within minutes, Tessa was ushering Erica through the bar—giving the nervous whiskey man a wide berth—and out the front doors. She bundled Erica into the car hastily and watched the car drive away before heading back to the motel room.

Vivian's fingers rubbed her handbag handles back and forth, back and forth, but Hannah's bottom lip was already thrust out, showing some pink. "What do you mean, leave the cars? How will we get to the cabin?" Then she perked up. "Hey, does that mean we're going to a hotel instead?"

"No," Tessa said flatly. "We're taking mass transit. You too, Vivian."

Hannah's face looked like Tessa had suggested she run naked through the bar. With her head on fire. *Mass transit?*

"I think someone's watching the car," Tessa said. "Do *you* want to go out there to check?"

Hannah shut her mouth but continued pouting.

"The parking lot is in back of the building, so she can't see us if we go out the front to the bus stop about a block away. We have to time it. I think the guy sitting at the bar might be spotting for her — maybe reluctantly — so I'll ask Evangeline to keep him busy while we leave. If anything, she can wrestle him to the ground if he tries to leave without paying."

Tessa went downstairs to borrow Evangeline's cell phone, which had internet access, and to speak to her about distracting the whiskey guy. Then Tessa came back to the room. "There's a bus that's supposed to come in seven minutes."

"Which means it'll be late," George said.

"You can all run, right?"

Vivian gave her a "Don't be ridiculous" look.

"Vivian, you just told me that everything that happened last year was 'exciting.'"

Now Vivian looked almost as mutinous as Hannah. "Fine." She reached down and yanked off her fine beige shoes. They didn't have a very high heel, but she wouldn't have been able to run in them. She shuddered as her feet touched the dingy carpet.

"I'll go downstairs to look outside to check if the bus is coming. When I text you, all of you hoof it out of here and run like crazy for the bus stop."

Tessa went downstairs, walked to the front door, and cracked it open, peering down the busy street.

The bus *was* late, but only by about four minutes. She saw it turn onto the street, several blocks away, and as soon as she saw the number on the front, she texted George's prepaid cell phone.

George, Hannah, and Vivian came rushing out of the stair-well and hustled down the length of the bar, looking like a scene from a sitcom—the music star, his daughter, and his lawyer's mother. "Hurry!" Tessa held the door open for them and then pointed them to the bus stop a block down the street.

The whiskey man at the bar stood up, but Evangeline approached with his tab, looking menacing. He hastily dug in his pockets, pulling out bills.

Tessa didn't see the rest, because she was running behind Vivian toward the bus stop.

Hannah reached the bus first, and as all of them climbed aboard, Tessa looked back at the motel. The bus doors closed. She paid their bus fare and watched as the man emerged from the motel, before quickly walking around the building toward the narrow driveway that led to the parking lot in the back.

The bus roared past the motel, but Tessa didn't see any cars coming out of the parking lot, didn't see anyone who would witness the bus or spot them on it.

Had she just been paranoid, or had there actually been someone in the parking lot? Had the whiskey-drinking man been forced to watch them and tell someone if they left?

More importantly, Tessa knew they hadn't been tailed after they left the leasing office of the mountain cabin for San Francisco and the motel. So if someone was in the back parking lot, how had they been found?

Chapter **13**

The telephone in the mountain cabin was so old, and the landline so bad, that listening to the earpiece was like listening to someone chomp cereal in her ear. "Charles?" Tessa asked through the static.

"Your connection is terrible," he said.

"Tell me something I don't know."

"The forensic accountant is here at the law firm with the results of his analysis of the spreadsheet Hannah got. How soon can you get here?"

Tessa groaned, but she doubted Charles could hear it over the static on the line. "Three hours?"

"What? I thought you said three hours."

"Yeah."

"Are you walking to San Francisco or something?"

"Or something."

He gave a frustrated noise and said, "I don't want to know," at the same time Tessa told him, "You don't want to know."

Awkward silence.

"Okay, three hours," he said.

"Three hours," she said at almost the same time. Again.

Tessa groaned again. To leave, they had to walk down the mountain to one of the few lights on Highway 17, so they could cross over to the northbound side where they would then walk to the bus stop and catch a bus to San Jose. In San Jose, they had to go by bus or light rail to Caltrain into San Francisco, and then by bus to the law office. That would get them there around six o'clock—about three hours from now.

In reality, it took them three hours and seventeen minutes, and Hannah complained for two hours and twenty-seven minutes of it. Even George had finally snapped at her to be quiet.

"We will get. The Moose. After. We talk. To Charles." Tessa had a hard time talking through her tight jaw as they stalked into the building. At least they hadn't been followed. It was easier for Tessa to know if they were being followed when they were on the light rail and the bus, and she'd seen no sign of a tail.

Still, she took precautions. She stopped at the security desk near the entrance. "Excuse me." She smiled brightly at one of the guards, whose nameplate read "Frank."

"How can I help you?"

"I'm expecting a ten-year-old girl to arrive. She may be with a parent, or she may be alone." Tessa hadn't wanted to say "father" in case the assassin found a woman to sneak her into the law offices.

"She should be easy to spot," Frank said. "We don't often get children in the building, since all the suites are businesses."

"If you see her, can you please ask her to wait here for me? And then could you please phone the law offices of Pleiter and Woodhouse? We'll be with Charles Britton, extension two-three-oh-two. Charles will come down in a few minutes to escort her up."

Frank nodded. "I know Mr. Britton. No problem, Miss."

"Desiree Britton," Tessa said. "I'm his cousin."

"And what's the little girl's name?"

"Hannah Mynheir."

Frank nodded as he wrote the names down. "Sure thing."

While they were in the elevator, Hannah leaned over to whisper to her, "You are freaky paranoid. But that was pretty smart."

"Why, thank you."

When they entered the law offices, Charles met them at the reception desk.

"Whoa," Hannah said. "Are you psychic or something?"

"Yes," he said.

Tessa glared at him.

His face relaxed into a smile and a dimple peeked out. "Frank phoned me to say you were coming up. There aren't any conference rooms available, so let's go to my office. The accountant is already there."

Tessa explained to Charles about what she'd told the security guard about "Hannah Mynheir" possibly arriving.

"Good thinking." His look of respect warmed her insides, even as she tried to inch away from him.

A slender man rose from the chair in front of Charles's desk, and for a moment, Tessa thought it was the same man who'd been with the assassin at the airport, just with his goatee shaved off. But a second look assured her this man was older with darker hair.

"This is Fisher Daley, one of the best forensic accountants in the business," Charles said.

"Good name for what I do, isn't it?" Fisher gave each of them a quick handshake, his movements a bit coltish, as Charles introduced them. He had a wide, friendly smile, and his eyes, behind glasses, were open and honest.

Charles introduced them all, and then found a few chairs to drag into his office so they could all sit down around the small meeting table in the corner. Someone had cleared the surface of the table, but stacks of paper were still piled up on every other flat surface in the office, including on the floor leaning against the wall.

On the table, Fisher laid a printout of the spreadsheet, but the numbers made Tessa's head swim immediately. She and George exchanged sympathetic glances. Hannah leaned forward eagerly.

"This particular spreadsheet was a little difficult to figure out," Fisher said. "I've seen others that were easier to map. But each gambler has his own system."

"So these are betting odds?" Tessa asked. Betting she understood. It was Uncle Teruo's favorite form of income, especially since he was most often the house.

"These are so much more than betting odds." Fisher sounded more excited than a teenager about to go to prom. "Like I said, it was hard to figure out. They didn't exactly spell out everything. But if you read between the lines, it can explain a lot of things."

"Does it prove the voting for the show is rigged?"

"Most definitely," Fisher said. "What's more, it practically spells out who's behind it."

"Is it the producers of the show?" George asked.

"Possibly one or two, or maybe even three of them. At first I thought a handful of them were organizing all of this, but then if you look at column BFJ23 ..." Fisher must have caught the look of blind panic on Tessa's face, because he gave a lightning smile. "Sorry, I get carried away. Basically, it points to twenty-four main players, and seven minor players."

"Thirty-one people are involved in this?" Charles said in disbelief.

"Not just any thirty-one people. The seven minor players could be anyone. I'm pretty sure at least two of them are producers of the show because of . . . well, I'm pretty sure two of them are producers. But those twenty-four . . ." He practically rubbed his hands with glee. "This is the closest we've ever gotten to them. We've been referring to them as the Double Zodiac."

He seemed disappointed at their blank faces. "Well, I guess you wouldn't have heard of them. They're a gambling syndicate. We don't know what they actually call themselves, but the Double Zodiac sounds kind of dramatic, don't you think?"

"You've dealt with them before?" Tessa asked.

"I've analyzed some of their data for the FBI," Fisher clarified. "They've been operating for at least five years. By now, they're all probably trillionaires."

"Tr-trillionaires?" George said.

"FBI?" Tessa asked. She hated the FBI, understandably because of their frequent investigations of her uncle, but also because Mom had always been adamant about not trusting them. Mom had never elaborated, but Tessa had a feeling it was something apart from their interest in Uncle Teruo. She always wondered if they had somehow interacted with Mom — or interrogated her — at some point in the past, before Tessa or Alicia could remember clearly or perhaps before they were even born.

And she could imagine how the FBI would salivate at the thought of getting another shot at the niece of the San Francisco yakuza boss.

"If one of the producers is working with the Double Zodiac, the FBI might be able to use him to finally get to them," Fisher said. "Unfortunately, this data doesn't name names."

"One or more of the producers is betting on their own show?" Hannah said.

"The producers and the Double Zodiac. All of them are making long-shot bets and rigging the voting. They will come away from this with a killing."

Tessa wasn't surprised that money was motivating them to rig a television singing competition. "This is a really elaborate scheme. They've done this before?"

"There's no proof, but it seems that way, doesn't it?" Fisher's eyes grew serious. "These men are dangerous. Some of my friends in the FBI told me stories about them. They are not nice people at all."

That pretty much described most of Tessa's childhood friends and many of her cousins.

"We know they're dangerous enough to hire an assassin," Charles said. He glanced at Tessa meaningfully. "We need to call in the FBI."

She tensed as if she'd been whipped with cat-o'-nine-tails. Calling the FBI was the last thing she wanted to do. But she had to think of George and Hannah. This gambling syndicate would hunt them down until they were no longer a threat—meaning, very dead.

"Okay," she said quietly.

Charles nodded, then turned to Fisher. "You have contacts at the bureau?"

"Of course. I'll alert them. Shall I have them contact you?"

"Yes, I—"

A knock at the door interrupted him, and Charles's secretary, Abby, peeked her head in. "Charles, your six forty-five is here, a little early."

He looked a bit disconcerted for a moment. "Uh ..."

"You mentioned you'd be done on time," Abby continued sweetly, swinging the door wide open. "And since there are no conference rooms available for her to wait in ..."

Abby stepped aside for a petite redhead who had full red lips and creamy skin. She was dressed like a lawyer, in an expensive skirt suit and conservative beige blouse, but she had curves that would have put Venus to shame. Her fiery hair was pulled up in a smooth chignon, and she walked with a precise step into Charles's office, not even hesitating when she saw everyone sitting at the table.

Charles rose to greet her. "Danica, a pleasure to meet you."

From behind Danica's back, Abby raised her eyebrows at her boss, and then closed the door.

Aahhh. This was Charles's *date*. Tessa hadn't known she'd be meeting him at the office.

"I'm just glad I happened to be in San Francisco this week." She had a slow, calm cadence to her voice, but she finished her words with a slight snap that marked her as someone who worked in corporate.

Tessa smoothed down her loose-fitting microfiber shirt and began to intensely dislike the woman.

"We just finished," Charles said.

We did?

"If you'd like, feel free to sit at my desk. I'll walk my clients out, and then we can go."

He wasn't going to introduce them? Tessa considered forcing

the issue just to be annoying, but one look at Danica's composed face convinced Tessa that doing so would only make herself look childish.

At that moment, Charles's desk phone rang. Charles picked up. "Charles Britton. Oh, hi . . ." His skin suddenly became paler than the papers on his desk. "That's all right. Thanks, Frank."

His intense gaze captured Tessa's. "The 'ten-year-old' is in the building."

Chapter **14**

W hat?" Tessa shot to her feet just as Danica Wyatt gave Charles a puzzled "Please tell me you're not a crackhead" look.

Focus, Charles. First things first. He ignored Danica's look and said to Tessa, "Your plan worked. Frank stopped her as she entered the building and asked her to wait while he called me, but while he was on the phone, he said she disappeared."

"That means she's on her way up." Tessa grasped Hannah and George by the arms. "Let's go. We have to get out of here before she enters the offices. Is there another way out?"

Charles shook his head. "Only the emergency stairs, but it sounds the alarm when you open the door."

Tessa shook her head. "If there's a panic, if there are too many people, she can just hurt someone and take off without anyone seeing her."

Hannah blanched at Tessa's blunt description but kept her head high as she waited for Tessa's instructions.

How had it gotten to this? How had the assassin found them?

And did it really have to happen just as he met his date for the evening?

Tessa hustled George and Hannah out of Charles's office. "What about Fisher and Danica?" Her voice seemed to stumble a bit over Danica's name.

"She doesn't know who Danica is, but Fisher ..."

The forensic accountant had stood, his thin body ramrod straight. "It's a hit man?" he guessed. "Hired by the Double Zodiac?"

Tessa shook her head. "He knows too much about her employers. She might take him out just for kicks and giggles."

"Hit man?" Danica's voice was strident. "What's going on?"

Charles turned to her. "Look, I know this is going to sound completely crazy, and I'm sorry."

"I get it. You really didn't want this date. You've got a bet with your friends for the worst date ever. Or the most gullible girl you can find."

"No, I promise ..."

"We have to go," Tessa said urgently.

"Just ... stay here. Don't show your face," Charles said to Danica.

Danica regarded him for a moment, and it looked as if she was torn between whipping out her crucifix to keep him away from her and laughing hysterically. Finally she said, "No way." She had a mulish cast to her jaw. "If you're not trying to pull my leg, and there's a hit man out there, I'm not staying here once the bullets start flying."

"No time to argue. Let's go!" Tessa shoved George and Hannah out of the office.

They ran down the carpeted hallway to the entrance foyer, but before they turned the corner, Tessa stopped them and peeked around the corner. She immediately jerked her head back, her mouth tensed in a tight line. "She just walked in," she whispered.

They heard the receptionist say in motherly tones, "Hello, are you lost?"

A light voice said, "No, I'm here to see Charles Britton. He's my uncle. He should be expecting me. Can I go straight in?"

Oh no.

"*That's* your hit man?" Danica had peeked around the corner and stared in disbelief at Charles.

"Look closer," he said.

She did, then straightened. The skin around her eyes had become pastier. "She's just like one of my cousins. She's proportioned like a child, but she's a lot older than that."

"She's really scary." Hannah's eyes were wide, her breath coming in short gasps. "She almost . . ." She swallowed.

Danica's eyes darted left, then right, then her face hardened, as if she'd put on a mask. "What's your secretary's name?"

"What?"

"What is it?" she demanded.

"Abby."

And in a flash, Danica darted around the corner and into the foyer.

"What is she—?" Tessa's face had gone deathly pale as she watched Danica approach the assassin.

"Hello," Danica said to the ten-year-old-with-a-switchblade. "I couldn't help overhearing. You're here to see Charles Britton?"

The girl nodded.

"I'm afraid he didn't tell me you were coming. I'm Abby, his secretary. Why don't you come with me, and I'll take you to his office?"

"Oh no," breathed Tessa. "If Danica tries to take her to another office, she'll know immediately and kill her."

But it was too late. Danica had taken the assassin's hand and was leading her behind the receptionist's desk in the opposite hallway. A wall separated the foyer from the hallways, so as Danica and the assassin passed out of sight, Tessa sent George and Hannah into the foyer, ships passing in the night.

"Go!" she hissed to Charles, then silently crept behind the pair down the hallway.

Charles ignored her and paused behind the receptionist's desk.

The assassin turned around and saw Tessa just as Tessa was sneaking past an open office door and one of the associates, Randy, spotted her. She must have looked rather suspicious, moving so stealthily behind Danica and a "young girl."

"Hey!" Randy called.

The assassin moved in a blur.

Tessa moved almost as fast.

The assassin had a knife pressed to Danica's side in a blink, but Tessa had launched herself at the woman at the same time. The two women went down and Danica staggered away, clutching her side, red staining her beige blouse.

Charles raced to Danica, and she grabbed his arm. "I'm all right."

The assassin was on her pink-sneaker-clad feet in a flash, aiming a kick at Tessa's head. Tessa blocked it with her arm and wrapped a hand around the woman's upraised knee, making the assassin lose her balance. She slipped her foot from Tessa's grip but took a step backward. It gave Tessa time to get to her feet.

"What are you doing?" Randy shouted, starting toward them. "Leave that little girl alone."

Oh no. Charles left Danica to grab Randy's arm. "That's not a little girl. She's got a knife."

Randy still fought Charles's grip, and Charles had to slam him against the wall. "Did you hear me? Can't you see the switchblade?"

Now he could — now they all could, because the assassin was swinging it at Tessa, who leaped and twisted to avoid it. Other people were drawn to the hallway, gathering in doorways and standing several feet away from the two fighting women, watching in surprise and disbelief.

Tessa managed to block a swinging arm and elbow the assassin in the temple. It didn't even faze the Thai woman. She rained blows against Tessa's side, making Tessa flinch and lose her grip on the woman's knife hand. The blade slashed downward.

Blood sprayed down Tessa's shirt, onto the carpet, but Tessa didn't even seem to notice. She feinted, then suddenly took a step and completed a twist. She now had hold of the woman's arm in a complicated grip. It happened in a split second.

The hallway filled with the sound of bones popping.

The woman didn't scream, but a muffled cry escaped her lips, her forehead creased with pain, making her look her true age. She ripped her arm from Tessa's grasp and aimed a kick at Tessa's unprotected knee.

Tessa rolled with the blow, but Charles still caught the grimace of pain on her face.

And before he knew it, the assassin was headed straight for him.

He tried to avoid her, but she was too fast — faster than any human he'd ever seen. With her good arm, she socked him in the kidney, causing pain to explode from his side, then aimed a kick to the inside of his knee.

The pain to his knee was the worst. He dropped to the ground, his cheek rasping against the carpet. He could smell the citrus-scented carpet cleaner, mold, and grease.

Footsteps ran past him, then faded.

"Charles!" Tessa was at his side.

He couldn't speak. His knee throbbed.

"Who was that?" people around him were asking.

Finally he croaked, "Is she gone?"

"She ran out the front," Danica said from his other side.

"I guess you were in her way," Tessa said drily.

In her way. He was such a chump.

He slowly rose into a sitting position, his hands around his knee.

Tessa's gentle fingers pried his hands away and felt his joint. "It might be okay. Did you hear or feel a pop?"

"No."

"May not be your ACL then. You'll need to see a doctor and stay off of it for a few weeks at least."

A few weeks? His diaphragm would have fallen to his knees if his kidneys weren't feeling as if a fist had squeezed them.

A few weeks off his knee. Just when Steven Nishimoto had invited Charles to his office tomorrow for a run.

Chapter 15

Mama was giving him the evil eye. And it was because she actually *liked* Danica.

She cut off glaring at him to smile at Danica, who reclined on Charles's couch, the shallow cut on her side bandaged up, though there was still red on her blouse. "You were so brave," Mama said to her.

"You know, I thought to myself, 'Today would be a good day to be skewered by a four-foot assassin.'"

Tessa and Hannah, sitting on the other couch, both laughed.

"And 'Apply to be a taxicab driver,'" Hannah said.

Danica smiled. "No, I already do that in LA. Drive brother to soccer practice. Drive Mom to the grocery store. Pick up boss's dry cleaning. Yes, I consider his suits a passenger."

"Well, I'm grateful you were here with your rental car so you could drive Tessa and George to pick up her Suburban and my car from the parking lot of that bar," Mama said. "Otherwise, who knows how long it would have taken my son to do it." She leveled another "How did I give birth to you?" look at Charles.

After the incident at the law office, since the assassin was neutralized—at least temporarily—Charles wasn't able to drive because of his injured knee, so Danica had driven Tessa, George, and Hannah to the Snuggle Up to pick up Tessa's and Mama's cars, and then they had all driven to Charles's house. They'd invited Fisher to join them, but he'd opted to go home instead. Mama had been delighted at the opportunity to feed people, and right now a Cajun shrimp casserole was baking in the oven.

"Speaking of the parking lot," Tessa said, with a wary look at Hannah. "How did the assassin even find us? I know we weren't tailed, not to the bar and not to the law offices."

Hannah correctly interpreted Tessa's look. "I promise it wasn't me. I haven't even used that new burner phone you gave me after the assassin attacked us in LA. I didn't sync it with my computer, either."

"You didn't log your computer on to any wireless networks, did you?"

"Only at the studio, and no one got onto my computer while I was online. I'm positive. Plus, most of the time I've been working offline on some encryption programs."

George, sitting in a recliner, suddenly turned beet red. "I, uh . . . I think it's my fault."

Hannah gave Tessa a "See?" look.

"You told me to use other people's phones to check my voice mail at home," George said, "but one time I forgot and used the burner phone you gave me. I hung up right away, as soon as I realized it, but . . ."

"Give me your phone."

George responded to the urgency in Tessa's voice and threw the phone to her. She promptly removed the battery and began systematically dismantling it. "You too," she said to Hannah, who handed over her phone. Within minutes, Tessa had neutralized all three phones—hers, George's, and Hannah's.

She sighed. "I'll need to get new phones tomorrow. But now I know how they found us. And why they haven't found the mountain cabin—there's no cell-phone service up there. They might even have lost the signal as soon as we headed up Highway Seventeen."

There was the sound of a key in the front door lock, and then Charles's younger brother Eddie burst into the foyer. "Mama, I'm—" He looked into the living room and saw the posse gathered.

Eddie was dressed even more disreputably than normal. His T-shirt and shorts looked like they'd been dug out of the dirty laundry from three weeks ago, and—great balls of fire—he smelled like a football locker room. Granted, Charles was sitting nearest the entry foyer, but still, Eddie positively reeked.

Charles adjusted the ice bag on his knee as he laid back in the recliner. "Eddie, this is Danica Wyatt, and that's George—"

"Awesome!" With his usual exuberance, Eddie bounded forward, bypassing Danica, who'd risen gracefully to her feet, to pump George's hand. "You totally rocked it on the show this week!" He turned to Hannah. "You're his daughter, right? On the show, he said you're a genius with computers."

Danica apparently just got a whiff of eau de Eddie. She looked as if she'd just stepped on a dead toad with bare feet.

"Eddie, what are you doing here?" Charles asked.

"What do you mean?"

Charles made an expansive gesture of his living room and

what he could see of the entrance foyer. "I'm happy to have you over anytime, but what did you need?"

Eddie's face grew more confused. "Dinner, of course. I always come over for dinner on Wednesday nights after MMA practice, since your house is closer to the gym than my place."

Charles looked at Mama.

"I didn't realize you didn't know," she said. "You've been working so late for the past few months."

Had his own brother really been coming here for dinner every week for months? Charles didn't know what to say. True, he'd had a heavy workload, but that was only recently, wasn't it? He started counting the months backward. No, it had been since the Denmark case. Nine months, at least.

"Well, we're all here now," Mama said brightly. "I better go check on that casserole."

Eddie had found his manners from where he'd stuck them under a rock, and now turned to Danica, who cringed away from him—or rather, his odor. Or maybe it was his sweat-stained shirt or the dirty athletic tape still stuck to his hand.

"Hi, I'm Eddie, Charles's brother. Do you work with George or something?"

"No, Charles and I had an aborted date tonight," she replied.

"Date?" Eddie swung around to give Charles a look that was somehow both disbelieving and disappointed at the same time. Thankfully, he didn't look at Tessa.

However, when he turned back to Danica, his demeanor was markedly cooler. "Oh. Well, uh . . . Charles is terrible with women."

Danica raised an eyebrow sharply. Tessa's mouth fell open. Hannah goggled at Eddie.

Only George wasn't surprised, but instead regarded Eddie with speculation. What was he thinking about?

"I'll form my own opinion, thanks," Danica replied frostily.

"Trust me, Charles is … stuck up." Eddie looked down his nose at Danica.

"Eddie!" Charles roared. "You can take your fraternal 'love' and your BO and leave my house."

"See?" Eddie said. "He can't even insult people properly."

"Edward Roderick Britton, get your behind into the kitchen right now!" Mama shouted. She apparently wasn't too busy to overhear everything.

"Yeah, we're just a crazy family. Sorry we ruined your week." Eddie skedaddled toward the kitchen.

Danica looked a bit like someone had just battered her over the head with a wet noodle before leaving the room. Which was sort of what had happened. She sat down. "Your brother is a little odd."

"He's a little off his game today," Tessa said. "Maybe too much Gatorade."

In the uncomfortable silence that followed, Danica said, "Well, I may as well get it out there. I know why you asked me out." She leaned back in her chair and stared at Charles, her gaze mildly challenging.

Tessa looked bewildered but didn't say anything. George looked a bit surprised, but he also didn't speak. Hannah however, had no compunction about demanding, "What are you talking about?"

Danica turned to her. "You didn't know?"

"Know what?"

Danica studied Charles for a long moment, her green eyes

surveying him. Finally she said, "Don't get me wrong. I actually would love another date—a real one, not one where I get stabbed."

She glanced toward the kitchen. "And I do like your mom, although your brother may have been hit in the head too many times tonight."

Charles noticed she refrained from mentioning Eddie's moldy-socks smell.

"But I also know, now, why you asked me on a date." Danica's eyes challenged him to deny it when she said, "You asked me because a certain number of producers of *Grab the Mic* have hired Rendell, Lerman, and Hunter, and one of the partners is my boss."

Tessa gave a sharp intake of breath. "You work for them?"

"I'm a legal secretary, although not for any of the attorneys who work with the producers of the show. But I did hear from Paul Harris's secretary that he was upset that a contestant was making trouble for his client." Danica glanced pointedly at George. "And now I see that someone hired an assassin, who would have killed the contestant if not for his bodyguard."

Danica leaned toward Charles. "Now, I won't disclose anything I'm legally bound to keep confidential for my employer, but do you mind telling me what the heck is going on?"

ے‌لم

She couldn't believe she was doing this. She was more nervous than if she were facing down three Chinese Triad gang members armed with only a toothbrush (which had really happened once).

Hannah noticed Tessa's nervousness. "They're not going to arrest you, are they?"

"They have nothing to arrest me for." Not exactly true. They had no proof of any crime they could arrest her for, and thankfully it wasn't illegal for her to be related to a gangster.

They followed Charles's secretary, Abby, up the same carpeted hallway they'd raced down only a few days ago. One or two of the people working at Pleiter and Woodhouse who walked past them gave Tessa strange looks. Understandable. Some of them probably still thought she'd beat up a ten-year-old girl.

Abby knocked on the door to Charles's office, and then Tessa entered the lion's den.

Fisher Daley, the forensic accountant, was there again, and he gave them a quick smile. Next to him was Charles, who rose from his seat at the small circular table, but he seemed to be avoiding Tessa's eyes.

And then a tall, balding man rose to his feet, cool eyes surveying her from behind thin wire-rimmed glasses. Tessa's step faltered. He looked familiar to her, but in a vague, wispy way, as if she'd seen him as a minor character on a TV show.

"Reuben Glenn, FBI," he introduced himself. His voice was higher pitched than she expected it to be.

Charles did the introductions, and Agent Glenn shook George's hand, then Hannah's.

Finally he shook Tessa's, and she noticed the widening of his pupils, the slightest movement of his Adam's apple. His hand gripped hers firmly, but also with the faintest tremor, and he didn't let go right away. He was ... attracted to her.

The realization made her pull her hand away sharply. She

should have been flattered. She'd seen that George appreciated her, although his flattery never crossed the line. But while she found George appealing, this man's interest made her recoil rather than feel flattered.

As Charles got more chairs, Agent Glenn sat and adjusted his glasses, organizing the papers in front of him. In some ways, he was a bit dorky, like Fisher. But while the accountant reminded Tessa of an awkward puppy, this man reminded her of a hyena. He might move like a Labrador, but she got the distinct impression that he had very sharp teeth.

And he'd noticed her reaction when she pulled her hand away. What Tessa was uncertain about was how he felt about that.

Agent Glenn cleared his throat. "I'm normally in financial fraud, but I was assigned to this case and happened to be closest to San Francisco. Agent Townsend, the head of this ongoing investigation, will arrive later tonight, but he has authorized me to speak to you about this gambling syndicate." The agent's glasses flashed as he glanced at Fisher. "Fisher tells me they have a rather fanciful name for the syndicate, so for simplicity's sake, I will refer to them as the Double Zodiac."

"I already explained my spreadsheet findings to Reuben," Fisher said.

Reuben? Fisher was close to this man, apparently.

"Fisher tells me the Double Zodiac may have hired a woman to attack you?" Agent Glenn said.

George nodded. "She looks like a ten-year-old girl, but she attacked my daughter once at the studio in LA, and then she arrived here a few days ago. She injured our friend, Danica Wyatt, before Tessa broke the assassin's arm."

Danica had been gutsy to do what she did. In fact, it was something Tessa might have done herself. The fact that Danica didn't have Tessa's special skill set made the move all the braver.

When she'd realized Danica was Charles's date, Tessa had felt the hiss of jealousy uncurling in her stomach, but she'd firmly squelched it. She wanted to be happy for him, had expected Danica to be sweet and charming, maybe someone like Vivian.

Instead, Danica had been calm, gutsy, and witty. She made Tessa want to be her friend.

Dream on. Talk about massively awkward.

Agent Glenn scribbled something down on his notepad, then looked up at Tessa coolly. "You are Tessa Lancaster, niece of Teruo Ota?"

"That has nothing to do with this," she bit out, while at the same time Charles said hastily, "That has no relevance in this case."

Agent Glenn put up a hand. "I didn't mean to imply anything. I simply wished to ascertain Ms. Lancaster's unique abilities as documented in her—ahem, previous case."

His words were apologetic, but somehow Tessa didn't get the impression he was actually sorry. It was as if he'd deliberately said it to see what their reaction would be.

Hyena, just as she thought.

And Charles's reaction bothered her too. If he was ready to date other women, what was he doing defending her? It didn't make her feel warm and fuzzy; it made her feel hot and buzzy. She didn't want him looking out for her.

"And why do you feel the Double Zodiac is after you?" Agent Glenn asked George.

In his rambling way, George explained about the email, blithely confessing all the illegal things Hannah did despite the fact that she kept kicking him under the table.

But when he got to the part about Hannah stealing the spreadsheet from the computer that tried to hack into her laptop, Agent Glenn nodded at her in admiration. "Very clever."

"That's what I told her," Fisher said.

"You did a good job figuring out that the spreadsheet was one of the syndicate's schemes," Agent Glenn told him. "You're worth every exorbitant penny we pay you, Fisher."

Exorbitant? Exactly how much had Fisher Daley cost Charles when he hired him to analyze the spreadsheet? She supposed Elizabeth St. Amant would pay that eventually, although maybe the FBI would foot the bill. It might make their interference worthwhile after all.

"It sounds like you've been after them for a while," Hannah said.

Agent Glenn nodded. "Agent Townsend has been in charge of the investigation since the FBI first discovered the existence of this syndicate. I was pulled in when the suspect in one of my investigations was thought to be intimately involved in the syndicate."

"What exactly do they do?" George asked. "When Fisher explained the spreadsheet, it seemed like they just gamble on stuff."

"They attract high-bankroll gamblers," Agent Glenn said. "They've made some infamous payouts over the years that keep gamblers interested in their activities. But they also make secretive side bets, and according to Fisher's analysis, they're rigging the outcome of this television show."

"Do they only do TV shows?" Tessa asked.

"No, they've done quite well on football and baseball. There's no evidence they influenced any of those games, but some of their supposed wins appear suspicious. We also suspect them of fixing fights—boxing, mostly, but also MMA, possibly, in recent years. We haven't seen anything to indicate they're involved in horse races or car races, although there was a lead on yacht racing in Monterey. Again, no proof for any of this."

Yacht racing. Tessa kept a mildly interested expression on her face, but her mind flipped back to her days on the street. Uncle Teruo loved the ocean, and his side interest was the yacht races along the California coast. Naturally, he ran some gambling rings related to the races. Was Kenta's brother Mits still involved in those?

She shrank from the idea of seeing Kenta again. The memory of her attraction to him had faded over the years, but she was uncomfortable with the simple fact that he had seen her at her weakest, at her most emotional, at Uncle Teruo's house last year when she had blown up at Charles. Kenta, who had come closest to being a friend, closest to being a lover, had witnessed her intense pain, something she had previously hidden from everyone, including her uncle.

She didn't want to look in Kenta's eyes and see his reaction to her now. Would he view her with contempt? With pity? Or worse, with the same longing yet steely self-control he had exerted the last time they'd talked? She didn't want his longing, not anymore, and yet she had always resented his self-control because it somehow made her feel devalued. Not worthy of acting on his emotions, of sacrificing anything for her.

Kenta and his brother Mits were close. If she went to visit Mits, she had to time it carefully so that she could avoid seeing Kenta.

"You said you saw the assassin with a man at the San Francisco airport," Agent Glenn was saying. "An investigator, Vernon Mead, correct? Have you seen him again since?"

"No," George said. Tessa also shook her head.

Charles leaned forward. "I spoke to *Entertainment Bay Area*, and they were happy to give us the original video footage they took. Unfortunately, it took them until now to send it over. I just received it today."

"I'll take it with me before I leave," Agent Glenn said. "We'll have the lab analyze it."

"The producers of *Grab the Mic* insist that they hired Vernon just to do background checks on me," George said. "And that they did the same for the other contestants. They said he had nothing to do with the assassin at the airport."

"Unfortunately, they could be telling the truth." After a pause the agent added, "Although I highly doubt that."

Maybe he wasn't such a bad guy after all.

"Did you find anything else out about the assassin?"

Tessa remembered what Nez had told her. She and Hannah exchanged a covert glance, although Hannah quickly dropped her eyes. Tessa also looked briefly at Charles.

He said, "We know she's Thai. That might not be immediately apparent from the video footage. Other than that, nothing."

He had protected her again. And again, it upset her when it should have made her feel relieved.

However, the reminder of what Nez had said about the assassin made her wonder if he'd been right, if the assassin had been hired by one of her uncle's *kobun*. It was a tenuous connection to the syndicate, to the yacht racing.

She'd have to follow the thread, even if it risked her uncle's displeasure.

Chapter **16**

When Charles saw Rick's name on the caller ID list, guilt squeezed his shoulders as if he'd slung a backpack full of rocks onto his back. Rick had called to talk to him, but Charles hadn't had time to visit his friend at the hospital lately.

Charles called him back immediately. "Hey, Rick, how're you feeling?"

"Still like a dump truck ran me over." Rick's voice sounded thready, although he was a little more energetic than when Charles had talked to him a few days ago. "I've got more chemo today, or maybe it's another scan. Who knows. I can't keep track anymore. You sound like you're in your car."

"I'm in a rental. I'm in LA."

"Defecting from Pleiter and Woodhouse?"

"Following a lead and then going on a date."

"Oh, ho!" Rick's tone was almost cheerful. "From my list?"

"I'm ashamed to admit it, yes. Danica Wyatt."

"I like Danica."

"You liked Marcy and Kayla too. And look how they turned out."

"No, I've actually spent more than two minutes with Danica. She's the younger sister of one of Annelissa's college roommates."

"So she's Annelissa's connection, not yours? No wonder Danica's normal."

"Hey, Kayla was pretty."

"And planning to take over the world someday."

Rick hastily changed the subject. "So what's the lead you're following?"

"It has to do with my client George Mynheir."

"I've been totally dissed. You still haven't brought George in so I can meet him."

"Tell you what, I'll do it in two days. I promise."

"I won't last another two hours. The hospital is trying to poison me with this Jell-O."

"Oh? At the office they're saying Randy McDonald poisoned you. He got two of your high-profile cases."

Rick made a frustrated grunt. "Randy needs to just go and play professional soccer in Europe or something like that. Enough of this lawyering stuff."

"Still smarting from that loss, eh?" Randy had beaten the pants off Rick at a soccer match only a few weeks before his collapse.

"I just wasn't playing my A-game at the time," Rick said quickly. "It was the cancer."

Somehow, Rick making fun of his cancer made Charles feel confined, filled with nervous energy and a need to go for a long run at top speed. "You'll feel better soon," he said lamely.

"Anything has got to be better than feeling like oatmeal

spilled on the floor."

"Oatmeal?" That seemed kind of random, even for Rick.

"And for the record, it is not my fault my youngest has been spilling oatmeal since I've been in the hospital."

"Hey, at least you don't have to watch marathons of *Sesame Street*."

"He's graduated to *Cars* finally, remember? Besides, I think I'd rather suffer through *Sesame Street* than feel like I'm something my kids dug up from the backyard."

"Wouldn't that mean you're fossilized?"

"Ha! Good one." Rick's breath seemed to be coming more quickly now. "Better go. Talk to you later."

Charles headed toward Rendell, Lerman & Hunter in the heart of downtown, a stone's throw from city hall.

He had just gotten off of the freeway when his phone, which was lying on the passenger seat, rang. The sight of Tessa's name on his phone still sent a spark through him. He had to stop that. His "Hello?" came out a bit harsher than he intended.

"Is this a bad time?"

"No, no. What did you need?"

"Could I use your panic room?"

"You wanting to use my panic room induces panic in me."

"Ha-ha."

"I'm not kidding."

"Look, it's for George and Hannah."

"I thought you guys were all safely holed up in your little mountain cabin." He suddenly realized there wasn't any static on the phone. "Where are you?"

"Uh ... at your house."

"What? Is Mama there?"

"She's the one who told me to call you."

He almost ran a red light but slammed on the brakes just in time. "Why do you need the panic room?"

"I told you, for George and Hannah."

"Are you telling me you're going to lock your clients in my panic room?"

"Uh ... no, I won't tell you that if you don't want me to."

He imagined her neck in his hands as he wrung the air. "Why do you need to lock them in?"

"I need to go somewhere, and I can't take them with me."

"Why not?"

"It's not like I'm going to get my hair styled, Charles." Her tone was acidic.

True. "So you need them protected while you're gone. What about the FBI? Can't they protect them for you?"

"Okay, disregarding my fantastic relationship with the FBI, if I went to Agent Glenn and said, 'Hey, will you babysit my clients for a couple hours?' he'd ask why. And I'm not about to confess to him who I'm going to visit."

Ah. That meant that the FBI would definitely be interested in exactly who she was visiting. "What do you need to talk to your, er, friends for?"

"Something Agent Glenn said about the Double Zodiac made me start thinking, and I want to talk to someone who might know the identity of someone in the syndicate."

That made sense, since the assassin sent after them had been hired by a yakuza. "Yes, you may use the panic room. Just don't set off the alarm, or the police will arrive."

"Okay."

"But don't disconnect the alarm either, or else if they need to contact the police, they can't."

"Okay."

"And uh ..." She wasn't going to like this. "Make my mama go in there with them. Better safe than sorry. And if she puts up a fight —"

"Don't worry. I was already going to do that."

The way she read his mind was sometimes rather frightening. "Mama's right there, isn't she?"

"Yup. I'll think of something, don't worry. When will you be back? Your mom said you're in LA, right?"

Was she concerned for him? He hoped so. No, he didn't hope so. "I've been following up on something that occurred to me yesterday morning while I was making a copy of the *Entertainment Bay Area* video for the FBI."

"That was a smart thing for you to do."

"Did you really think I'd hand over the video without making a copy?"

"No, I guess not. What was it that occurred to you?"

"We assumed the investigator Vernon Mead was hired to investigate George because the producer's lawyer said so and because Vernon Mead works for a San Francisco investigative company. But the papers I got from Crossman's Investigations don't say exactly what he was hired to do."

"Oh." He could almost imagine her pink lips open in surprise. "You're right. We just assumed. So what if he wasn't hired to investigate George? Then what was he hired for?"

"That's what I was thinking. So I called the private investigator I had hired earlier, Kurt Proctor, and asked him about

Vernon. He talked to Vernon's ex-wife, who sounds like she's amazingly like your sister, Alicia."

"Ah. Then talking to her was like rubbing a cheese grater against your cheek."

"You know, I could have done without the visual."

"Sorry." She didn't sound sorry at all.

"Vernon apparently has money problems. He hasn't paid last month's child support. His ex gave Kurt the names of three of Vernon's closest friends—two of them live in the San Francisco Bay Area, but one, Rory Bickham, lives in Los Angeles. Kurt talked to the two local friends, who both said that Vernon started acting secretively in the past month, spending less time with his Bay Area friends and more time with Rory down in LA.

"Kurt is currently checking deeper into Vernon's finances to see where his money is going. But Rory happens to be one of the legal counsels at a small independent film studio, so Kurt thought it might be better if I talked to him about Vernon."

"Makes sense. You're going to see him today?"

"I made an appointment to talk to him this afternoon at three."

A slight pause, then she asked, "What are you going to do for the next three hours?"

He gave a silent grimace. She had to ask that. "I'm having lunch with a friend."

Her "Ooohhhh" was pregnant with meaning. Then silence.

He lasted for about fifteen seconds. Then he finally blurted out, "It's Danica. You liked her, right?"

"It doesn't matter if I like her, Charles," Tessa said carefully.

Oh. Of course. "Yeah. Um, I'll talk to you later."

"Good luck with Rory."

"Sure."

He clicked off his Bluetooth headset with a bit more force than necessary. Stupid women problems. He ought to just become a monk.

He arrived at the Rendell, Lerman & Hunter law offices within a couple minutes and was soon entering the pretentious entryway. After he asked for Danica, he took a look around the waiting area, with its bold colors on the wall, large abstract art paintings, and fashionable furniture.

"Going for round two." Danica appeared from the door behind the receptionist's desk, her purse over her shoulder. She was wearing a cream-colored business suit this time, but her red hair was still pulled back into a sleek bun, giving her a more austere appearance.

He couldn't help thinking that Tessa, with her golden-brown hair cascading around her shoulders, attracted him more.

Oh, brother. This date was already not going well. Out loud he said, "Hopefully this date will end better. Where did you want to go for lunch?"

"If you don't mind a bit of a drive, I have a favorite restaurant."

They made nice, friendly conversation on their way to his car in the parking garage beneath the building. She plugged the restaurant's address into his GPS. They made more nice, friendly conversation as Charles pulled the car out of the parking garage.

Okay, it had only been ten minutes, and he was already kind of bored. Why was he bored? Danica was sweet. She didn't have a snarky mouth like *some* people. She didn't have gangster relatives like *some* people. She wasn't an ex-convict like *some* people.

Unfortunately, he was almost relieved when his phone rang. He glanced down at where it rested near the gearshift.

Rory.

He fumbled for his Bluetooth headset, couldn't find it, and finally hit the speaker button on his phone. "This is Charles Britton."

"Rory Bickham, here. Look, Charles, I know what you called me about."

Charles frowned at the phone but said nothing.

"It doesn't take a math genius," Rory continued. "You work for Pleiter and Woodhouse in San Francisco, so this has got to be about Vernon."

Charles had to hit his brakes, causing a faint squeal of his tires, to avoid rear-ending an SUV in front of him. Man, he was not driving well today. "About Vernon—" he began, but Rory interrupted him.

"I know how it looks, but I'll swear to you, Vernon did not do it."

Charles didn't know how to answer that. He glanced at Danica. She saw the perplexed look on his face, then circled her hand in the air to silently tell him to keep going.

"All I have are your assertions, Rory. Why should I believe you?"

"Look, you and I both know this is not worth going to court over. The girl wasn't harmed. Everything is fine."

"You said Vernon didn't do it."

"He didn't. It's complicated. Look, I'm leaving the office. I'm on my way home right now because I forgot some papers in my safe. Why don't you meet me there? We can have a nice conversation in private."

What in the world was Rory talking about? Besides, Charles was on a date. "No, Rory—"

"Look, I'll do you one better. Vernon is coming to my house. He'll be there in an hour or so. You can be here when he gets here and talk to him yourself."

Charles's private investigator, Kurt, hadn't been able to find Vernon at all, whether in San Francisco or Los Angeles, and they hadn't seen him since the video was shot at the San Francisco airport. Here was Charles's chance to actually talk to him ...

No, he was on a date. "Rory—"

Suddenly Danica touched his wrist and nodded vigorously at him. She mouthed, "It's okay. Let's go."

"Okay, Rory. What's your address?"

Danica input the address into Charles's GPS, and Charles disconnected the call.

"This has something to do with George Mynheir, right?" she said.

Since she'd been nearly julienned by the assassin, Charles had told her about the email Hannah had received and the illegal gambling. "Vernon was seen with the assassin up in San Francisco, but we haven't seen him since. Rory is Vernon's friend down here in LA. I was supposed to meet him at three today."

"What was Rory talking about? What did Vernon do?"

"That's the thing. I have no idea."

"Is Vernon an assassin too?"

"No. He's an investigator up in San Francisco. Why are you willing to go see him with me? This is hardly the way to make up my last date with you."

"Well, obviously this is important." Her green eyes were wide as she stared at him. "An assassin tried to kill George and

Hannah, and if you don't find out who's behind it, they'll send another one after them. That's much more important than a date."

Charles had to respect her for that. Their conversation might be as exciting as watching the grass grow, but she had a good heart. He wanted to be attracted to her. If he was asked to draw the perfect woman for him to marry to further his career, he would draw Danica.

It certainly wouldn't be the ex-yakuza currently locking her clients and his mama in his panic room.

ﻌ

Rory lived in a nice neighborhood in the LA suburbs. Occasional foreclosed houses, usually spray-painted with graffiti, were interspersed between the well-kept homes. Rory's pale-beige ranch-style home wasn't huge, but it wasn't a stand-alone apartment either.

Parking on the street was difficult, so Charles slid his car into the empty driveway. He called Rory. "Are you home already? I parked in your driveway ..."

"I'm just pulling in now. No worries. I'll just park behind you."

Charles looked in his rearview mirror and saw an electric green Mazda inch up behind him. He pulled forward as far as he could to allow Rory to double-park behind him and not stick out into the street.

Rory was a short man with more energy than should be allowed in a human being. He bounced out of his car, took a step toward them, took a step back to his car, pulled out his briefcase, stepped toward them again, stepped back to his car to retrieve his keys, then walked to them with his hand outstretched, forgetting to close his car door. "Rory Bickham. Nice to meet you."

"Charles Britton. This is my secretary." Charles gave Danica a meaningful look even as he omitted her name, and she nodded.

"Now I know it looks bad," Rory said as he headed from the driveway up the front walkway toward the door, "but—"

A sudden crash inside the house made them all freeze.

"Wh-who's in my house?" Rory seemed undecided between fight or flight. He took one step backward, then one step forward.

"Is your wife home?" Charles asked.

"No."

Another crash.

Charles pulled Rory and Danica back around the corner of the garage so they weren't visible from the front windows.

"Oh, my gosh, oh, my gosh." Rory's legs wouldn't support him, and he sank to the concrete of the driveway, his back against the garage door. "There are thieves in my house. I need to do something."

"Don't be idiotic. What if they have guns?" Charles said.

"Oh, my gosh, oh, my gosh." Rory started hyperventilating.

"What if it's the assassin?" Danica whispered.

"What assassin?" Rory squeaked.

"She has a broken arm," Charles said.

"Oh, that's right."

"She could still be in there!" Rory hissed. "Who are you people anyway?"

If the assassin was inside, she wouldn't stick around long after making such noise, especially since no one was home.

Charles scanned the front yard for a weapon in case she came running out the front door toward them. He saw a hoe leaning against the far corner of the garage and grabbed it, handing it to Danica.

"I don't believe in violence," she said primly.

"What?" She'd obviously never been faced with Chinese mafia thugs whose sole intent was to break all her fingers. "What about the assassin at the law office?"

"I was distracting her so you could escape. I didn't expect ninja woman to start a brawl in the middle of the hallway."

"Ninja woman?" Rory shrieked.

"Shhh," Charles hushed him.

Great. Charles was stuck outside a house with a possible assassin about to escape, armed with only a hoe, and flanked by Mr. Basketcase and Miss "I don't believe in violence." If Tessa were here, she'd tell him to go to the backdoor, and she'd take the front, and they'd gate-crash the party.

Then again, maybe he'd leave with fewer broken fingers without her here.

"I'm calling the police." Rory tried to dial, but his fingers were shaking too much. Well, at least he was good for some—

A sudden high-pitched squeal came from the house ... which modulated into a giggle.

Rory dropped his phone, not even noticing as it splintered on the driveway. "That's my wife!"

Ah. Okay. Totally different scenario. Charles set the hoe back down.

Rory was on his feet and barreling toward the front door before Charles could say, "Honey, I'm home." Charles and Danica followed him.

Rory jammed his key into the front lock and whipped open the door ... which bounced against the wall and slammed shut on him again. Growling, he opened it with a tad less force the second time.

A pretty brunette stood in the living room wearing nothing but whipped cream. Next to her was ...

Vernon Mead.

Also wearing nothing but whipped cream.

What a waste of whipped cream.

"Ewewewew." Danica turned away. "I totally could have gone my entire life without seeing that."

"Lulu!" Rory roared. "And ... Vernon!" And he launched himself at his friend.

Vernon, luckily, didn't lose much of his whipped-cream loin-cloth as he fell to the floor. Rory slipped off him and slid onto the carpet. Charles spotted Vernon's pants near the door and tossed them to the man, who immediately pulled them on.

Lulu had grabbed the only other piece of clothing in the room, which, unfortunately, was a diaphanous nightie. She dropped it immediately for a throw blanket off the couch. "Rory, what are you doing home early?"

"Vernon, what are you doing here early?" Rory demanded.

"The answer's a bit obvious, don't you think?" Charles muttered.

Lulu's face fell. "I only wanted to try something I saw on YouTube that involved a guy, a flight attendant, and a can of whipped cream."

Rory had gotten to his feet, and he again launched himself at Vernon, his hands aimed for the taller man's throat. But again, the whipped cream made Rory's hands slide right off.

Vernon sidestepped, and Rory landed in another heap on the floor.

Charles went to stand between Rory and Vernon. "Rory, don't do anything you'll regret."

"Regret? I regret ever being friends with this slime," Rory spat. "Vernon, you deserve to have to pay every penny that girl wrings out of you. Get another lawyer."

"You're Vernon's lawyer?" Charles asked.

"Not anymore."

"But Rory," Vernon said, brushing whipped cream out of his goatee, "what about the lawsuit?"

"What lawsuit?" Charles and Danica asked at the same time.

"Last month, he had sexual relations with a minor he picked up at a San Francisco bar," Rory yelled.

"She had a fake ID," Vernon protested.

Oh. So it had nothing to do with the studio. Still, Charles needed answers about that. "Vernon, what were you doing with that little girl in the San Francisco airport?"

"I didn't do anything! That's disgusting! I was only supposed to escort her to . . ." His pale eyes narrowed as he surveyed Charles. "I know who you are."

Rats.

Vernon straightened, although looking dignified with whipped cream sticking out of his armpit was difficult. "I was only helping that little girl out of the taxi," he said coolly. "I'd never seen her before in my life."

"That's a lie. What were you hired for?"

"To do a background check on George Mynheir, your client, Mr. Britton."

Nothing. He'd come all this way for nothing but to gain a sudden and intense dislike for whipped cream.

"You're lucky his ninja woman isn't with him," Danica suddenly said, her eyes blazing. "Next time, she's going to kick your whipped-cream-laden—"

"Time to go." Charles grabbed her and pushed her out the door, flicking the lock and slamming the door behind them just as another of Rory's outraged cries reverberated through the walls. Someone ran into the door from the inside, fumbling with the locked handle. Then someone else banged into the door from the inside, and there were sounds of a scuffle.

"What happened to 'I don't believe in violence'?" Charles asked her as they hurried to the car.

"Shouting threats isn't the same thing," Danica said with a sniff.

Then they stopped dead in their tracks.

Rory's Mazda was blocking their car in the driveway.

can't believe you're locking us up." Hannah stood in the doorway to Charles's panic room.

"I'm not locking you up. You're locking yourselves in," Tessa said. Vivian stood next to Hannah, working the touch pad to lock them inside the room.

"Why can't I go with you?" Hannah whined.

"Because where I'm going, you definitely can't go." Although it would have been amusing to see Mits's face if Tessa showed up on his doorstep with Hannah.

"Have you seen this room? I'm going to be bored silly."

"No, you won't." Vivian didn't look up from where she was programing the touch pad. "I'll teach you to knit, and your father will practice his song for the next show."

Hannah gave Tessa a wide-eyed "Save me!" look.

"You can use Charles's computer." Tessa gestured to the machine that was set up in the corner and hard-wired to the Internet via a secure feed.

"It's ancient."

"It's also probably being monitored, so don't do anything illegal, okay?"

"Aw, man—"

Vivian finished with the keypad, and the door closed in Hannah's face.

It felt strange to not have Hannah and George with her for the first time in a few weeks, but Tessa didn't let up her vigilance, especially now that the FBI was involved. She drove the Suburban to a VTA parking lot, then took a series of buses around San Francisco. When she was sure she didn't have a tail, she took a bus to San Francisco Japantown.

Mits Akaogi took care of his mother in the house his father had left to her when he died several years ago. Mits's brother Kenta lived only a few streets over in a house he'd bought, and he came over frequently to help with their mom. Both were loyal *kobun* to Uncle Teruo, and Kenta had already risen to a high position of responsibility despite his relatively young age of thirty-six.

As she hiked the steep hill to the Akaogi home, Tessa scanned the street for Kenta's car, in case he had driven straight to Mits's house before heading to his own. No powerful black Lexus sat next to the curb. It wasn't sitting in the restored Victorian's tiny driveway either, but Kenta usually didn't park there, since it would block in Mits's car if he had to drive their mother somewhere.

She passed beneath the cherry blossom tree that sat next to the stairs that rose to the front door. After she rang the doorbell, she took a step back on the front step and looked toward the front bay windows, which were curtained.

Within minutes, a hand cut through the curtains to peek out, and she saw Mits's bright black eyes. She waved at him.

He opened the door for her seconds later, his wide smile making his eyes disappear in his face. "Tessa, long time no see." His husky voice seemed deeper than the last time she'd talked to him, over a year ago.

He didn't hug her, but she felt his pleasure at seeing her in his welcoming gesture as he opened the door wide so she could come in and by the way he kept grinning at her. He was only three years younger than she was, but she had always felt much older than he was, almost like an aunt.

"It's good to see you, Mits. How's your mom?" Since he was considerably shorter than his older brother, Tessa felt like she towered over him a bit.

"Feisty, as usual," he said with his typical good humor. What a contrast to Kenta's serious demeanor. But it was good to see Mits hadn't lost his humor, especially after taking care of his mother for so long.

"Mits, who is it?" The voice called from the kitchen at the back of the house. "I can't leave the *mochi*."

"Mrs. Akaogi, it's Tessa Lancaster," she answered.

"Tessa! I heard you were out of prison. Why haven't you come to see me sooner? Come into the kitchen. Mits, come put on the teapot."

Tessa moved from the postage-stamp foyer through the postcard-sized living room and into the envelope-sized kitchen, which was warm from the sunlight streaming through the wide windows over the antique sink. She remembered helping Mits install those windows. They'd removed the original tiny panes and cut through the wall to fit in the gigantic glass segments overlooking the back porch, which was covered in pots of flowers and one huge pot of bamboo.

Mrs. Akaogi stood at the antique kitchen table, her hands busy shaping sticky rice dumplings. The glutinous dough was still hot and steaming, so she worked quickly to form half spheres the size of Hostess Ding Dongs, stuffing each with sweet red-bean paste.

Her smile was identical to Mits's as she looked up, but she didn't stop making *mochi* balls. What shocked Tessa was that her hair had gone completely white. It had been ash-brown — or at least dyed ash-brown — the last time she'd seen her.

She should have visited sooner. Seeing Mrs. Akaogi reminded Tessa of the passage of time, how it went so quickly. She often forgot because it had seemed to go so slowly when she was in prison.

"Mits, start the water for tea," Mrs. Akaogi said.

"Mom, you keep forgetting I bought us this electronic hot-water pot." Mits went to a sleek white electronic water dispenser that looked out of place on the tiled counter. He scooped green tea into a black iron pot and, with a touch of a button, steaming water dropped into the pot from the overhanging spout.

Mrs. Akaogi waved her hand dismissively at the pot, spraying a fine mist of cornstarch from the *mochi* dough into the air to rain on the kitchen floor. "I keep forgetting. I'm too used to putting on the kettle."

Mits just rolled his eyes behind his mother's back.

"Come help," Mrs. Akaogi demanded of Tessa, and after she washed her hands at the sink, Tessa stood next to Mrs. Akaogi to help form *mochi*.

She remembered being with her mom and doing this a few

days before New Year's with a table full of aunties. Then the *mochi* was plain, but Mrs. Akaogi had a sweet tooth and made *mochi* year-round, usually with a variety of sweet fillings. Tessa's favorites were peanut butter or strawberry jam, but today Mrs. Akaogi was making the *mochi* with the more traditional adzuki red-bean paste.

Tessa rubbed cornstarch on her hands, grabbed a bit of hot dough, pressed a pinch of adzuki bean paste into the middle of it, and then formed the dough around the adzuki, pinching the sticky dough closed. The heat made her fingers and palms sting.

Mits reached in to grab a finished *mochi* dumpling. "Hey, you can't eat unless you help," Mrs. Akaogi said.

"*Mochi* is women's work," he said matter-of-factly — not derisively, but just as a statement of how things were. Neither Tessa nor Mrs. Akaogi responded, because he was right. Tessa had never seen an uncle or a male cousin help with the *mochi* forming. In the old days, the *mochi* dough had been pounded by hand by the men, but now the *mochi* dough was made with a machine that looked a bit like a rice cooker. As far back as Tessa could remember, only women had made *mochi*.

"Besides, I am helping," Mits continued through a mouthful of sticky dough. "I'm waiting for the tea to steep."

"It's probably oversteeped by now," Mrs. Akaogi said sharply.

Mits moved to the counter, and Tessa heard the sound of tea being poured into cups. In a moment, Mits had placed two handleless earthenware cups of tea on the table, a little apart from the cornstarch and *mochi*.

"How have you been?" Mrs. Akaogi asked Tessa.

"Fine. I started my own bodyguard business."

"Yes, I heard." Mrs. Akaogi's voice was interested, but it also had a sharp curiosity edging it. "You're no longer working for your uncle?"

"I'm not."

"Hmm." They formed *mochi* in silence for a while. "People wondered, you know, if something had happened between you two."

"No one asked uncle?"

"Would *you* ask your uncle?"

"Yes."

Mrs. Akaogi sighed. "Yes, you would. Well, the rest of us don't speak our minds very often. And your uncle has said nothing."

He wouldn't, because he wouldn't think it was anyone's business.

Mrs. Akaogi had already done most of the *mochi* before Tessa'd arrived, so they finished within a few minutes.

"Have you eaten lunch?" Mrs. Akaogi asked as they washed their sticky hands at the sink.

"Say no, Tessa." Mits sat at the table and now sipped tea from his mother's teacup.

"You already had lunch," Mrs. Akaogi said. "And don't drink all my tea. I want some."

"But I'm hungry again." He passed her the teacup.

Tessa picked up her own teacup but put it down again quickly. The ceramic had become hot from the tea, and her fingers were still sensitive from working with the *mochi*. Mrs. Akaogi, on the other hand, was immune to the heat and sipped her tea contentedly as she sat at the table surrounded by little *mochi* dumplings.

Tessa instead grabbed a dumpling and bit into it. It was still warm and gooey, the rice dough only faintly sweet, while the red-bean paste had been generously sweetened. *Mmm.* She hadn't had *mochi* in a long time. "You still make the best *mochi*," she told Mrs. Akaogi.

"Not as often as I used to." She sighed. "Doctor said I have to cut back on my sweets. These are the first I've made in months."

"You're not diabetic, are you?"

"No, but the doctor said I'm putting on too much weight." She patted her soft stomach.

"I told her she needs a new doctor." Mits stuffed another *mochi* in his mouth.

Mrs. Akaogi stood. "Can I get you lunch?"

"Yes," Mits said quickly.

"I wasn't talking to you."

"Yes anyway."

She glared at him.

He grinned at her.

"How about miso soup?" Mrs. Akaogi asked. "You go into the living room while I heat it up for you."

Years of living with her husband and her two sons, who were all in the yakuza, had honed Mrs. Akaogi's hostessing skills. She knew Tessa hadn't come for the *mochi*. Although Tessa hoped she could take a few home with her.

Tessa took her cooling cup of tea to the living room while Mits absconded with his mom's cup and followed her. They sat on two recliners by the antique fireplace, and Mits placed his cup on a small side table crammed with tiny porcelain Japanese figures of old men with fish they'd caught, bears standing on their hind legs, and dragons curling around themselves.

"Mits, do you still do the yachts?"

His eyes narrowed as he regarded her, still jovial but now

wary. "You don't work for Uncle anymore. Why do you want to know?"

"Have you ever heard of a gambling syndicate with twenty-four members?"

Suddenly his face was wiped of all humor. "You don't want to go there, Tessa," he said quietly.

"Is Uncle—?"

"You know I can't say anything about it."

This was beyond frustrating. "They're rigging a TV show in LA. One of them—or maybe one of their associates—made a mistake, and the daughter of a contestant found out about it."

"Tessa, what does this have to do with me?"

"The syndicate hired an assassin the yakuza has sometimes used. A Thai woman, four feet tall, often dresses like a child."

Mits had stilled, and his eyes were dead. He didn't answer her.

"She's attacked me twice." Tessa raised her arm, briefly.

Mits's interest sharpened. "Does she know who you are? Whose niece you are?"

"I doubt it."

"It wouldn't matter if Uncle found out."

That surprised her. "Do you really think so? I'm the one stepping in the gambling syndicate's affairs." Unless Uncle wasn't involved in the syndicate. That would explain why he might be angry if his niece was attacked. "He's not involved. I'm right, aren't I?"

Mits sighed and looked away. Yup, she was right.

But why this assassin? Random chance? Unless what Nez said was right. "A yakuza is involved in this. Without Uncle's knowledge."

Mits pressed his lips together.

"Mits, that is seriously bad."

He laughed shortly. "That's an understatement."

"How did you find out about it?"

At first she thought he'd continue to stonewall her, but then he admitted, "By accident. I wish I hadn't."

"Why didn't you tell Uncle?"

"I don't have proof."

It must be a very high-ranking *kobun*. "You can't tell me—?"

"No, I can't. Stay out of this, Tessa."

"No, I can't," she said quietly.

Suddenly, the sound of a key in the front door. She automatically turned to look toward the foyer.

Kenta strode into the house, his tall frame making the home look almost like a dollhouse. He spotted Tessa and froze.

His eyes flared as he saw her, but not with anger.

She leaped to her feet, her heart throbbing hard and fast in her chest. "Hello, Kenta."

"Tessa."

She had expected the same old pull toward him, but it wasn't there. She was ashamed to be caught pumping his brother for information, but being in the same room with Kenta didn't make her want to draw closer to him.

Not the way she always wanted to draw closer to Charles.

That thought made her set her cup of tea down before she dropped it. "I should go."

"Yes, you should," Mits said with a meaningful glare.

"Don't go," Kenta said, his deep voice rumbling against the low ceiling. "Stay for lunch."

"Tessa, you're not going?" Mrs. Akaogi entered the living room, wiping her hands on her apron.

"I'm sorry, I'm on the clock. I have clients I have to get back to." She gave Mrs. Akaogi a quick hug. "I'll visit again soon." And she would, she vowed to herself. "Thanks, Mits."

He nodded to her, his old smile returning, although not as sunny as it had been before.

"See you, Kenta." She had to move past him to get to the door, but he touched her arm. It didn't move her the way it used to.

"You'll call if you need anything?" he said.

"Of course." She was honored he'd think of her, especially because their relationship—whatever it had or hadn't been—couldn't really go anywhere. He was a high-ranking *kobun* and would probably marry for advantage, not for love.

And she realized she no longer loved him.

She was just out the front door when she suddenly remembered something and poked her head back into the house.

"Mits!"

He had gone back to the kitchen already—following the smell of the miso soup—but he came back out into the living room to gape at her. "What?"

"Do you have a laptop I can borrow?"

Chapter **18**

Vivian had attacked her with those knitting needles again.

Not literally. But she had Tessa on the couch in Charles's living room, once again fighting with two sticks and a length of string.

Tessa fought to get the tip of the needle through the loop, but the loop was so tight it was strangling the other needle.

Vivian watched her. "You haven't really been practicing, have you?"

"I can't exactly knit on the job." There, she formed another stitch. Whew.

This time Vivian had lent her a pretty yarn that was a mix of sky-blue, lavender, buttercup-yellow, grass-green, rose-pink. "Make a scarf for your mother," Vivian had told Tessa as she practically wrestled her onto the couch.

"When does this start to get soothing?" Tessa asked as the yarn fell off the tip of her needle again.

Vivian was knitting a gorgeous scarf in deep jewel tones, and she seemed to be working effortlessly. "How long did it take you to learn how to take down a two-hundred-fifty-pound man?"

"Uh ... not long. I practiced."

"Exactly."

Tessa started to rise and set the knitting aside. "I think I should go check on Hannah—"

"Sit!" Vivian barked.

Tessa sat.

"She's having the time of her life with that laptop you brought home for her and the copy of the *Entertainment Bay Area* video that Charles made." Vivian finished a row and turned her work.

Tessa was still doing the knitted cast-on, also known as row one. She sighed.

"To be honest," Vivian said, "after a while, I got tired of listening to George practicing his singing."

"I'm sorry I put you in danger. Again."

"It wasn't your fault."

"It wasn't George's. I should have been checking with him and Hannah every day about their phones. They don't think like I do. That's what they're paying me for."

"You're too hard on yourself."

"I feel like I've been messing up a lot with this job." The yarn fell off the tip of Tessa's needle again.

"You're understandably distracted."

"Distracted? What do you mean?"

"By Charles, of course."

"Vivian, I don't want to talk about this—"

"I know you don't. So just listen instead." Vivian pulled out more jewel-colored yarn from the skein. "Charles did something wrong. Fine. I don't know if he's even asked for your forgiveness for it. Fine."

"What do you mean, fine? It's not fine." The tip of one of Tessa's needles scraped against the side of the other.

"You are extremely hurt by it all. That's because what he did caused a debt."

A debt. Yes, Tessa felt like Charles owed her. Not just an apology, but an eye for an eye. She wanted him to feel the pain she felt, to make him pay for the debt.

"Darlin', it's the same debt that Jesus paid for your sins," Vivian said.

Didn't Tessa already know this? Hadn't she prayed the prayer because she had almost physically felt the weight of her sins pressing down on her? She had sinned against Jesus. Charles had sinned against her.

"I'm not Jesus," she said. "And I'm certainly not going to die for Charles."

"No. But the debt still has to be paid, doesn't it?"

The debt, this pain inside of her. "It's not a debt. It'll just go away eventually."

"But I don't think that's the same thing as forgiving him."

Forgiving him? Erasing everything that had happened between them? Going back to how they had been? Growing closer. Growing similar. Growing into better versions of themselves.

She longed for it. But at the same time, she didn't want it. The pain inside her would never let her be the same again.

"I think you think your anger at him is hurting him," Vivian said, "but I think it may be hurting you more."

This was starting to sound crazy and confusing. Tessa didn't want to deal with it. It reminded her of her sessions in prison with the counselor who told her how she should feel about her father.

At the thought, the rage boiled up in her stomach again, became a living thing, encompassed her thoughts until Charles and her father were the same.

Her plastic knitting needle snapped.

"Oh, dear." Vivian immediately stood up.

Tessa looked at her hand and saw blood running down her palm in a scarlet stream, down her wrists. Suddenly Vivian was there, taking the broken needle, pressing a cloth to Tessa's hand to staunch the blood.

"Do you know what makes me sad?" Vivian said. "Your anger and resentment have changed who you are. I miss the Tessa I met last year." Her hand cupped Tessa's cheek.

At Vivian's touch, something flowed into Tessa. A wave of emotion that filled her eyes and squeezed her throat, that caged her lungs and stopped her heart.

"I got an email from my father," she breathed.

Vivian folded her in snickerdoodle-scented arms. "Oh, goodness. No wonder you've been so mad at Charles."

Tessa didn't cry, not exactly. She just sat in Vivian's embrace and breathed in and out. But each breath out was harsh and sharp, and each breath in was painful and rough.

She didn't think. She didn't allow herself to think. She just concentrated on breathing, on keeping herself from shattering.

"I don't want to forgive him." She wasn't sure if she was referring to Charles or her father.

"Are you kidding? None of us want to forgive." Vivian's arms tightened. "You choose to do it like you choose to rip off a bandage or dig out a thorn."

That was a good analogy. Except it was ripping a bandage off her soul, digging a thorn out of her heart. "Even if I forgive him, I'll never be the same again."

"No one expects you to ever be the same again."

Tessa didn't feel like she'd found any answers, only lots of questions.

She pulled away from Vivian but still felt their bond, like they were two needles knitting the same scarf.

Vivian reached over, picked up Tessa's discarded knitting, deftly replacing the needles with a new set, and handed the knitting back to Tessa.

So Tessa went back to knitting the blasted cast-on.

Thankfully, Hannah rescued her a few minutes later. "Tessa!" She bounded down the stairs.

"Be careful." Tessa turned in time to see Hannah taking the last few steps three at a time. She could just see her slipping and falling and breaking her neck.

Oh, man, now she sounded like a parent.

Hannah darted into the living room, her father following at a slower pace. She laid the laptop on the coffee table in front of them. "So I have good news and bad news."

"Bad news first," Tessa said.

"I managed to retrieve that email from your dad, but I couldn't trace where it came from."

Tessa had been telling herself not to get her hopes up, but she had to tug to keep her stomach from sinking. "You couldn't find any information about it?"

"Whoever sent it deleted the account and any information pretty thoroughly, and I think it was sent from another country, not the U.S."

If it wasn't sent from the U.S., then it probably wasn't a

yakuza who'd sent it. But what did that mean? "Does that mean it's a legit email?"

"I didn't say that. It could still have been spoofed by someone trying to get at you."

And Tessa definitely had plenty of enemies.

And one missing father.

"Okay, now for the good news," Hannah said. "This is a still of the video from the airport." With a few taps and swipes to the touchpad, she zoomed in on a white tag hanging off of Vernon Mead's luggage. "That's an old luggage tag, dated about three months ago. He flew to San Francisco from Nevada."

"Was he in Nevada on a job?" That wouldn't really help them much.

"I wasn't sure, so I checked his company server files for his current job information—"

Which had probably been entirely illegal.

"—but there wasn't anything about Nevada. Then I checked on social networking sites and found him on Facebook!" The screen changed as she tapped and swiped. "Voila! Who's awesome?"

His Facebook photo showed a younger Vernon Mead, sans goatee, with more hair than he had now. "You are," Tessa agreed. "But I still don't know how this helps us."

"I got to thinking about the man who logged on to my computer in Oakland, the one I captured on my webcam."

"Charles said there was no record of him at Vernon's agency."

"Right. But remember, the private investigator Charles hired was asking questions at the studio. Someone had to have followed the PI when he met with Charles in San Francisco, and then the next day, follow Charles to the park when he met us. But the day before, when my webcam took the video, the guy was at my house in Oakland. He'd have had a hard time following Charles in San Francisco and being in Oakland. That's a lot of driving."

"So you're thinking it was a two-person job."

"And I wondered if maybe his associate is someone he's known for a long time. I figured it wouldn't hurt to try. I searched Vernon's Friends list for people who went to his high school." She gave a snort. "It was so easy. He has his Nevada high school publicly listed on his info page, and he had all his old friends on a list labeled 'High School Friends.'"

"Wait a minute. For Facebook, you're not supposed to be able to see what list someone adds a friend to. Did you hack into his account?" Tessa demanded.

Hannah froze a moment. "Uh ... okay, forget about that part. We don't need it anyway." She scrolled down the computer screen. "Look what I found on his Facebook wall, and it's completely public," she assured Tessa as she caught her glare.

The screen showed a post on Vernon's Facebook wall from someone named Campbell Rollins. It was dated over a year ago.

Hey, Mead, happy birthday! Remember your first birthday in computer club freshman year? Ha-ha! I think the school still bans chia pets from the computer lab in case they're hiding flash drives. What idiots. I'll call you when I get back from Cabo!

Hannah tapped a few keys on the laptop, then said, with a flourish of her hand, "Meet Campbell Rollins. Yeah, I'm super awesome."

The computer now displayed the Facebook profile of the scruffy man.

"So that's his name. Campbell Rollins."

"All anyone would have to do is go through Vernon's Friends list," Hannah said. "I looked at their info. Campbell is a janitor."

"But he has the money to go to Cabo."

"According to his Facebook wall, he's gone at least once a year, sometimes twice."

"If he's not really a janitor, what does he do?"

"According to what I've been able to find out about them, in high school Vernon and Campbell were in computer club their freshman years, but not any other years."

Hannah brought up a photo she'd pulled off the Web that looked as if it had come from Vernon's Nevada high school's alumni website. It was a black-and-white group photo that looked like it had been scanned from the school yearbook. Tessa could make out Vernon and Campbell near the back, looking a bit grumpy. Campbell was about fifty pounds lighter but still had the same nervous look in his eyes, and Vernon looked almost the same, again without the goatee.

"And that's a clue how?" Tessa asked.

Hannah looked at her in disbelief. "Seriously? You don't see it?"

"See what?"

"I was in computer club in junior high, but only for my first year." She made a ta-da motion with her hands.

Tessa still didn't get it.

Hannah made a disgusted sound. "I left the computer club because they were lame. Remember how Campbell called their computer club idiots? All my computer club wanted to do was hack into the school mainframe, which was so dumb. I'd done that when I was ..." She broke off when she saw the frown on her father's face and the glare coming from Tessa. "I mean, I never broke into the school mainframe. Ever."

"So you left computer club because you were too smart."

"I left computer club because I was too *illegal.*" She said it without guile.

"Hannah!" George looked toward the ceiling and grabbed his hair with his hands.

But Tessa was finally starting to get it. "You think Vernon and Campbell left computer club because they also felt they had bigger fish to fry. Campbell is a hacker."

"But then, why would he have a Facebook page?" Vivian said. "That seems counterintuitive for someone whose entire existence is to not exist."

"Some of the best hackers love having a double life," Hannah said. "A perfectly normal Facebook life and then a secret life where they're only known by their hacker name."

"But Vernon is a private investigator," Vivian said.

"He could still do some hacking on the side. Or it could be just Campbell doing the hacking."

"What would they hack?"

"They could have created that program I was telling you about weeks ago that could send false votes to the computer that tallies the results of *Grab the Mic.*"

Tessa stared again at the photo of Vernon and Campbell.

"These are the guys rigging the voting."

Chapter 19

Charles had done more unmanly things in his life. Like the time he cried when Carly Looman broke up with him in fifth grade. Or the time he'd been sitting on a rock, resting during a hike with Eddie, and a lizard somehow found its way into his shorts and he'd squealed like a girl.

But tonight, he hadn't been able to kiss the girl. And that made him feel like a complete loser.

Danica had been willing. After the late lunch Charles had treated her to—he owed her after the entire whipped-cream incident—he'd driven her back to the parking garage of the building where her law offices were. He parked his car next to hers. She'd stood by her open driver's-side door, chatting with him about what a lovely time she'd had.

And then she'd taken a step, a tiny step closer to him. She'd lifted her chin, exposed the long column of her neck, and smiled that mysterious woman-smile that usually sent his blood simmering.

Nothing. No simmering. Not even a little steam.

She waited. Looked deep into his eyes. He looked back.

Even swayed closer to her. Here was his chance, handed to him on a silver platter. This woman actually liked him. She didn't think he was a complete idiot or a jerk. Wanted to get to know him better. Was obviously attracted to him. Was a knockout herself.

Best of all, she'd make his coworkers crazy-jealous of him.

He'd put his fingers on her waist. Felt her muscles melt under his touch. He'd leaned in, smelled her sweet perfume—something he'd smelled before, nothing exotic, nothing like the rain-and-cherry-blossoms scent of Tessa ...

Why had he thought of Tessa??

Charles realized he'd been psyching himself up to kiss Danica, he'd been making a supreme effort, and now it was ruined.

But why had he had to make such an effort to begin with?

He'd kissed her cheek, friendly and impersonal. He tried to make up for it with his words. "Thanks for everything you did for me today. You're amazing."

Danica was only partially mollified. Her face smiled at him, but her eyes were a little hurt. His first impulse was to tell her that it wasn't her fault, that it was his for thinking of another woman while he was with her, but he'd hesitated and lost his chance, and thankfully realized what a complete moron he would have sounded like if he'd said that.

As if he could sink any lower. He was neck-deep in swamp water.

A delayed flight later, he was back in the Bay Area in a fog of self-recrimination, insults to his manhood, and general "You suck" thoughts. Now that he was home, he really didn't want to wake Mama up, didn't want to have to find a way to lie to her about his day.

Besides, she'd known about his date and would be positively gleeful to hear it went badly.

He turned off his car's headlights and ignition and coasted into his driveway. He was amazed at how easy it was. He ought to sneak into his house in the dead of night more often.

He had his house key between his fingers, the rest of the keys on his keychain muffled in his fist. He silently activated his car alarm. After toeing off his shoes, he grabbed them, stuck his briefcase under his other arm, and walked, in his socks, up the front walk to his door.

He was amazed at how smoothly his key slipped into the dead-bolt lock. He had expected a lot of noise, but there was only the faintest click as the dead-bolt slid back. The lock on the doorknob opened even more softly.

Charles opened the door slowly, listening for any telltale squeak, but the hinges were still quiet from when he'd oiled them a few months ago. He only opened the door enough so that he could slip inside —

Wham! Something that felt like a baseball bat jammed under his chin, knocking sharply against his throat and taking away his breath. He fell back against the closed door, his keys, shoes, and briefcase dropping. His shoes made a dull thud against the tile, and since they fell just before his briefcase, they softened the sound of its fall. His keys, however, tinkled as they skidded over the floor.

Suddenly the bat — no, it was a forearm pressing against his Adam's apple — stiffened and withdrew. "Charles?" whispered a sharp voice.

Rain and cherry blossoms. And a hint of yarn.

Charles didn't think. He just felt the tide of something surging up from deep within his belly. It made his hands reach up and cup her face so he could kiss her.

The kiss was like a long, sweet breath, a deep, hungry gasp after being underwater for too long. He kissed Tessa hard, driven by the frustrations of the evening, fueled by the longing that had been building in him for months. Years. His entire life.

She gasped but didn't move away. She wouldn't have been able to — nothing could have torn him from her in that moment. This kiss was the focal point of everything he'd ever wanted, of every risk he'd never taken, of every hope he'd been afraid to hope.

At some point the kiss softened. He knew this because her lips softened under his, and her hands at his waist were as light and tentative as butterfly wings. His hands slid down to her throat, where her racing pulse beat under his fingertips. He filled one hand with her hair, silky and smooth, flowing over her shoulders, not held by pins or product.

And she smelled divine. Like clean spring rain. Like spicy cherry blossoms. Like a warm blanket in front of a fireplace.

She smelled like Tessa.

And she was exactly what Charles wanted.

The moment he realized it, he tried to pull her closer to him, but she suddenly stiffened and jerked away. His waist felt cool where her hands had been. His body felt empty.

He could just see her eyes gleaming in the glow from the nightlight in the hallway. He heard that her breathing, quick and fast, matched his own.

"Tessa ..." he whispered.

She took a few more quick breaths. Then she said, "I ... I can't."

And she turned and hurried up the stairs, leaving Charles feeling like his soul had been ripped in two.

⚓

They were gone by the time he woke up the next morning. Mama explained that Tessa had given in to Hannah's whining and had allowed them to sleep over at his house the previous night, but Tessa had woken up the Mynheirs early to take them back to the mountain cabin.

"And why were your keys on the floor, Charles?" Mama had asked while scrambling his eggs in a pan, adding way too much Tabasco sauce. "I almost slipped on them when I came down to make your breakfast this morning."

Charles was in a daze all morning at work. He was also a bit nauseated, maybe because of the excess Tabasco in his eggs.

The queasiness faded by the time lunch rolled around, and he went to meet the marathon running group at the track.

He needed this time. He needed to run from his problems, run from his ghosts. And then, maybe later tonight or tomorrow, he'd visit Rick in the hospital, see how he was doing.

Steven gave him a friendly nod. "How's the knee?"

"Finally feeling better." Charles was careful as he did his pre-run exercises but felt no twinges in his joints. When regretfully canceling their previous running meeting, he had avoided mention of the word *assassin*, saying instead that a "tiny little thing" had hit him in the knee while racing past him.

Jeff arrived and started the group off on a warm-up jog. Without even consciously thinking about it, Charles found himself running next to Steven.

"How was your weekend?" he asked.

"I was at work." Steven sighed. "Sometimes I wish we were still just a small company. Fewer headaches."

Charles paused, then answered truthfully, "I'm pretty sure anything I say will cross the running group's rule of 'no business discussion.'"

Steven laughed. "It's hard, isn't it? Most of my days are spent at work, so I'd think most of my concerns and conversation would involve work. And yet I can't talk about it here. I already talk about work too much to my wife, so why can't I discuss it with fellow professionals?"

"They're probably afraid I'll start trying to sell you insurance or something."

"I just realized I don't know what you do."

"I'm an attorney with Pleiter and Woodhouse."

"Oh." It was a "That's interesting and possibly useful" sort of *oh*; not an "Okay, that's nice; let's change the subject" sort of *oh*. Steven said, "I've heard of Pleiter and Woodhouse."

"Their reputation is one of the best in the Bay Area. They were my first choice when I finished my clerkship after law school."

"How long have you been with them?"

"Almost eight years. I made partner a year ago."

"Congratulations."

"Thanks."

There was a short silence, then Steven said, hesitatingly, "The main reason I was stuck at work all weekend was some sticky legal issues."

"Oh?"

"The issues took a lot of time, and I have to admit, they're more difficult for me to understand than my advanced math classes in grad school."

Charles laughed. "I'm the opposite. Law school was a breeze compared to my calculus class my freshman year in college."

Another short pause, then Steven said, "If I wanted legal advice, could I hire you for a short time?"

"You don't have to hire me. I'd be happy to give advice if I can."

"I can't do that."

"I would think sweating together for five or six miles creates at least a tenuous bond of friendship, don't you?"

Steven laughed. "Maybe we can talk about it this week. Lunch sometime?"

Charles expected angels to begin singing. This was an opportunity he'd been hoping for, and it had dropped in his lap. What had he done to deserve this? But he kept his voice neutral as he said, "Sure. After the run, I'll give you my card."

The warm-up over, Jeff started leading the team in a few speed-work exercises. Charles began breathing harder as his heart rate crept up. His heart-rate monitor said his heart rate was at 85 percent. Chatting with Steven was impossible, since Steven ran the speed-work exercises at a faster pace than Charles did. Besides which, if Charles didn't save all his breath for his lungs, he'd probably end up heaving all over Steven's shoes.

But Charles needed the exertion. He needed time with his own thoughts. He needed his body completely exhausted so his thoughts could run through his mind unfiltered and honest.

He'd kept thoughts of Tessa at bay for most of the day, but he couldn't hold them back anymore. He couldn't lie to himself—he wanted Tessa. He might even love her. He couldn't keep himself away from her. Even Danica, the perfect woman, couldn't tempt Charles, which meant he really had something fundamentally wrong with his sanity.

And Tessa had responded to his kiss. True, she had pushed him away and then run off as if he had the plague, but up until that point, she'd felt the same things he had.

But the myriad reasons he couldn't get involved with her were still there, louder and clearer than ever. And now that Steven had expressed even a small interest in Charles's abilities as an attorney, could he really afford to even date, and possibly marry, Tessa? It could negate the success of landing Steven Nishimoto.

It sounded terrible when he put it like that—it made Charles sound terrible. But how could achieving success at his job be bad? He loved his work. He'd known without a doubt that it was what God wanted him to do from the moment he decided on attending law school. Why would God want Charles to fail when he'd just given Charles so much?

During the cooldown, Steven slowed down and paced himself with Charles. "I forgot to ask you about your friend who's in the hospital."

"Oh, he's doing okay. He's undergoing chemo, but he's keeping his hopes up."

"I heard that's the best thing, a positive attitude. After all, none of us knows what happens after we die, so why spend time worrying about it?"

Charles remembered a Bible verse he'd only read a few times: "Let us eat and drink, for tomorrow we die." Was that what people who didn't believe in God thought? Just be happy now because who knows what happens after death? Was this what

Rick thought? Why hadn't Charles made more of an effort to speak to him about Jesus?

The run ended, and Charles handed Steven his business card. "If you change your mind about talking to me, I won't be offended," Charles assured him. "It's only business."

"I appreciate that." Steven sounded sincere as he said it. "And I hope your friend gets better quickly."

"Thanks," he said, then headed to his car.

That last reminder of Rick made Charles turn right instead of left out of the community center parking lot. Sure, he had a lot of work to do before his meeting at three, but he wanted to visit Rick. He owed it to his friend.

The hospital seemed busier than usual when he walked in, but he knew the way to Rick's room, and those hallways had less people. Just as he approached the room, the door suddenly flew open, and Annelissa came running out, nearly running into Charles.

He reached out to grab her before she lost her balance. Her eyes were overflowing with tears, and she was sobbing so badly she couldn't speak at first.

A weight thudded against his diaphragm.

"What is it?" he asked.

"How did you know?" she gasped between sobs. "I was just about to text you."

"Know what?"

"The chemo isn't working." She choked on a sob. "Rick just slipped into a coma an hour ago."

Chapter **20**

Charles had kissed Tessa senseless.

Completely out-of-her-mind, out-of-her-body, out-of-the-universe senseless. Kissing someone had never felt like that before. All Tessa had been able to feel was Charles's hands, his lips, the warmth radiating from his body. He'd smelled sharply of musk, which had made Tessa feel like she was drowning in a warm, scented sea.

Even now the memory brought back the rush, the roar in her ears like an ocean wave, the tilting under her feet. She'd been awake praying, not for forgiveness—she hadn't been able to reach the point where she could pray that—but for the willingness to obey.

And then she'd heard an intruder downstairs. She should have stayed in bed.

But she would have missed the most incredible moment of her life.

Remembering her sleepless struggle and straining prayers were what brought her out of that overwhelming kiss and why she'd eventually been able to push Charles away. Her mind had been whirling, caught in his spell, reveling in it and wanting to give in to it again, and yet another part of her still wanted him to suffer as she had suffered. And a third part of her wondered when, if ever, she'd be able to let go of everything—her resistance to him, her bitterness, her hurt.

This wasn't how she wanted it to be.

Even now, her emotions were a jumble, but she needed to focus. She was on a mission. If she came face-to-face with Charles again, it would only ruin everything. She'd want to pull his head down and kiss him again.

And then slap him.

She really wasn't used to being this irrational.

Tessa drove to the parking garage of the building where Pleiter & Woodhouse had their law offices and parked in the shadows, trying to hide the Moose. Then she found Charles's Audi and hunkered down between two other cars nearby so he wouldn't see her.

Tessa was a bit embarrassed when the owner of one of the cars she'd hidden between came out to drive away, but she scurried between the next two cars and could still see Charles's car clearly. Vivian had mentioned he left for his running group around 11:30. It was almost time.

Finally, at 11:32, she saw him dash into his car and drive away.

She immediately dialed his secretary, Abby, and hoped she hadn't yet gone to lunch.

"Charles Britton's office," came Abby's pleasant voice. "How can I help you?"

"Hi, Abby. It's Tessa. Will you be around for another few minutes? I had a question to ask you about my billing."

"Oh, certainly. Are you on your way here?"

"Actually, I'm walking into the building from the parking garage right now."

Abby met her in the reception area of the law offices. "You had a question about billing?"

"Yes, it's a bit delicate, so I didn't want to ask Charles. He isn't here, is he?"

"No, he just left for his running club. You must have just passed each other down in the parking garage." Abby escorted Tessa back to her desk next to Charles's office.

"I was wondering about the expense of the forensic accountant," Tessa said. She wasn't exactly sure how to bring up the suggestion that they bill the FBI rather than Elizabeth St. Amant, so she thought she'd ease into the topic. She could have asked Charles rather than Abby, but again, there were the kissing and slapping urges she had to fight, so she'd opted for a little cloak-and-dagger today.

"Oh. The cost of that will be added to the next monthly retainer bill, so you won't need to worry about it right now."

Wait a minute. Monthly retainer bill? Charles had told her he waived her retainer fee.

What was going on?

Forget the forensic accountant's bill and the FBI. Why hadn't Tessa been receiving a monthly retainer bill? And how could she get Abby to tell her more?

"Will, uh, the amount for the forensic accountant be automatically withdrawn from my account?" Hopefully that question made sense to Abby. If the retainer bill was paid manually, Abby would wonder why Tessa thought the funds would be automatically withdrawn. Tessa hoped her bill wasn't paid that way.

"Oh no. While your retainer bill is deducted automatically, special fees require you to approve payment from your bank."

So each month, she had a retainer bill that was paid automatically. Which she had never seen or paid herself.

Who was paying that retainer fee?

"Abby, when was the last payment I made? I don't remember."

"I can look it up for you." Abby clicked her mouse and typed Tessa's name. "Last month, the fifteenth was a Saturday, so payment was deducted on the seventeenth."

"If I wanted to change bank accounts, what would I need to do?"

"I'd have to send you to our financial department to do that."

"What would I need?"

"You'd need your current bank account number. Here, let me show you." Abby brought up a screen that showed Tessa's client profile and pointed to a bank account number on the screen. "This is your current bank account number. You'd also need your client number, which is this number here. And then you'd need your new bank account number. If it's a different bank, you'd also need the bank routing number. Let me write all of this down for you."

As Abby wrote down the information on a piece of paper, Tessa tried to maintain a grateful, polite facade.

Because in seeing the bank account number, she'd recognized it.

It belonged to her Uncle Teruo.

ﻋﻞ

"Vivian, he lied to me. Again."

Tessa's fingers dug into her phone as she sat on a bar stool in a Los Angeles hotel the following day. She kept George and Hannah in sight a few feet away, where they sat together at a small table, celebrating George's additional week on the show with a humongous ice-cream sundae.

"Darlin' —"

"No, technically he's *been* lying to me. Ever since last year when I was forced to have him on retainer, and he told me he waived my retainer fee. He told me to my face that I didn't owe him anything because I'd saved your life. And then he turned around and billed my uncle. My uncle!" The pain ate away at her stomach like battery acid.

"Now, Tessa, think about this. Would Charles have been able to bill your uncle if Teruo didn't want to be billed?"

That was a good point. Which meant ... "So that's why Uncle Teruo agreed to stop badgering me to come back to work for him. Because he felt okay about me being a bodyguard so long as I had a lawyer on retainer. And he was paying Charles's retainer fee. And Charles lied to me about it, even after he knew how I felt about what he'd done during my trial. He continued to lie to me."

This was what happened when Tessa allowed people to get close to her. She'd worshipped her father, and he'd disappeared. Then she let Aunt Kayoko close to her heart, closer than her own mother, and she'd been taken from Tessa by a heart attack. And then Tessa had started opening up to Charles, had started to feel something stir deep down inside herself where she hadn't felt much since Aunt Kayoko died.

But the difference was that Charles hadn't left her. He'd deceived her when he hadn't told her that he had been at her trial. He'd betrayed her when he'd let her continue their relationship in ignorance that he'd had a part in her sentencing, even though by that point he'd started to know her. He'd lied to her about the retainer fee, even knowing that she hadn't wanted any financial support from the yakuza because she wanted to put that life behind her.

"And I was even praying," Tessa raged. "I was even praying that God would help me be willing to forgive."

"Maybe that's why this is all happening," Vivian said.

"What? That doesn't make sense."

"No, it doesn't. And yet it kind of does, if you stop to think about it."

"What? How does it ...?" Tessa's head throbbed.

"This reminds me of when Charles came home—"

"Vivian ..."

"Oops, maybe let's use a story about Eddie instead. Oh, I know the perfect one. We had a tree house, and Eddie had strung up a short zip line from the second floor balcony to the tree-house roof. The zip line wasn't very high off the ground, and there were bushes underneath it, so I didn't worry too much about his safety. He made handles from an old bike he took apart and had the best time sliding from the balcony to the tree house. But to get the handles back to the balcony, he had to tie a rope to them. That way he could stand on the balcony and pull the handles back. So I told him, 'Eddie, before you slide to the tree house, always make sure the line to the handles is clear,' and he always said, 'Yes, Mama,' like I was some overanxious mother hen, which I thought was very unfair of him, because I hadn't objected to that darn zip line in the first place—"

"Vivian, is there a point to this?"

"Oh yes. So naturally, he never checked that the rope

attached to the handles was clear. And one day he jumped from the balcony and got midway and suddenly stopped because the rope had tangled around the slats in the balcony and gotten stuck. He was dangling in mid-air and couldn't go forward or back. He began yelling, and I came out and stood beneath him and laughed my head off."

"How motherly of you."

"Oh, he deserved it. I made him dangle for a good fifteen minutes before I sacrificed some clean blankets and put them under him so he could let go and fall safely."

And here Tessa had been thinking Vivian was such a comforting, encouraging mother.

"My point is, Eddie gave lip service to me every time he said, 'Yes, Mama,' when I asked him to check the rope. How often have you given lip service to your mother?"

"Uh …" Foremost in her mind was the time Mom found that butterfly knife in Tessa's dresser drawer and almost sliced off a finger. Tessa had promised to get rid of it, but she only moved it to the closet instead.

"Lots, right? Honey, children think they're very clever about appeasing their parents, but parents have lip-service radar."

Was that like didn't-brush-her-teeth radar or was-out-with-friends-instead-of-at-school radar, or perhaps more like is-wearing-dirty-clothes-because-she-forgot-to-do-laundry-this-week radar?

"Well, now, since we all gave lip service to our parents, think about how easy it is to give lip service to God."

"I don't talk back to God. He doesn't tell me, 'Make sure you check the rope' or 'Get rid of that butterfl—er, contraband.'"

"Haven't you ever promised him you'll do something and then not done it?"

"Yeah, but I try not to do that. God knows I'm not perfect."

"But I'm pretty certain God would want you to at least try to obey. So when you say, 'I'll do this,' I can imagine God saying, 'Will you, now? Even if I make this difficult for you?'"

"Are you saying this is God making things difficult for me?"

"No, but God does allow difficult things to happen and can use them for good."

"Good?" Tessa fought to breathe, each inhale a labor of her lungs. "Vivian, I feel like I've been hurt all over again."

"Do you see why I told you that you can't just let this fade away?" Vivian said quietly. "The debt has to be paid. You have to forgive Charles."

There it was again, the debt Tessa had to take on herself. She was in too much pain to take on any debt. "I can't do it."

"No, I can't imagine you can. But you have reserves of strength from the Holy Spirit. Sometimes you have to reach for help outside yourself."

Tessa didn't know how. And it was all messed up in her head, mixing with zip lines and butterfly knives.

"Oh, I hear Charles at the door. He's finally home from work."

"I'll let you go."

"You should talk to him—"

"Later." Much later, like maybe next year. "I'll talk to him later. Not now. Bye."

Tessa stared down at the cell phone in her hand, then up at George and Hannah, who were finishing off their ice cream. Tessa's emotions were like the leftover sundae toppings that sat in the puddle of melted ice cream in the bottom of their bowl, all swirling together. She realized that seeing how much George loved Hannah was difficult for Tessa because it reminded her of how her own father had failed her.

She felt like she was just one huge, painful sore.

The hotel bar didn't have many people in it, so she almost immediately noticed when a man entered the room and made his way toward her. Wilson Weiss, one of the producers of the show. As she recalled, he'd been the one to tell Hannah to lie to the press and say that she wanted her father to get married again.

He seemed to be smiling at Tessa, but in a rather nasty "I just crawled out from under a rock" way.

"Miss Lancaster," he suddenly called.

Tessa didn't look at him, didn't flinch, didn't even stiffen her shoulders. Just kept watching George and Hannah and their melting ice-cream sundae. But inside, she felt a bubbling, foaming wave of panic. He knew her name. He hadn't before. How did he know her name?

"Miss Lancaster?" He was getting closer. When she continued to ignore him, he said, "Or is it Miss Ota? I certainly don't want to call you by the wrong name, but I thought you had your father's last name, not your uncle's."

By now he was close enough that she couldn't ignore him, since he was speaking directly to her. She gave him a cool look, although her insides were churning. "Took you long enough to figure it out," she baited him. "You must have checked with every nanny agency in LA."

Color began to creep up his neck, and his brow clouded. "I'm not going to let you ruin this show."

"How can I ruin it? I'm not even on it."

"I will not have the taint of your mafia connections on my show."

"Again, how can I taint it? I'm not even on it."

"The contestants and their families are under close media scrutiny," he snapped. "There'll be more videos like the one from *Entertainment Bay Area*, and next time they may show more than just your tattoo."

"People have much better things to do than try to figure out who I am when they see a glimpse of me on gossip TV."

"If one person figured it out immediately, you can bet others will!" He seemed suddenly aware of his raised voice and, after a quick glance around, adjusted his tie and sniffed. "If a little administrative assistant like Charlotte Quilly recognized you and came to us complaining about your underworld connections, other people will too."

Who was Charlotte Quilly?

Then the answer came to Tessa. The admin for Erica's lawyer. The woman whose negligence had almost gotten Erica beaten up by her abusive ex-boyfriend. How did she know about Tessa's tattoo?

Unless Tessa's shirt had ridden up at some point after she'd crashed her car and fought Erica's ex, Dan. And then Charlotte Quilly must have seen the video and the part of it where Tessa's tattoo showed when her backpack had pulled the back of her shirt up.

Tessa slipped off the bar stool and glared at Wilson Weiss. She was wearing combat boots today, so she had a slight height advantage and stared down her nose at him. "I don't work for you; I work for George. And there's nothing in his contract that says you have any say over who he hires as a bodyguard. And yes, his lawyer looked over his contract and checked."

Wilson had opened his mouth but shut it again.

"My 'underworld' connections have nothing to do with my job. But I can't say the same for you and your fellow producers."

"What are you accusing me of?" Wilson demanded.

"I'm not accusing you of anything, just like you haven't accused me of anything." They'd just been doing a verbal dance around each other with barbed words.

She walked away from him outwardly calm, but inside she was screaming. Charlotte Quilly had made sure the producers knew who Tessa was. At least one of the producers was in league with the Double Zodiac. So now the gambling syndicate knew who Tessa was too. The same gambling syndicate that had hired an assassin to take out Hannah.

Charlotte Quilly had certainly had her revenge on Tessa, but she hadn't only ratted Tessa out.

She'd put Tessa's family in danger.

Chapter 21

After flying back to the Bay Area with George and Hannah, Tessa immediately drove them to San Jose and her mom's house, letting herself in the front door. "Mom!" She was probably already at work.

"Aunt Tessa?" Paisley wandered into the living room from her bedroom. She looked like she'd just gotten out of bed, but she also had a pallor to her skin, heavy-lidded eyes, and sluggish movements.

She coughed, and her breath rattled in her throat. "You better stay back. I'm sick. I came home early from school today."

"You remember Hannah, right? This is her dad, George Mynheir."

It was a mark of how sick Paisley was that she didn't recognize George's name and only murmured, "Hi."

"Go back to bed, Paisley."

"I'm glad you're here. Mom has been texting and calling me since this morning. She tried buying a coffee this morning, and her card was denied, and she somehow thinks it's your fault."

"She always thinks it's my fault."

"Well, she wanted to call you, but you switched phones again, so she didn't have your number, and she kept calling me to remind me to tell you all this when I saw you next. And I kept telling her that the next time I saw you would probably be the same time she did, but I guess I was wrong. Good night." Paisley zombie-walked back to her bedroom.

Well, Tessa's family seemed okay for now, but Alicia was going to go ballistic when Tessa said she wanted them all to move into the mountain cabin with her, George, and Hannah, at least for a little while. Why did Tessa's job seem to always put her family in danger?

"Do you think there's still cookie dough in the freezer from when Paisley and I made it last time I was here?" Hannah asked. "I'm kind of hungry."

"Go ahead and look. If there is, feel free to bake a few." She looked to George. "Think you can supervise? The oven is gas, and there's a wok inside that needs to be taken out."

"Sure." He and Hannah headed into the kitchen.

Tessa headed to her own bedroom at the back of the house to pick up some extra clothes for herself. She opened her dresser drawer ... and froze.

Before she'd gone to prison, she'd been so insanely paranoid that she had started certain habits with her things that would enable her to know when her room had been riffled through. She kept an innocuous empty water bottle on top of a stack of T-shirts in her dresser drawer so that if someone looked through her clothes, the bottle would move. She hadn't believed she was in imminent danger like when she'd worked for her uncle, but force of habit was hard to break, so she often still set the water bottle in place without thinking about it.

She was glad she did, because the bottle had moved.

It was now resting on the edge of the stack of shirts. Her mother didn't touch her clothes. Neither did her sister or niece.

Tessa scanned the rest of her room. She didn't have extensive experience in this kind of stuff, but when she had worked for her uncle and been ordered to look through someone's home — which she'd done more times than she cared to remember — she typically went through drawers, the trash, the laundry. So when she set up precautions with her own stuff, she had guessed at what someone would move if they searched her room. Even after getting out of prison, she had fallen back into the same habits she'd once had because she couldn't quite get rid of her admittedly freaky paranoia.

She slowly opened her nightstand drawer, where she kept an envelope of cash on the right side. She'd deliberately rested some rubber bands on top of the envelope. They looked like they were randomly scattered on top, but she had placed them in a certain design, and since they were rubber, when she opened the drawer — which wasn't often — they usually didn't move from their place on the envelope.

The rubber bands had been moved.

Maybe Paisley had come in and looked for some cash.

Tessa opened the envelope, but it still had the full $120 she kept in it.

That meant someone had picked up the envelope but not taken any cash. Whoever had been here had been looking for something else.

Tessa's breathing started to pick up.

Tessa had also often looked through people's shoes in their closets, because they often hid valuables in the boxes or inside a shoe, so she had a pair of boots in a shoebox, and she deliberately kept the right boot stacked on top of the left boot. She figured that someone searching inside the boots wouldn't pay attention to if one boot was on top of the other.

But when she looked in the shoebox, the right boot was still stacked on top of the left boot. Either someone hadn't searched her shoes, or they'd unwittingly put the boots back the way they'd been.

She also kept a trench coat on a hanger in the center of her clothes bar, directly under a bracket that held up the shelf above it. If someone moved her clothes to search the wall at the back of the closet, she'd know about it.

But the trench coat wasn't moved either. Hmm. Strange.

Suddenly a suspicion sent a jolt of electricity through her. She hurried to Paisley's bedroom and knocked on the door, opening it a crack.

"Huh?" In her bed, Paisley propped herself up on her elbow.

"Paisley, what time did you come home from school today?"

"Uh ... maybe eleven. Nobody else was in the school health room, so the nurse was nice enough to drive me home."

"Did you come in through the front door or back door?"

"Front."

"Did you go to the back door at all?"

"Nope."

"Thanks. Go back to sleep."

Paisley flopped back onto her pillow, and Tessa closed the door.

Tessa headed through the kitchen to try the back door.

It was unlocked.

Mom could have forgotten to lock it before she left the house this morning, but she rarely forgot.

Someone had searched through Tessa's room just this morning but had been interrupted when Paisley returned home from school. The intruder had escaped out the back door.

A chill shuddered violently through Tessa's body. The Double Zodiac hadn't wasted any time. They'd found out who Tessa was, discovered she lived with her mom, and immediately came to search through her room. And they had almost been caught by her niece, which might have put Paisley in danger.

Tessa's immediate reaction was to gather Paisley, George, and Hannah and get out of the house, but she forced herself to calm down and think.

The intruder hadn't hurt Paisley, although he could have. So the Double Zodiac hadn't ordered anyone to harm them ... yet. He'd been searching for something, but what? Tessa only had questions, no answers.

She reached out to firmly lock the back door. She'd stay here until Alicia and Mom came home. She had to think about what to do, how to handle this.

Her sister was going to go Freddy Krueger crazy if Tessa tried to force her up to the mountain cabin, which was even worse than when she went Michael Myers crazy.

Hadn't Alicia been trying to get ahold of her? Tessa considered not calling her at work, because with the day she was having, she didn't want to listen to her sister blame Tessa for something random like her credit card not working, but she found herself dialing Alicia's number anyway.

"Alicia Kingsley," her sister snapped into the phone.

Oh, brother. Sounded like Alicia's day hadn't improved since she was denied her morning coffee. "It's Tessa."

"Finally! I wish you'd remember to let your family know

when you switch cell phones. I don't understand why you need to do it so often."

"It's to protect my clients, not to deliberately make your life miserable." Her relationship with Alicia hadn't really improved in the past year, but for some reason, Tessa wasn't as instantly peeved at Alicia for being her normal crabby self.

"Well, you always seem to make my life miserable anyway." Alicia gave a short, frustrated huff. "Have you looked at your bank accounts?"

"Uh ... no."

"Used your credit card lately? I suppose not."

"Not since ..." She thought back. "Yesterday morning." But it had been a prepaid credit card, and her name wasn't associated with it.

"Well, Starbucks wouldn't give me a coffee this morning because my card was denied. And it's your fault."

Here we go again, Alicia's mantra. "How is it my fault?"

"It has to be your fault, because not only is my credit card canceled, Mom's and my bank accounts have been drained."

"What?"

"I'll bet Mom's cards are canceled too. What did you do?"

"How is this my fault?"

"It's always your fault when something horrible like this happens." And Alicia hung up abruptly.

Had this been Tessa's fault? Or was it some weird identity-theft thing that had happened to only Alicia and Mom?

The house began to fill with the smell of baking chocolate chip cookies. Tessa took a couple deep breaths to calm herself as she dialed her bank's telephone number.

She tapped in her bank account number for the automated

system but was automatically shunted to a customer service representative.

Her stomach began to feel queasy.

"Hello, this is Sarah Smith. Could you please repeat your account number?"

After Tessa verified her identity, Sarah said, "Miss Lancaster, I see your account has been flagged for insufficient funds."

"What?"

"When you withdrew funds yesterday, your balance dropped below the minimum required balance of—"

"I didn't withdraw any funds yesterday."

Sarah gave an uncomfortable cough. "My records show you did. You emptied your account entirely, but you didn't close it. Would you like to do so now, or would you like to add funds to your account to raise the balance to the minimum required level?"

Tessa barely heard her. Someone had drained her account. And her sister's and her mother's, if Alicia was to be believed. And canceled Alicia's credit card and possibly Mom's.

Who were these people that they could do that?

She hung up the phone without answering the customer service rep.

This was a warning. They wanted the email. And the spreadsheet Hannah had stolen.

Now that the Double Zodiac knew Tessa was connected to George and Hannah, they were simply pursuing this new lead, this new avenue of finding what they had lost.

According to the gambling odds, George would make it through one more round this coming week before being cut the week after. Tessa wasn't entirely sure the Double Zodiac could pull that off, because Hannah said George was by far the favorite in all the unofficial internet polls. However, once he was cut, Tessa figured people would only complain loudly before forgetting about it.

Whoever had been in the house hadn't harmed Paisley. If the Double Zodiac was intent on cutting their losses and getting rid of George, they would have instructed their hireling to attack first and ask questions later—at least that's what Tessa would have done. But perhaps since George was so close to his prescribed exit, they decided to keep him around for another week.

Tessa hoped this was true.

Regardless, even though the gambling syndicate had sent this shot over the bow, so to speak, to indicate they had the power to destroy her, she wouldn't let them harm George or Hannah or her family. She hadn't been her uncle's enforcer for nothing. She never backed down, especially not when the enemy had issued a clear challenge.

Until Wilson Weiss had told her that Charlotte Quilly recognized her tattoo in the video, it hadn't even occurred to Tessa that someone could identify her that way, least of all an administrative assistant. But now that she was aware of the possibility, it occurred to her that if one of her uncle's respected *kobun* was really one of the Double Zodiac, he could have seen the video and tattoo and identified Tessa Lancaster as Hannah's bodyguard long before this.

Charlotte Quilly had perhaps not seen the video right away, but she had recognized the tattoo immediately. That meant that none of the people in the Double Zodiac knew the design of her tattoo. If they had, it wouldn't have taken this long for them to come after her. That eliminated some of Tessa's suspects, but the Double Zodiac could still have yakuza in its ranks.

While most yakuza had tattoos, not many of them had seen Tessa's. She didn't make a habit of parading around with her torso exposed.

However, that dragon tattoo around her midsection was similar to Uncle Teruo's dragon, which he'd had tattooed around his waist as well. How many of his *kobun* had seen her uncle's tattoo? She would guess very few of them, and only his most trusted.

She had a feeling Mits was wrong, and the yakuza who was part of the Double Zodiac was not one of her uncle's most-trusted *kobun*. It was someone else, someone not as close to Uncle Teruo. Someone who hadn't seen his dragon tattoo and who wouldn't recognize Tessa's tattoo as being similar to Teruo Ota's.

While it wasn't probable that one of uncle's closest, most-trusted *kobun* was in the Double Zodiac, Mits had still heard one of their names associated with the gambling syndicate.

And each of those *kobun* had sons or nephews who wouldn't be averse to using their powerful relative's name to get what they wanted.

Tessa knew exactly how to find out who it was.

Chapter **22**

Ever since she'd noticed the misplaced water bottle, Tessa had forgotten to think about how she felt about Charles, hadn't remembered to think how she'd feel when she finally talked to him again. But the reality was so much worse than anything she could have expected anyway.

For one thing, as soon as he entered his home and saw her, as soon as he saw them all sitting in his living room, he'd grown taller, straighter, stronger, a Spartan ready to fight to the death to protect his own. His stance seemed to say, *You are all welcome into my home, and I will protect you.* And that was just incredibly sexy to Tessa.

At the same time, she approached him awkwardly, stiffly. Her jaw was tight, as if aware of how reluctantly she spoke to him. "I need your help."

"Yeah, all the people in my living room clued me in to that." He smelled more strongly of his cologne than he had the night he'd kissed her. She missed the masculine tang of his musk.

"Hi, Charles," Vivian said from the sofa, where she was chatting with George and Tessa's mother, who didn't look terribly happy about all this. Tessa's sister, Alicia, looked as if she'd bite off the head of anyone who spoke to her, which didn't bother Paisley, who was passed out asleep on a recliner, a blanket thrown over her and a mound of used tissues on the floor near her feet. Hannah typed away furiously on the laptop Tessa had borrowed from Mits, trying to find the Lancasters' pilfered funds.

Charles touched Tessa's elbow. "Let's go into the kitchen."

She knew she shouldn't be alone with him, but it was noisy here in the foyer, and there were things she had to say to him that she didn't want her family or her clients — or even his mother — to overhear. She followed him to the far corner of his spacious kitchen, out of sight and sound of the living room.

"Have the FBI contacted you lately?" She crossed her arms over her torso.

"They discovered Campbell Rollins, but Hannah had already found out about him, so it wasn't anything new."

"They didn't tell you anything else?"

He gave her a look. "Agent Townsend seems like a decent guy, but I got the distinct impression that Agent Glenn wouldn't tell us anything if he could help it. He wasn't overly friendly."

No, he hadn't been. There had been that brief flare of desire in the agent's eyes when he first looked at Tessa, but nothing since then.

She noticed that Charles's eyes looked sunken in. "Are you all right?"

"Long days at work," he answered, although his gaze was intense as he looked at her. "And I've been spending time at the hospital each night."

"Your mom told me about your friend Rick. I'm sorry."

His gaze skittered away, and the bags seemed to deepen under his eyes for a moment. Then he turned back to her.

She realized he was remembering their kiss. Well, she hadn't forgotten it either, but she'd also spoken to Abby in the meantime. Had Vivian told him about what she'd talked about with Tessa?

"I'm assuming you need me to protect your family now too?" he asked. "Although Alicia looks like she could use a Valium."

Tessa couldn't help a short breath of laughter.

"What happened?" he asked.

"The Double Zodiac knows who I am."

"It took them long enough. I'm surprised they didn't figure it out sooner."

"The problem is that they're more technologically skilled than I could have imagined. They canceled my sister's and my mom's credit cards, and they drained all our bank accounts."

He goggled at her. "All?"

"The only things I have are the prepaid credit cards I bought. Luckily I'm paranoid, but it's still not enough."

He took a step toward her. "I can lend you—"

"Thanks. I'll let you know if I need it." She turned and looked out the window over his sink into the inky blackness of his backyard. She suddenly realized how exposed she was and closed the blinds. She stepped back, leaning against the countertop. "Move out of range of the window," she told him.

He did, but the move placed him closer to her, so close Tessa breathed his air, felt the space between them pulsing with crackling energy. Her breath quickened before she could control herself.

His arm went around her waist, and then he was kissing her.

It was even more intense than before. There was that roaring in her ears, that pulsing of her blood, and all the while his hand burned against her waist. She couldn't help it when her hands moved to his back, when her fingers twisted the fabric of his fine cotton shirt, feeling his muscles move as his breathing heightened.

But then ... but then ...

She didn't know how she did it, but she put her hands against his chest and pushed, hard. Hard enough to send Charles crashing back against the edge of the kitchen counter.

He stumbled, trying to stand, completely shocked. She realized Vivian hadn't spoken to him about their conversation.

"I spoke to Abby," she said. "My uncle has been paying you." She was surprised at how monotone her voice sounded, even to her own ears.

Comprehension dawned in his eyes. He straightened. "Yes."

"Why'd you lie to me — "

"He asked me to."

Yes. Of course he would. Tessa had been thinking about Uncle Teruo more often lately, and she realized she'd forgotten how hard it was to resist him when he wanted something.

"He told me not to tell you he was paying my retainer fee because you'd be upset."

"That's an understatement."

"I tried to waive the fee, but he wouldn't hear of it. He said he wanted everything aboveboard. Completely legitimate."

An arrangement Charles probably couldn't refuse, especially if he didn't want to anger both the San Francisco yakuza boss and the senior partners of his law firm.

She recognized this fact logically in her head, but she couldn't make it penetrate the numbness and coldness in her heart.

"He did it because—"

"He wants to control me," she said.

Charles paused before he said, "I think he did it because he cares for you, and you wouldn't accept his help."

It was true. She'd done all she could to prevent her uncle from trying to help her, because she had wanted to separate herself from him, from the yakuza, from a lifestyle that no longer understood her.

But though she had realized that just because her uncle didn't understand her new faith didn't mean he didn't love her, she'd always assumed it was a more careless, offhanded love. But maybe she was wrong.

"I need to see him tonight, but I can't leave my clients or my family unprotected."

"What do you need to see him about? This retainer business? Even if you fire me, he'll just find some other way to support you, so why not let me help you?"

"No, not the retainer business. I know the identity of one of the Double Zodiac."

Charles's gaze sharpened, but he didn't ask how. "Will your uncle be upset?"

"Maybe. But he has to know."

"And you can't exactly take your clients and your family along with you."

"I could probably take my family, although Alicia would try to freeze me with disapproval. But no, not my clients."

"Be careful." There was an odd tone to his words, and she could hear what he didn't say: *They'll try to follow you.*

She nodded.

She considered telling him she understood, if only in her

head, about Uncle Teruo and the retainer. She considered explaining to Charles the mess of emotions inside herself that related her father to Charles. But she wasn't quite ready. A strong part of her still had a tight hold of her bitterness, and she couldn't pry it loose yet.

As she turned to go, she called over her shoulder to him, "I don't think they're in real danger, but keep them close to the panic room."

He didn't answer her, and that somehow made her feel empty.

على

Maybe because she was tired, maybe because she was worried about her family, maybe because she had to deal with a mess of emotions so deep-seated that she couldn't shove them aside, but for whatever the reason, she didn't see the tail until she had already turned toward her uncle's house.

When she'd left Charles's house, she had deliberately headed toward Fremont before turning around to swing back. She'd been looking for a tail but hadn't seen one. Until now.

Drat.

Her brain scrambled through escape routes until she realized that whoever was tailing her could just lie in wait outside her uncle's house on Sea Cliff even if she did manage to ditch them now. They knew where he lived. At least, the FBI did, and she assumed they were the ones following her.

Because if she were an FBI agent who knew that *Grab the Mic* was being rigged by the Double Zodiac, that contestant George's bodyguard was the ex-convict niece of the San Francisco yakuza boss, and that said niece had just snuck out of her lawyer's house alone, at night, even *she'd* follow her.

And if they weren't FBI, she wasn't about to lead the Double Zodiac to Teruo Ota's house either. With their yakuza tie, she couldn't let them see her going to her uncle.

She couldn't let *anyone* see her. If the FBI were following her, she didn't know what legal implications entering his house might have. It could give the FBI a reason to bug his house. Suspicious activity and all that.

She knew of only one way she could get to her uncle's house without being seen. An old foot trail ran along the cliffs below Uncle's home. She and her cousins had used it frequently when they were younger, but the last time she'd been at Uncle's house and peeked over the balcony, the trail had been overgrown, obviously unused for years.

The closest accessible trailhead was almost two miles away from Uncle's house, so it typically took about an hour for Tessa to traverse the trail. The problem was that one long section of the trail was below the tideline. If the tide was in, that segment of the trail would be underwater and inaccessible.

Tessa wished she had a smartphone so she could access the tide charts. Was it in or out at this time of night? How much time did she have?

Regardless, first, she needed to shake her tail and get to the trailhead without being followed.

She thought there were at least three cars working together, handing off the tail to each other, a very professional job, which might be another reason Tessa hadn't spotted them until she was almost at her uncle's house.

To complicate matters, she had to make sure that if FBI cars were planted along the route to Uncle's house, she didn't overlook them.

Tessa stepped up the aggressiveness of her driving, darting in between cars, getting as far ahead of all three cars as she could. The problem was that it was later at night, so there was less traffic, which made it harder to leave her tails in the dust.

She sped down the Embarcadero, then jammed the gas up the steep hills. She caught a glimpse of the red car behind her, but ahead she saw the black and white of a one-way street sign.

She turned onto the street, going the wrong way.

Three cars were in the two lanes, and all were headed directly toward her.

The first of two cars in the right-hand lane yanked the wheel and went bouncing up onto the curb. The driver of the car behind that one saw Tessa and hit his brakes, his car skidding and spinning sideways as he tried to avoid a direct collision.

The only vehicle left was a small car with an engine so loud Tessa could hear it over the Moose's engine. She wanted to pull the Suburban into the lane with the car that had spun sideways, but there wasn't enough time to fully clear the car, and the driver seemed to be in too much shock to pull out of her way.

At the last moment, the driver of the third vehicle veered away from Tessa, scraping against some cars parked along the left side of the street. Tessa swerved to avoid the stopped car and then sped away from all of the vehicles behind her, as well as the cacophony of car alarms and horn honking.

Oncoming drivers managed to avoid Tessa as she continued to barrel down the one-way street, and she didn't see anyone behind her. She laid on her horn and slowed a little as she reached each cross street, but the cars on those streets were apparently intimidated by the size, weight, and age of the Moose and let Tessa go even when they had a green light.

Tessa glanced along the side streets to see if she could see any of the cars that had been tailing her paralleling along one of the other streets, but she didn't see anyone.

She finally pulled off the one-way street and drove randomly up and down, block after block. When she still didn't see the tail, she made her way to the trailhead.

The foot trail wasn't really a trail anymore, and the trailhead was not public access. Tessa parked along the small, lonely street a few houses down from the trailhead, which was in the backyard of 261 Winter Court.

She paused several long moments, listening to the crashing of the ocean waves, soaking in the otherwise-silent evening, letting her heartbeat slow after her crazy drive going the wrong way down the one-way street and from being on high alert as she drove the rest of the way here, trying to make sure she wasn't followed.

Then, in the rearview mirror, Tessa saw a shadow turn onto the street. Obviously it was a car, but its headlights were off, and it was only visible in the faint front porch lights of a few houses.

Suddenly she realized she hadn't checked the Moose for a tracking device.

Too late now. She had to move. She had to lose them on the trail.

She climbed out of the Suburban and scurried into the shadows of the bushes that lined the street, heading for the trailhead. She turned onto the cracked cement driveway of number 261 and sneaked around the side of the house to the backyard.

She darted across 261's manicured lawn as fast as she

could, then climbed over the low fence that circled the yard. She skidded down the steep hill face, grabbing at scrub brush and exposed roots to slow herself. Then her feet touched rock, and Tessa bore her weight down to stop herself before she slid straight into the churning waters of the San Francisco Bay far below.

The trail wound along the cliff, sometimes within five to ten feet of the water. The ocean was closer than Tessa remembered it being. If the middle segment of the trail was underwater, she'd have to decide if she wanted to give up for tonight or swim and risk being dashed against the rocks or swept out to sea.

She kept glancing above and behind her. She thought she saw a figure far behind, picking his way more slowly along the trail. She began to run as fast as she dared. At a certain point, the trail seemed to disappear in front of Tessa, but she climbed up about seven or eight feet to a narrow ledge that she then crawled along before dropping back down to the rocky trail. It would take her follower a little time to figure out that trick.

If she could get far enough ahead of him, the trail wound around a corner just before the point where she could climb off the trail and into her uncle's backyard. The house was out of sight of the trail, and no one would see her enter it.

Tessa reached the middle length of the trail. It wasn't completely underwater, but it was close enough to make her pause. Water sluiced over the rock, receding for several seconds, then pounding up again.

She stepped forward.

Icy water soaked her socks and pants completely, taking her breath away. She grabbed the cliff face, clinging to roots and branches and rocks as she made her way forward. She planted each foot so that the tips of the incoming waves wouldn't pull her feet out from under her.

It seemed to take forever, although only the first few yards of it were bad. The rest was a bit higher than the waterline, and she could move faster, though she was still hindered by her soaked clothing.

When she reached the other side and looked back, she didn't see anyone on the trail behind her.

Finally she came to the bend in the trail and turned to see Uncle Teruo's house ahead and above her. Overgrown brush and weeds blocked her way, but she climbed over and through them, vaguely remembering the twisted path that was the easiest way up.

Just before she reached the fence that separated Uncle's yard from the steep cliff, she heard a pistol cock. She stopped climbing and looked up into the barrel of a revolver, wielded by one of her uncle's guards.

"Hi, Jared," she said calmly.

The older man's eyes nearly popped out of his head. "Tessa!" He holstered his gun and reached down to help her up.

"Give me your jacket."

He shrugged out of it and handed it to her. She wrapped it over her head, then reached a hand toward him. "Get me into the house, fast."

She felt a bit silly running through the shadows on the lawn toward the darkened back door but felt instantly better when the door closed behind her, shutting out the bitterly cold night, and the light turned on.

"Jared, get her some towels." Uncle's gravelly voice called from the doorway to the room.

He stood dressed in his old blue *hanten* coat, which was starting to look a bit ratty now. He'd donned split-toe socks with turtles on them so his feet wouldn't be cold in the house slippers he wore, and he had on dark green, striped pajamas.

"I'm sorry, Uncle." Tessa realized her teeth were chattering. "I was tailed …"

She didn't notice that Jared had disappeared until he was suddenly at her side with towels. She didn't want to move because she was muddy, but Jared helped her remove her shoes. He had to untie them for her, because her hands were too numb. Funny how she hadn't noticed that on her frantic flight here.

Uncle threw a blanket around her and led her to the bathroom, which had an *ofuro*, a Japanese sunken bath, filled with burning hot water.

"I'll get you some clothes." He left her.

Tessa undressed and was careful to soap up and wash off the mud and dirt in the small shower in the corner of the room. After rinsing, she slowly entered the heated bath, gritting her teeth and grunting as the hot water made her cold limbs sizzle with pain.

Soon the water began to feel good, but Tessa didn't sit for long. She toweled off and donned the clean set of her aunt's flannel pajamas she found outside the door along with a dressing gown.

She padded to Uncle's office, which was toasty warm thanks to the sunken fireplace in the center of the room. Uncle sat cross-legged on one of the tatami mats that circled the fireplace.

He was reading some papers while stroking a cat. The firelight glinted against his salt-and-pepper hair.

Tessa knelt and bowed to him formally, then sat cross-legged kitty-corner to him. "Since when have you owned a cat?"

"Since it came into the house a couple weeks ago and wouldn't leave." Tessa was surprised to see a smile on his lips, softening his square jaw.

She studied the contented tabby, which looked as if it had some pretentious long-haired descendants. Aunt Kayoko had always liked dogs.

"Uncle, you made arrangements to pay Charles my retainer fee," Tessa began.

He didn't seem surprised she knew. "Do not blame the boy. I asked him not to tell you."

"Yes, I know. Uncle, it was sneaky."

His dark eyes blazed when they looked at her again. "How else am I to care for you? You refused all my offers of help."

"I want to be legitimate. I think I had the FBI after me tonight. I don't know what would have happened—what they would have done—if they saw me enter your house."

"Possibly nothing. Why would they have been following you?"

"There's a gambling syndicate after my new clients. One of my clients discovered that the TV show *Grab the Mic* is being rigged."

"Rigged?" Uncle Teruo pouted briefly. "That's my favorite show."

She blinked at him.

"Well, it is," he said defensively.

"Do you know anything about the Double Zodiac?"

"What?"

She'd forgotten that Fisher had told her that name, that others might not know it by the Double Zodiac. "A gambling syndicate of twenty-four members."

"Ah yes. They have no name that I know of."

"Do you know anyone in the syndicate?"

He studied her silently, his face impassive.

She continued, "I heard rumors the yakuza were in the syndicate, but it's become obvious you are not involved." Because he'd have tried to speak to her about it once he knew Tessa was protecting George and Hannah. "But rumors said that Hitoshi-san was in the syndicate."

Uncle's bushy eyebrows rose high on his forehead. "Impossible."

"I don't think he's involved." If Hitoshi-san, one of her uncle's most powerful *kobun*, were involved with the gambling syndicate, he would have instantly recognized her tattoo in the video segment on *Bay Area Entertainment*, and the Double Zodiac would have figured out her identity long before this. Tessa knew Hitoshi-san was familiar with all of her uncle's tattoos, since Hitoshi and her uncle were old friends. One night a few weeks after she'd gotten the dragon tattoo, she'd arrived at Uncle Teruo's house and found the captain having a leisurely drink with her uncle. When Hitoshi-san asked to see her new tat, she had assumed Uncle Teruo had told him about it.

Tessa continued, "But I think Hitoshi-san's son Bennett is one of the syndicate and has been using his father's name to get what he wants."

Her uncle's face grew stormy. "This is not the first time Hitoshi's son has done this."

"If something happens, if Bennett is arrested, will this have repercussions for you?" That was the million-dollar question. Would the connection between Bennett, Hitoshi-san, and her uncle cause problems for him? At the very least, an arrest would bring intense shame on Hitoshi-san's family.

Uncle shook his head. "I am not involved in this syndicate. The FBI is investigating?"

"Yes. My clients' lives are in danger unless the syndicate is stopped."

Tessa's uncle folded his hands across his slightly paunchy stomach. "They are my competition, so I am not unhappy."

Great, Tessa thought sarcastically. It was so good to know she would be behind the continued success of yakuza illegal gambling.

"You'll need to cancel the bank account you're using to pay my retainer fee. If anything in my life or finances is looked into by either the FBI — now that I've put myself on their radar — or the gambling syndicate, they may find out the account belongs to you."

"It is too old anyway. I should have closed it before this." He struck a small bell gong, similar to the one used by Buddhist monks, that sat on the edge of a mat near the fire, and Jared entered the room. "Close this account at First Kohei Bank." He rattled off the account number, and Jared nodded before closing the door.

"Anything else?" he asked drily.

"And um . . ." She sighed. "The syndicate drained my, Mom's, and Alicia's bank accounts."

"What?" he thundered. "You didn't think to tell me this before?"

"They also canceled Alicia's and Mom's credit cards."

"They have stolen from my flesh and blood?"

It sounded exceptionally bad when he put it that way. "I guess."

He frowned fiercely into the fire, his breathing deep and heavy. "I will take care of it," he said bitingly.

Tessa knew he meant more than making sure they had money. This was an insult he wouldn't take lightly. "Remember, the FBI is involved."

His expression was amused. "Are you worried? I will be careful."

She bit her lip. "I need to get back to my clients."

He nodded. "Jared and Tim will drive you."

Meaning, one would be her driver and one would be a decoy, and between the two of them, no one would see her leave her uncle's house or be able to track her back to Charles's place.

She got on her knees and bowed formally. She was about to rise when her uncle reached out a large square hand and placed it over hers on the mat. His skin was rough against her knuckles and very warm. He squeezed her hand gently.

"It has nothing to do with my wanting you to work for me again," he said softly. He was talking about paying Charles's retainer fee for her. "I only want to help you, as I would help my daughter."

The words were full of meaning, respect, and love. Uncle would never speak this way about any of his captains, about any of the other cousins. For her, he had reserved a special place, that of the daughter he'd never had, and it was an honor he gave to her as he would give someone a kimono of gold.

"Thank you," she breathed, overwhelmed.

One last squeeze of her hand, and then he released her.

All year, Tessa had been trying to keep as far from the yakuza as she could, because she had feared Uncle would try to buy her loyalty. But his motives ran deeper, purer.

She was floored. This was the closest he'd ever come to telling her he loved her.

Chapter **23**

Charles sat at Rick's bedside, not wanting to leave, not wanting to stay.

Since Rick had slipped into the coma, he'd had regular seizures, each one more intense than the last. His breathing had grown more labored, his heartbeat slower, his brain activity weaker.

Charles had been here every night after work, just sitting, sometimes talking. Annelissa had turned into a pillar, still and fragile where she sat in the other chair next to Rick's bed.

Rick never woke up. Charles wondered if he had been hoping Rick would, because as he sat there, Charles became more and more aware of the guilt burning a hole in his stomach.

They'd been friends for years, and Charles had never once talked to him about his relationship with Jesus. Not even in casual conversation.

Rick had always been vocal about the fact he was an atheist, and he and Charles had enjoyed arguing about it, neither of them winning or convincing the other. But apologetics weren't the same as talking to his friend about how he'd felt Jesus's arms holding him the night he'd cowered with Eddie in the bedroom listening to his daddy beat Mama to unconsciousness in the living room. How the words he read in the Bible every morning were slowly leeching away the bitterness and rage in his heart against his father. How his mama's prayers for him sometimes made his body tremble as if he'd touched the hem of God's cloak. No, Charles hadn't told Rick any of that. Instead, he'd argued with him because that was an intellectual pursuit the two of them enjoyed. Charles hadn't wanted to make Rick uncomfortable with the emotional aspects of his faith.

And now it was too late.

This evening seemed exactly like the night before. Rick was still and weak. Annelissa held his hand like always.

But then Rick's breathing slowed, became more labored. Annelissa sat up straight, reached for Charles across the bed, and clutched his hand hard. Her breath started coming in sobbing gasps.

And then Rick's heart stopped beating. The steady whine of the heart-rate monitor blasted through the room. Nurses rushed in, but he was already gone.

Charles sat in the corner of the room while a flurry of hospital personnel moved around Rick's bed.

His friend was gone.

The pain crushed his rib cage, pulverized his breastbone, crunched his clavicle, worked its way up his body. The tears running from his eyes seemed inadequate, a mere mist sprayed on the fire of his grief.

It had happened so fast. It had happened so fast.

Charles hadn't spent enough time with Rick. He hadn't appreciated the time with him to the fullest. He'd missed out on asking him about his kids, his dreams, his hopes.

He had failed him.

He'd been too focused on himself, on feeling included at the law firm, feeling respected and approved of—all the things Charles had never received from his father. He thought he'd dealt with that wound, but remnants of the scar still drove him, focused his thoughts and desires.

Surely it wasn't wrong to love his job, to be good at it. He thrived on the intellectual stimulation, the puzzle solving, the challenge. But recently, maybe he'd only been looking at the gift God had given him, and not at the Giver, as Mama would say.

Charles had been striving to land Steven Nishimoto as a client, to find the perfect wife to further his career, to cut from his heart the one woman who made him feel alive.

What was all his striving for if he went the same way Rick did? In one failed heartbeat?

He saw himself in a hospital bed, asking himself, *What have I done with my life?*

But by then it would be too late.

What was the purpose of anything he did? Why did he even bother?

Then Charles looked up, saw Annelissa sitting in the chair by the bed, still looking like a glass statue. He went to her and put his arm around her. And she began to cry.

And Charles cried with her, gave her as much comfort as he could with his arms, his tears ... and his prayers.

He couldn't verbalize what he felt, but his heart cried out, and he somehow knew God heard him. God saw Annelissa. God knew Charles's own dark thoughts.

And Charles vowed he would not live with any regrets. If anything, Rick's death taught him that time passed too quickly to not take full advantage of every moment. He'd had his chance with Rick, and he'd blown it.

The nurses had left them. Annelissa turned to him. "Charles, I want you to go."

"No, you need someone here with you."

"No, I don't want you here for this."

"For what?"

"Rick was an organ donor. They're going to take him away soon. I don't want you here to see it."

Annelissa was so strong, but her strength was precarious. She didn't want Charles here to see her like this. It would only make it harder for her.

"Okay." He picked up his briefcase and his suit jacket, and then his eye fell on the bedside table.

A Bible was on it. Not surprising; every hospital room had one. But Charles recognized this Bible. He recognized the tattered edge colored red from when he'd spilled red paint on it, and the cut on the cover where Eddie had accidentally sliced it with a pair of scissors.

It was Mama's Bible.

"Has my mama been here?" His voice came out in a croak.

Suddenly Annelissa's eyes grew soft, her face less taut, more serene. "She's been visiting for a few weeks. She talked to Rick and me. I didn't quite agree with everything she said, but it seemed to give Rick peace."

Peace. Had Rick found ultimate peace? Charles knew the answer wasn't quick and easy, wasn't necessarily a pat happy ending.

But now Charles at least had hope, whereas he'd had none in the weeks after Rick slipped into his coma. Had his mama taken over when Charles dropped the ball?

The thought made Charles ashamed of himself.

He'd always thought he would have more time.

‿॰ी‿

Charles went to running group because he had no reason not to go, even though being around people was the last thing he wanted. The office was somber, and he couldn't stand the oppressive atmosphere anymore.

He had ghosts to outrun.

He arrived a little late on purpose. He joined the group just as they started on their warm-up lap, slipping in behind everyone else.

He ran harder than he'd ever run before, but somehow the health of his body, the heaving of his lungs, the pounding of his heart seemed meaningless.

How long would he feel like this — so hopeless, so aimless, so numb?

Steven came up to him at the end, his face concerned. "What's wrong?" he asked softly.

"My friend ..." Charles swallowed. "He died two days ago."

Steven clasped Charles's shoulder, hard. "I'm sorry."

Charles shook his head but said nothing.

"Is there anything I can do?"

Charles was about to say, "No," but something made him burst out instead, "Tell me there's at least hope that Rick is with the God who loves him."

Steven's face grew pained. "Charles ... I don't believe in a God."

Somehow that admission was like a blow to Charles's stomach. "You don't? What do you believe?"

"I believe that there's just ... nothing. That life ends."

The thought of that blackness, that nothingness, made Charles's throat close up.

"Rick is no longer in pain," Steven said, his voice strangled.

"You can't know that."

Steven's eyes grew sharper, harder. "You think there's a hell?"

Charles thought about it for a moment. He was done giving the Sunday school answers he'd grown up with. What did he really believe?

He remembered Annelissa's tears, the comfort he gave her, the comfort he received with the silent prayers of his heart. He remembered the verses that seemed to groan out of him as he'd held her in that hospital room.

For God so loved the world that he gave his one and only Son, that whoever believes in him shall not perish but have eternal life.

I am the way and the truth and the life. No one comes to the Father except through me.

They weren't just Sunday school answers. There was fire in them.

Charles turned to Steven. The man's uncomfortable, slightly derisive expression made Charles hesitate before he spoke, aware that his answer would be more than words. But he was past the point of living for what he thought he should be living for. He needed to live for what God wanted him to live for. That was the only thing worthwhile in this life.

And he felt an otherworldly burning in his chest to say the words.

"If I believe that there's nothing after I die, or that there's no hell and everyone goes to heaven, then what's the point of my life? What's the point of suffering or becoming a better person? What's the point of Rick dying?" Charles swallowed. "No. No. I believe there's a heaven, and I believe there's a hell. And I know that's an unpopular opinion to have these days, but I don't care. Rick is gone. Life is only a blink, and I've realized it's too important to me to want to waste it anymore."

Steven's face had become hard. "I never expected you to have such a close-minded opinion."

"You asked me what I believe, and I'm not ashamed to say it. What's the point of doing and saying what everyone else does and says if you're going to kill off a part of your soul? I'm not afraid to be unpopular."

Steven stared hard at him. "You're grieving—"

"I am grieving. But I'm also free." He turned to go, then said to Steven. "If you want to still have lunch this week, let me know. But if I don't hear from you, it's fine."

He no longer cared about landing Steven as a client.

He wouldn't turn to look back at his life with regrets.

George had made it to the final four.

And now his life was forfeit.

Problem was, Alicia's was too. Because Tessa was going to *kill* her.

"That is a death trap." While standing outside their little mountain cabin with Tessa, Alicia pointed a manicured finger at it as if it were Dracula's castle.

Sure, it was a little small, but it was only a little bit more cramped than Mom's house. Besides, Tessa liked it. It had pretty blue trim, the back deck was made of wide, unfinished hardwood, and there was an unhindered view of the woods from three sides of the cottage.

"And I am not staying another day in there!" Alicia marched toward the Moose, which was parked in the driveway, and yanked at the driver's door handle. It was locked. Alicia's hand slipped, and she staggered back a few steps in her two-inch high-heeled shoes.

Tessa crossed her arms as she watched her. "Shout a little louder and wake the neighbors who are *half a mile away*."

It was actually close to eight in the morning, and most mountainfolk got up early, but Alicia's tone could have burned toast.

Paisley, used to her mom's "emo attacks," as she called them, dipped her head from where she stood in the open front door so she could see the front window, which was fitted with twelve thick panes of (only slightly dirty) glass. "I like it. It smells nice."

It smelled like fir and oak and moss. Tessa smiled.

"It smells like mold, dirt, and slugs," Alicia said.

"It smells like bleach and vinegar since Grandma started cleaning," Paisley answered.

"It's only for a little while longer," Tessa said to her sister. "The FBI is investigating the Double Zodiac, and once they get them, we'll all be safe." She couldn't believe she was saying that about the Feds. "Come back inside. It's cozy now that George has a fire going in the fireplace."

"No. I'm sick and tired of those pokey four walls." Alicia's ire obviously warmed her against the bracing morning air, although Tessa had started to shiver. "I want to ... Oh, I don't know ... Go to work so I can feed my child?"

Through the open front door, Tessa could hear Hannah say,

"I wouldn't mind it if it had internet." She was sitting on the sagging couch—aka her father's bed—playing a video game on Mits's laptop. Paisley left her post at the door and sat down next to her.

Alicia raged. "You and George got to go down to LA—"

"He couldn't miss the final four show, and I couldn't trust the studio bodyguard they assigned to him."

"—while we were holed up in that horrible little panic room, but at least the panic room is in *civilization*!"

Vivian Britton had actually "cheated" and had let Alicia, Paisley, and Mom out of the panic room for most of the day while Tessa took George and Hannah to the live edition of *Grab the Mic*, but since they'd all still been alive when Tessa and the Mynheirs got back from Los Angeles, Tessa hadn't been too upset.

"But to be forced from there to this *shack* is simply not to be borne!"

Tessa had to grit her teeth to prevent herself from rolling her eyes. Alicia was really going at it this time. And from her language, Tessa suspected she'd been reading a lot of historical romances lately.

Mom had just started cooking breakfast on the ancient stove while Alicia was having a meltdown outside, and now the scent of bacon and eggs wafted through the open doorway and wrapped around Tessa. Her stomach growled, but Alicia was still too far away to smell the food.

"Alicia, please come inside."

In response, her sister started walking down the narrow road that snaked its way toward Highway 17, tottering slightly on the heels she usually wore to work, the only shoes she'd thought to bring with her when Tessa had forced them to come to the cabin with her, Hannah, and George.

George came outside and joined Tessa as she stood and watched her sister stalk away. "It's been four days since your family joined us here in the cabin. Shouldn't the shock have worn off by now?"

"It takes at least a week," Tessa muttered.

At that moment, one of Alicia's heels snapped off and she fell down. Tessa and George ran to her, but by the time they reached her, she'd already gotten to her feet. She shoved them both away when they tried to help her. "Go away!"

"Alicia, you can't walk all the way to the highway with only one heel."

Alicia probably wouldn't be able to find her way to the highway, period, because the roads this far into the mountains were a maze, but Tessa refrained from saying so.

"I'm tired of that horrid house—"

"Alicia Yukiko Lancaster Kingsley, get your skinny behind in this house right this moment!" Mom's voice carried just as well as Alicia's. She stood outside the house, hands on hips, with her spatula sticking out at a tangent from one fist. "My eggs are getting cold."

"Really, Mom?" Alicia demanded. "That's all you can think about?"

"It's better than shrieking like an *oni*." Mom glared at her oldest daughter.

Alicia did kind of look like the Japanese goblins that Tessa had seen pictures of when she was younger. *Oni* were usually brightly colored, and right now, Alicia was plum purple.

Only Mom could ever get Alicia or Tessa to obey in the middle of a tantrum. Alicia limped back, passed her mother, and walked into the house with as much injured dignity as she could manage with one broken heel.

They had a stifling breakfast that looked a bit odd with Alicia sitting there in her business casual clothing as if she were about to leave for her biotech job. Tessa avoided her sister's eyes. Before leaving San Jose, Alicia had told her boss she had a family emergency, but she hated inactivity, and she'd been unable to do anything here at the cabin, since Tessa had forbidden use of the landline phone, which crackled worse than a walkie-talkie; there was no cell phone service; and it wasn't possible to telecommute for the type of biology research Alicia did, even if they had had internet access. So Tessa understood that Alicia was chafing from both inactivity and stress at the thought of the workload piling up for her back at her lab.

If she ever made it back to the lab.

At the end of breakfast, Mom stood and shot Alicia a hard look. "Alicia, help me wash dishes."

Alicia shot daggers at Tessa with her eyes. "Fine." She stood, but then the grumbling started.

"This well water is going to ruin my manicure ... If we had internet access I could at least get some paperwork done ... Look at that, I have a bite on my arm. When did that happen? Probably from a spider while I was asleep."

Tessa escaped out the back deck after Alicia exclaimed, "There are cobwebs under the sink!"

Taking a deep breath, Tessa stared into the forest. And then she saw movement.

About four hundred yards down the hill, near a large fern.

Tessa's heart pounded in her chest, and she ducked and ran back into the house, slamming the door closed.

"Get away from the windows," she ordered.

Alicia put her hand on her hip. "Why?"

George surprised them all when he roared, "For cryin' out loud, will you stop being contrary and just listen for a change?" He grabbed Alicia and plunked her down on the floor next to one of the large multipaned windows on the side of the house.

The living room took up the entire east side of the house and had three windows—the front, side, and back. Tessa drew the curtains closed on the back windows and hissed, "Hannah! Paisley!"

The two girls immediately ran to close the curtains on the side and front of the house, staying out of sight.

Tessa peeked through the curtain of the back window.

They looked like hunters. They were dressed in camo, but not military outfits. No helmets, no bulletproof vests or body armor. They had hunting rifles, not AK-47s, and they moved quickly through the trees, circling the house like a pack of wolves. No attempt at stealth anymore.

They weren't an ex-SWAT or ex-military team. So they probably didn't have grenades or tear gas. But they would surround the house in a few seconds, regardless.

Tessa picked up the phone connected to the landline. No dial tone. She crawled to the kitchen, past Mom, who was huddled next to the sink.

Tessa opened one of the dark-paneled cabinets and reached behind the flour and sugar for the false back. She'd put false backs in all the cabinets so they'd all look alike. But only this false panel slid away, allowing her fingers to grab the satellite phone.

It took a few seconds for it to connect, and she peeked out the window closest to her while she waited. She could see one guy in front, one on the side. That made a total of six—that she could see.

She dialed the local sheriff's office, which was only four minutes away and one of the reasons she'd chosen this location. "Sheriff Carter? This is Desiree up at the Roberts' cabin. I don't know what's happening, but there are men with guns surrounding us. I think they think we're someone dangerous. Please come quickly!"

She then dialed the police station, a little farther away at eleven minutes when she'd clocked the drive in her Suburban, and repeated her message.

Hannah's eyes were huge as she stared at Tessa. "Will they get here in time?" she whispered.

"Yes." Tessa infused as much firmness as she could in her voice. "Okay, you know the drill. Take the others with you."

Hannah nodded and motioned to Paisley and Mom. "Into this bedroom. Tessa already barricaded the windows and door in there." She began to crawl toward one of the bedrooms.

George grabbed Alicia, who was now pale and tense, and urged her to crawl toward the larger bedroom.

Tessa moved toward the front door and grasped the medium-length oak walking stick she'd planted to one side of it before she peeked out the front window. The man stationed there had paused at the edge of the forest on the opposite side of the road. What was he waiting for?

She thought she knew.

They suddenly crashed through the front door, but Tessa was prepared. She smacked the first one across the bridge of his nose with the staff, following it with a sharp jab to his kidney. He went down, blood spurting from his nose into his eyes.

She tried to knock the second one over the head, but he brought up his gun in time to stop the blow, so Tessa aimed a kick to his knee. Unfortunately, she wasn't able to get as solid a hit as she wanted.

He swung at her with his gun, and she ducked.

She whipped the staff around and whacked the second intruder hard in the ribs. He grunted and staggered, and she knocked him out cold with a blow to the temple.

The next attacker to try to enter the cabin was gigantic. His blond head brushed the ceiling. Tessa jabbed at his solar plexus, but he swerved, avoiding the blow, and grabbed the staff, jerking it out of her hands.

Tessa picked up a kitchen table chair and used the legs to entangle his arms. She took advantage of her leverage to try and wrest his gun from his hand. They swiveled like dancers, moving deeper into the kitchen with each step. But while she crashed painfully against the kitchen table, he merely frowned and knocked the entire table aside with his body.

Suddenly Tessa heard the sound of cracking glass. One of the attackers was trying to knock out the panes of the living room's back window.

Tessa saw that Alicia had been slow in crawling after George and was still a few feet away from the bedroom door, but when Alicia saw the man in the back window, almost on top of her, she screamed and scrambled away from him on her hands and knees. That took her away from the bedroom and closer to the front door.

"Alicia!" George yelled at her from the bedroom door.

The old-fashioned glass of the windows was thick, and the attacker was having a hard time breaking it. He began using the butt of his gun, but Tessa didn't spend too much time worrying about him getting in.

He was in for a nasty surprise.

"Alicia, get to the bedroom!" Tessa shouted. While she was yelling, her attacker knocked the chair out of her hands. Tessa aimed a few kicks to the giant's thighs, surprising him. She felt his muscles flinch. The blows may not have seemed overly painful to him, but he would soon find it harder to keep his balance on his bruised quads.

Meanwhile, the attacker at the back window smashed the last pane of glass. Alicia, still on the floor, continued shrieking. Tessa saw a blur out of the corner of her eye as her sister jumped to her feet and ran toward the front door.

"Alicia!"

The hunter began swinging his leg over the low windowsill and then leaped into the room—except he bounced right back out again with a sharp cry. The steel wire she'd strung over the windows had sliced deep into his arm, had cut his hip, and had almost caught his neck. Blood spurted onto the shattered glass that covered the floor.

The giant was too strong for Tessa. She couldn't win this battle. She struggled a moment longer, getting him into position, then twisted to his side, captured his arm, and flipped him over her hip.

She'd aimed it perfectly. His head hit the solid, old-fashioned porcelain sink, cracking it and knocking him out.

Wait a minute, where was Alicia?

Tessa raced to the open front door in time to see one of the attackers grab Alicia around the waist, struggling because she was flailing so wildly.

At that moment, the sheriff's Jeep roared down the driveway and came to a screaming halt in front of the cabin. "Hands up!" Sheriff Carter yelled as he opened his door and positioned himself behind it, his gun pointed at the hunter holding Alicia.

Tessa saw the blur behind him a moment too late. "Sheriff—!"

The hunter who had been waiting in the woods on the opposite side of the road shot the sheriff in the back. He fell to the ground.

Alicia screamed.

The attacker holding Alicia turned to Tessa, who was still standing in the doorway, shocked. "All we want is the girl." He'd slung his rifle over his shoulder and now pressed a wicked-looking hunting knife to Alicia's side.

In the hunter's grip, Alicia stared at Tessa wide-eyed, her hair a crazy tangle on her head.

"I'll kill her," the man said. "I can gut her in less than a second."

Tessa had never been frozen in horror before this moment. She could barely breathe. *Alicia!*

And Alicia opened her mouth to snap, "Don't you dare give him what he wants!"

For a split second, Tessa felt like she was looking at a mirror image of herself.

She stepped back to close the door, but somebody was in the way.

"Let her go!" said a teenage voice.

"No!" Alicia and Tessa screamed at the same time.

Tessa tried to shove Paisley back into the cabin, but Paisley grabbed the doorframe and dug in her heels. "I'll go with you! Let her go!"

But the hunter sneered at her. "Nice try. You're not the girl."

"Yes, I am — !"

The sound of a rifle shot filled the air. It took Tessa a second to realize it had been fired by the man still across the street, now partially hidden by the sheriff's car.

Paisley flinched and then grabbed her upper arm, blood pouring between her fingers.

She turned deathly white and exclaimed, "That hurt!" Then she fainted.

The hunter with Alicia jabbed the knife into her side, making her cry out, and Tessa saw blood stain Alicia's shirt. "Give me Hannah."

Tessa was shoving Paisley's body back into the cabin so she could shut the door, but suddenly two legs leaped over them and ran out of the cabin.

"No! Hannah!"

The hunter released Alicia, who fell to the ground clutching her side, and grabbed Hannah as she ran toward him.

The girl looked like she was going to be sick. She gave Tessa a last look — a last fierce look — that said, *Find me!*

And then the man had her around the waist and was shoving her into the sheriff's Jeep. The man who'd shot the sheriff joined him, and they roared away.

Chapter **24**

The FBI tech looked up from his laptop at Agent Townsend and shook his head. "The file can't be copied, only moved."

He'd been trying to copy the spreadsheet Hannah had stolen, which she'd put on a flash drive. She'd given Tessa the flash drive a few weeks ago, and Tessa had buried it in a plastic bag out in the woods.

This explained why after Hannah was kidnapped, the Double Zodiac had called Tessa's cell phone—they'd probably gotten the number from Hannah—and demanded the flash drive in return for Hannah's life. Hannah hadn't gotten duplicated information. She had the only copy of that spreadsheet.

"Did you trace the call?" George demanded of the FBI techs.

"No, sir, the call was too short—"

"Well then, what good are you?" Townsend exploded.

While the FBI agents tried to placate him, Tessa walked to the ambulance parked to one side of the tiny cabin where Paisley and Alicia were being patched up. Paisley had only been grazed by the bullet. Tessa assured her niece that that had been the hunter's intention, just to scare her, although privately Tessa wasn't so sure about that. Alicia's stab wound was small, but since the knife had cut some of her abdomen muscles, the EMT wanted to take her to the hospital. Alicia, however, refused to go until she knew what was going to happen next.

Alicia sat on the edge of the ambulance, a little white around her mouth but otherwise looking like her normal, cranky self. Paisley leaned against the ambulance next to her, her arm bandaged up.

Tessa and Alicia looked each other square in the eyes.

Before today, Tessa had never seen that look in her sister's eyes. All that remained of it now was a shadow of the expression Alicia'd had when she'd told Tessa not to give Hannah to the hunter. It was a deep-seated courage that came out in stress, a pure virtue Tessa recognized.

"Thanks," she told Alicia.

Her sister knew what she was talking about. "You're welcome."

"Do I get thanks too?" Paisley asked.

"No, you do not," Alicia snapped. "We already discussed your crazy behavior."

Paisley scowled. "It wasn't crazy. It was the right thing to do."

Alicia and Tessa shared another look over Paisley's bent head. Despite her sharp words, Alicia respected her daughter for what she tried to do. So did Tessa.

Tessa was distracted by her thoughts. *Is Hannah okay? Oh, God. Please let her be all right.*

At that moment, Charles drove up, parking next to the ambulance. He saw Paisley's blood dotting Tessa's shirt and blanched.

"It's not mine," she told him.

"You're all right?"

"I got shot!" Now that she'd been given a painkiller and her wound had been dressed, Paisley was positively excited about it.

"I got stabbed," Alicia said sourly.

Seeing they were obviously both okay, Charles turned to Tessa. "How did they find you?"

She licked her lips, then looked up at him. "The only person who's ever called this cabin was you, when you asked us to come to your law offices to look over what the forensic accountant had discovered." At the time she'd been distracted by how long it would take them to get down the mountain without her SUV, since she hadn't gotten it back yet from the Snuggle Up. At the time she'd forgotten to ask him if he'd remembered the security instructions she'd given to him. "When you called me, did you remember to use someone else's phone?"

"Yes. I used the phone in Rick's office. I figured they can't monitor all the outgoing calls from the law office."

Tessa winced. "If anyone knew Rick wasn't at work, the call from his phone would stand out, and they'd investigate who you called."

Charles acted as if he'd been punched in the stomach. He bent over and rested his hands on his knees for a moment. "Oh, my gosh. I'm so sorry."

"I looked around the woods," Tessa said. "It looks like they've been camping near the cabin since the day you called us."

"Don't tell George." Alicia glanced to where he was still arguing with the FBI agents, although Mom was there trying to get him to calm down.

"Aunt Tessa took out *four* of them," Paisley said.

"Yes, we heard you the first five times you said it," Alicia said.

"Where are they?" Charles asked.

"Three were unconscious when the police arrived, and they've been taken to the hospital. My gut says they're just freelancers sent to snatch Hannah and deliver her to whoever hired them. I'm not sure they'll be able to say much about their employer. The fourth man got cut up in my booby-trapped window, but he ran away. The FBI is sending for dogs to track his scent. He was bleeding."

"Maybe one of the men *will* know something."

"It might be too late by then. The Double Zodiac called my cell phone. I didn't recognize their voices, so they weren't the hunters I talked to here. They want the flash drive."

"Where? When?"

"They didn't say, but they'll make the exchange somewhere far from where they've got the computers they're using for the gambling, as well as far from where they're holding Hannah right now."

Charles glanced at the dozen or so agents busily looking around the cabin and working in the temporary truck they'd set up on the street. "They're looking for her?"

"Yes, but I don't know if they'll find her in time. Or what they intend to do to keep the syndicate from getting the flash drive."

"Look, the FBI is working on it now," Charles said. "Alicia and Paisley are injured. Let's keep the body count low."

"You're really going to trust the FBI?" Paisley asked in disgust.

Alicia glared at Charles. "They couldn't care less about the body count. They want the Double Zodiac." Thanks to Mom, Alicia and Paisley were as distrustful of the FBI as Tessa.

Charles leaned back from all three women, hands raised. "Sorry, forgot. Mafia family."

Mention of it suddenly made Tessa still. "Wait a minute. Uncle."

Charles asked in a low voice, "Would your uncle help find her?"

Alicia's face was grim. "Our bank accounts were drained, and his great-niece was shot. You bet he'll help."

"But the FBI is investigating this," Tessa said. "We don't want Uncle stepping right into their way."

There was thoughtful silence, then Charles spoke up. "I have a solution. But I won't do it unless you agree to let the FBI handle this."

"You really trust them?"

"Your uncle might have the social net wide enough to be able to find where the syndicate is holding Hannah. But if you don't want him further involved in this, you'll have to trust the FBI, because they have the technology to be able to save her and investigate the syndicate."

Charles was right. And while it pained her, Hannah was more important than Tessa's prejudices. "Fine. What's the solution?"

"I'll tell the FBI that I found her location. I have no direct connection to your uncle," Charles said.

"Do you still have the satellite phone?" Alicia asked her.

Tessa nodded.

"Call Uncle." She flicked a glance first at the empty woods on the other side of the street, then at the FBI. "I'll keep watch."

&

"Three minutes?" Tessa wasn't sure if she'd heard the FBI computer tech correctly.

He nodded. "Once the computers are triggered, they'll destroy all the data within three minutes."

"You can tell all that just by scanning the building?"

"You wouldn't believe what I can do just by scanning the building."

Space was cramped in the FBI mobile command post that had been placed several blocks away from the South San Francisco warehouse where the Double Zodiac had relocated their computers. Beside her, Agent Townsend was watching her warily but without the hostility she would have expected from an agent who had gotten dead-on accurate information from an unknown source and now had the niece of a mafia leader and her attorney in close quarters with him. Tessa still didn't trust the FBI, but perhaps they weren't *all* out to get her.

"That spreadsheet must have some long-shot bets they don't have records of anywhere else." Fisher Daley had been called in again now that the FBI understood the value the syndicate placed on the spreadsheet.

"The setup here isn't their master system," the tech said. "That would be hidden somewhere else — could be in Europe for all we know. This setup is made to integrate the spreadsheet they'll get from the flash drive. Then they'll break all of this down and probably take it back to LA, since that's where the studio is."

"All this just for that little spreadsheet?" Tessa asked.

"It's not just a 'little' spreadsheet. And their system is very complicated, which is why they have the self-destruct trigger."

"So what are you going to do now?"

"We have a duplicate flash drive with a virus that will disable the self-destruct trigger." Agent Townsend nodded to an agent who was donning a bulletproof vest. "An agent is going in with the flash drive—"

"No, no, no," Tessa said. "They'll just kill him and take the flash drive, and then they'll kill Hannah."

"My agent is entirely capable—"

"So am I, and I have a better motive for walking up to the front door with their precious flash drive that may not get Hannah killed so quickly."

"What?" Charles had been sitting to one side, but now he rose to his feet, his brows knit. "You're not going in there."

"You're not going in there," Agent Townsend repeated after him.

"I'll pretend to be going in rogue. My story is that I don't trust the FBI—for obvious reasons—and so I'm offering the flash drive to them in exchange for Hannah. They'll keep me alive long enough to at least plug the flash drive in. Then you guys can come in with guns blazing."

"That's the most asinine plan I've ever heard," Charles said.

"My agent can go in and do the exact same thing," Agent Townsend said. "You two are in this mobile command post so you don't try doing things on your own, clueing them into the fact that we've found their center of operations. I'm not about to send you walking up to their front door."

"Yes, they'll get your little virus into their system whether I or your agent takes it in, but your agent is expendable," Tessa said. "If I go in, they're never going to think Teruo Ota's niece is in league with the FBI. I am not expendable, and they won't shoot me right away." She made herself sound more confident than she felt. "I am Hannah's best chance. If your agent goes in, they'll probably shoot him, and then they might shoot her *before* they install your virus."

"You have no guarantee they won't shoot you," Charles said.

"Think of who I am. They'll be less likely to shoot me than an FBI agent."

She knew Agent Townsend found her reasoning plausible.

"Sir," Agent Glenn spoke up. "I don't think this is a good idea." His dark eyes rested on Tessa for a moment.

She shivered.

Agent Townsend regarded her. She knew what he was thinking. The last thing he wanted was two civilians dying.

But he didn't know her capabilities. She would do everything she could to stay alive and keep Hannah alive until the FBI was able to follow her in. And she was certain she could do it. Hannah understood her. Hannah would listen to her.

"Fine," Agent Townsend said.

"Sir," Agent Glenn protested.

"No way," Charles said.

"I don't see any other lead investigators in here," Agent Townsend said, his voice raised.

That ended the discussion.

The FBI would be able to hear most of what was said through remote audio listening devices the agents had already planted near the warehouse, so Tessa wouldn't need an earpiece, which was a relief. She didn't want any FBI equipment on her when she walked in.

The tech handed her the flash drive, no words of "good luck" or caution. She didn't care.

But she did care that as she started walking away from the

mobile unit, Charles ran after her. He kissed her hard and briefly. "Come back," he said.

"I will."

She was about to say more, but Agent Glenn approached, his expression unfathomable despite the witnessed kiss. "I'll escort you until about a block from—"

"No," she shot back.

"But—"

"What part of *no* do you not understand?"

He shrugged and walked back to the mobile unit. Tessa realized that Charles was gone too.

She turned and walked toward the warehouse alone.

It was about five blocks from the mobile unit, so by the time she entered the deserted parking lot, hopping over cracked cement, she was sufficiently chilled from trudging in the cold air. Any minute now …

She heard someone approaching behind her and waited for him to speak, but instead, a hard blow to the back of her head sent her careening forward to the ground.

Her vision throbbed in and out, and pain made her entire head feel as if it were on fire. Her hands curled into fists, but she made herself relax them. She had to be captured so they could get the flash drive.

A hand grabbed her upper arm and half-dragged her into the warehouse. She heard the metal door slide open, then shut.

Inside it was dark and chill, even colder than the air outside. She was propelled forward and noticed the air growing warmer as she stumbled onward.

Her vision was starting to clear, and she saw tables set up with several computers, each hooked into massive power cables that rose up out of the concrete floor. The warehouse was littered with old wooden shipping crates but was otherwise empty, so Tessa could see the far end of the building even through the gloom. Lots of tall shelves were on that side of the warehouse, stacked with things with wires sticking out of them and other machine parts.

Hannah sat next to the tables of computers in a chair, her legs and arms tied with zip ties. Her lip was cut and swollen, and a handprint stood out on her cheek. Tessa's jaw clenched, which made her head throb more.

Her captor threw her to the floor several yards from where Hannah sat. Hannah's eyes widened when she saw Tessa, but she didn't say anything.

"She just waltzed in," said a familiar voice.

Tessa turned and saw Campbell Rollins, the scruffy man who'd hacked into Hannah's computer in Oakland and who'd approached them near the park. He looked at Tessa with sneering hatred. "Yeah, remember me? Not so tough now, are you?"

She'd like to see how tough he was when she wasn't holding back.

"Go ahead," said a man standing at the computers. Tessa looked up and saw Vernon Mead. He wasn't even looking at her, too engrossed in the computer he was typing at. "She doesn't have anything we need."

"I have the flash —"

She didn't get the chance to finish. Campbell ran up and laid a solid kick to her side.

She grunted in pain. She nearly twisted to catch his leg so she could flip him onto his back.

No, she had to let them do this. She had to keep them

occupied until they took the flash drive and uploaded the virus, long enough for the FBI to come so she could save Hannah.

So instead of retaliating, she curled up.

He kicked her again and again. During one of the kicks, his foot hit at just the right angle, and Tessa felt her rib crack. She gave a muffled cry. It felt like a bomb had exploded in her abdominal cavity.

Campbell kept kicking her. She heard his high-pitched laughter, interspersed with his quick breathing.

"Stop it!" screamed Hannah.

Finally, mercifully, he stopped. Tessa lay on the icy cement, her eyes screwed shut because the pain was so intense. She couldn't have moved if she'd tried.

"Tie her up," said a new voice.

In the dim lighting and because of the blow to her head, she hadn't noticed the third man in the warehouse.

Campbell roughly grabbed her wrists and zip-tied them together, then her feet. She subtly tested the ties. Her ankles were loose.

She managed to open an eye and peer over at the computers.

A Japanese man stared down at her impassively. She had never seen him before, but his face was familiar. Then she realized he looked like Hitoshi-san, her uncle's *kobun*, whom she'd met several times. She'd never met his son Bennett.

Until now.

He must have helped them find this warehouse, which was probably the reason Uncle Teruo had been able to find the temporary computer system setup so quickly.

Bennett leaned down to speak to Tessa. "I know why you're here. Your uncle sent you. What he doesn't know is that I couldn't care less about his people or about my father. And when your uncle sees your body, he'll get the message loud and clear."

What had she walked into? It sounded like Bennett had a feud with the entire yakuza. But at least it also sounded like he would never believe she'd cooperated with the FBI.

"I have the flash drive," she said weakly. Not all of it was feigned. Her lungs burned as if she'd inhaled an entire fireplace.

"Of course you do." He began probing her clothing. She gritted her teeth as his fingers groped where they didn't need to go. He quickly found the flash drive in her jacket pocket.

"You idiot!" Bennett suddenly roared, and then he was on Campbell, slapping his balding head. "You broke it!"

Oh no. Oh no. Could they still plug it in? Would they be able to download the virus? Had all this been for nothing? Was the FBI listening? Did they know the drive had been broken during the beating?

"Mead told me I could," Campbell sniveled. "I couldn't touch the girl, but I could get whoever came in after her."

Sadistic snot. Just give her some time, and she'd show him she could give as good as she got.

Bennett tossed the broken flash drive to Vernon Mead, who looked at it and made a frustrated noise. "I'll need to take it back to LA to try to get the information out of it. Man, we set all this up for nothing."

"They're expecting this information in a few hours," Bennett said.

"We'll have to tell them what happened."

"Can I kill them now?" Campbell's voice was eager.

A long pause. Then Bennett gave Tessa a nasty smile. "Yes, go ahead."

It was as if her vision expanded. She saw everything in high definition, from the lines on Bennett's mouth to the pimple on Campbell's nose. She slowly flexed some muscles and relaxed others.

Come and get it.

Campbell approached slowly, apparently wanting to savor it. She glared at him, then spat at him. Hopefully it would make him go after her first rather than Hannah.

It worked. His sneer became ugly, and he drew his foot back to kick her.

In a flash she swept out her feet and knocked him to the ground. His head bounced hard against the concrete. She bounded onto him, slamming her elbow into his face, smacking his head into the concrete again. He went limp.

She reached for the gun she'd seen peeking out of Campbell's jeans.

Bennett had straightened in surprise, but he'd been slow to reach for his gun. He had it out now.

"Don't shoot!"

Wait, that voice sounded like ...

Charles entered the warehouse, hands raised high.

No.

She was about to cry a warning to him, but he cast her a hard, nervous look, and she swallowed her shout. She hadn't revealed to Bennett that she had Campbell's gun, so she kept it hidden, still kneeling on the floor.

"My name is Charles Kingsley," he shouted to them as he slowly approached the table with the computers, his hands still raised. "I'm her brother-in-law. Don't plug in the flash drive. It's got a virus."

Bennett's gaze was vicious and narrow, but he didn't speak.

He appeared to believe Charles's story. Probably because he knew Alicia's married name was Kingsley.

Charles continued quickly, "Teruo didn't send her. She came on her own. He just wants her back safely."

Bennett gave a short, arrogant snort but kept his gun pointed at Charles. "What'll he give me for her?"

"This." Charles opened his arms wider so that his jacket fell open. Tessa saw the flash drive hanging from a lanyard around his neck, and she could tell he wasn't wearing a vest, which made her heartbeat pick up. He probably hadn't wanted the letters "FBI" emblazoned across his chest, nor would he want to appear overly bulky from wearing a vest beneath his shirt.

But what was Charles doing here?

Bennett gestured to Vernon, who circled the table of computers and approached Charles warily.

Charles aggressively closed the distance between them and gave Vernon a rather evil smile. "Hello, Vernon. No whipped cream this time?"

Vernon turned red, then hastily whipped the lanyard off of Charles's neck and scurried back to the computer.

"Check it for a virus," Bennett ordered, his gun still trained on Charles. He was close. At that distance, he'd never miss if he fired at Charles.

Vernon muttered under his breath, "Who's the hacker here?" but Bennett apparently chose not to hear him.

In a few seconds, Vernon said, "It's clean. It's the real deal."

What? Charles had given them the spreadsheet?

Then they had no reason to keep him alive.

"Charles!" she shouted, just as Bennett raised his gun and fired.

Charles crumpled.

Hannah screamed.

Bennett would go after her next. Tessa raised Campbell's gun and fired.

She hadn't fired a gun in eight years. It felt unusually heavy in her hand, and the recoil jarred up her shoulders, pushing her backward.

Bennett's gun hand swung wide. She'd hit his wrist, as she'd planned. Good to know her aim hadn't gotten any worse.

She sighted down the barrel of the pistol.

Saw Bennett's wide eyes.

Couldn't pull the trigger.

He bolted toward the back of the warehouse.

Vernon had frozen at the sound of her gun going off, but now he fell on the computers, typing frantically.

No. He was setting the self-destruct trigger.

She aimed at him but hesitated, because she didn't want to hit the computer. He ducked, saw her hesitation, then continued typing, his head behind a monitor.

She squinted through the smoke and fired at a table leg.

She missed.

She fired again and winged it.

She had to do this!

One more time.

The leg exploded in a shower of wood splinters. The table began to tilt slowly, weighted down by all the computers. Vernon grabbed the opposite end of the table and kept it from falling by pressing down hard.

No! She aimed for Vernon's kneecap, but then heard a moan.

Charles was still alive.

He dragged himself over the concrete floor, closer to Vernon and the computers. What was he doing? Trying to get the flash drive?

She struggled to crawl toward him with her hands and ankles still bound.

Charles reached his hand toward the table, his fingers groping, but he was still a couple feet away.

And then she saw he wasn't wearing his normal watch.

At that moment, the computers began to beep a different sound.

"No!" Vernon cried. He tried to reach the keyboard to type, but the table started to tilt.

The beeping grew louder.

The warehouse doors crashed in. "FBI!" She could feel the vibration through her body as boots pounded on the concrete toward them.

Vernon let the table go and tried to run, but FBI agents swarmed him just as the computers crashed to the ground.

A few bounced over Charles's limp form. He was no longer moving.

"Charles!" She tried to crawl toward him, but an FBI agent was hoisting her up, carrying her out of the warehouse. Out of the corner of her eye, she saw Hannah also being carried out.

"Charles!" She was being carried farther and farther from his inert body.

She never told him she forgave him.

She never realized she loved him.

Chapter 25

What was with all the white?

Charles squinted at the ceiling, which was such a bright white it practically glowed. The white stabbed into his eyes.

Then he realized he really wanted to throw up. Except he couldn't, because his stomach felt like a predator alien had reached in and pulled out his spine.

He couldn't even move his head because his vision was spinning too much.

"Erp ..." he groaned.

And suddenly Tessa was in front of his left eye, and Mama was in front of his right eye. "Charles!" they both said.

He winced. "Inside voices, ladies."

"Oops," Mama said.

But Tessa just smiled.

Tessa was smiling at him.

And then, in front of his mama, no less, Tessa reached out to cup his face and kiss him.

"Blech," she said with a grin. "You have postsurgery breath."

"I'll give you a proper one later." He tried to shift in the bed and was rewarded with stabbing pain. "I got shot," he said dumbly.

"I know," she said. "I was there."

"How can you two react so calmly?" Mama said disgustedly.

"How bad was it?" he asked.

"A few major organs, nothing that extensive surgery couldn't fix," Tessa replied.

"It feels a lot worse than that."

"It *was* a lot worse than that," Mama snapped, exasperated. "Don't do that ever again or I'll kill you myself."

"I don't intend to get shot again, Mama."

There was a knock. Charles turned his head slowly, which caused the room to revolve slightly. He blinked several times, certain he was hallucinating. "Steven?"

It was strange to see Steven in a business suit rather than his running gear. He was holding a pot of something leafy and green. "I hope it's okay I'm visiting. I called your office, and your secretary told me you were here."

"Sure. Mama, Tessa, this is Steven Nishimoto, CEO of Neesh. This is Vivian Britton and Tessa Lancaster."

"Your secretary said you were in an accident?" he asked.

"Yes," Tessa said quickly. "He just got out of surgery, and the doctor said he'll be fine." She glanced at Mama. "Vivian, let's get a cup of coffee."

After they left, Steven sat down next to the bed. "I hope you'll feel better soon."

"I'm sure I will." Actually, he had no idea. How long did it take to recover from a bullet wound?

There was a strained silence, then Steven said, "At running club today, Todd was farting the entire time."

Charles laughed, but then gripped his side from the pain. When the pain was manageable, he said, "I'd hate to be downwind."

"Everyone was trying to avoid running behind him, so they ran too fast or too slow."

"What did he eat?"

"Apparently, his wife's chili."

They chatted about running club, typical guy stuff that didn't really say anything. Then Steven said, "I hope we can still have that lunch."

Charles stared at him. "I have to admit, I thought you wouldn't want to do business with me."

"I've thought about it a lot." Steven looked down at his clasped hands for a moment. "Don't get me wrong, I still don't agree with you about heaven or hell, but I respect you for holding to your opinion and being strong enough to express it. I realized I want a lawyer who's not afraid to tell me what he thinks, whether it's good news or bad."

"I'll definitely tell you what I think. But I might offend you because of my beliefs about God."

"I can handle that. That impresses me more than if you just said what I want to hear."

Steven didn't stay for long after that, but only Tessa returned to the hospital room after he'd gone.

"Where's Mama?"

"She's chatting with a nurse who loves to cook."

He winced. "What kind of food?"

"Filipino."

He moaned. "I don't want to know what kind of fusion

dishes she'll come up with. I survived the bullet, but she'll kill me with her cooking."

Tessa took his hand, leaned toward him. "You knew they'd kill you as soon as they got the flash drive." Her voice was thick. "Why did you do that?"

He had no shame—maybe because of the lingering effects of the anesthesia—and he wasn't about to not say what he felt. Life was too short. So he was honest. "Because I'd rather be killed trying to save you than do nothing and let you die."

Tears began streaming down Tessa's face.

"I don't want to be like Rick," he said. "I don't want to waste any more time."

She looked into his eyes, and he drowned in her gaze, in her amber eyes that were glistening with tears. "We won't waste any more time," she promised.

"Good." He yawned. "Because now I need some sleep."

EPILOGUE

Congratulations to the winner of *Grab the Mic*!" Vivian cried out, raising high her frosted glass of virgin strawberry daiquiri.

"To George!" Tessa joined her family as they toasted George, who had just walked in Charles's front door.

He turned pink, then gave a hearty laugh. "Looks like you all started the party without me while Charles was picking me up from the airport."

"Paisley!" Hannah pushed past her dad and went to hug Tessa's niece. "Can I see the scar? Is it cool?"

Paisley pushed up the sleeve of her shirt, showing the puckered scar, which was still vivid pink. "But now I won't be able to wear sleeveless dresses." She frowned.

"Are you kidding? Guys love those sexy, injured spy chicks. Hey, did I show you the new computer Dad got me?" Hannah unslung the laptop case from her shoulder. "Have you played the new Angry Birds yet?" They wandered into the living room.

Charles came into the house, still walking a bit slowly. He'd just been cleared to drive again, which was why he'd insisted on picking up George from the airport.

Tessa and Charles's families crowded around George, asking him about the concert tour he'd just returned from, but Charles's eyes found Tessa's, and he walked directly to her. "Hannah talked the *entire* ride from the airport."

"I can try to make you a virgin strawberry daiquiri," Tessa said. "Although mine aren't as good as your mom's."

"As long as it's cold and sweet."

He followed Tessa into the kitchen, but as soon as they were out of sight of the living room, his arms were around her and his mouth was on hers.

His lips were warm, contrasting against her lips, which were cold from drinking the daiquiri. His hand was on her back, pulling her close, and she wrapped her arms around his neck.

He smelled of his expensive cologne, but his natural musk came through—slightly sharp, slightly tart—and wrapped around her. She wanted his scent to linger on her skin.

"Scandalous," she murmured. "Your mama's in the next room."

"Let's not think about family right now." He kissed her again, a longer, lingering kiss.

She could have stood there forever, but she didn't want her mother to come into the kitchen and find them. Or worse, Uncle Teruo, who had put in a surprise appearance. She pulled away and began making his daiquiri.

He sighed but stood behind her, wrapping his arms around her waist. His touch was gentle as his fingers strayed to her rib. "Feeling okay?"

"A little achy today. Mom says it's because it's going to rain."

He paused, then said softly, "Agent Townsend was at the airport."

"What?" She tried to turn around, but he held her fast.

"I like holding you."

"That's nice, but mention of FBI agents usually requires explanation."

"He was with George. They managed to get the show's ex-producer, Holmes Taggart, to give up the names of the last of the syndicate members. They've found all but nine of them now."

"Bennett?"

"Found him in Las Vegas."

Tessa hadn't realized she'd been tense until his hand massaged her lower back, and she felt her muscles relaxing.

Then Charles held up his wrist. "And Townsend gave me the watch."

"Oooh, I want to see."

"They took the technology out of it."

It looked like an ordinary watch, not as expensive as his Rolex, but not cheap, either. "They put that little transmitter in here?"

In the warehouse, when Charles had been struggling to crawl to the table with the computers, he'd been trying to get the wireless receiver in his watch close enough so that the FBI techie could hack into Vernon's system and prevent the self-destruct trigger.

"Does this mean it's finally over?" Tessa found herself asking.

"Is anything really ever over?"

She knew what he was talking about. She had shared with him her pain over her aunt's funeral, her feeling of abandonment by her father. He had actually cried as he apologized for what he'd done, and she hadn't found it unmanly at all.

But the process of forgiveness, even for someone she loved, wasn't like flipping off a switch. There were times when something he said made her withdraw. Times when she didn't feel as close to him. Times when a flash of memory made her gasp until the tightness went away.

"No," she said. "I guess nothing is ever really over."

He placed his lips against the side of her neck. "Something occurred to me when I was driving George from the airport and trying not to go out of my mind from Hannah's talking."

"Mmm."

He was trailing kisses down her neck now.

"That email you got from your father."

She stilled.

Dear Tamazon . . .

"We never found out who wrote that," Charles said.

She couldn't move for several long seconds. "Who do you think wrote it?" she finally asked.

"I'm not sure. Yakuza, maybe."

"I don't think any of them would know about Dad's nickname for me."

"I don't think it's spam."

That Charles was saying this seemed to make the email more real. Tessa realized that a part of her had been stubbornly holding to the spam theory because she hadn't wanted to think about the alternatives.

She turned in Charles's arms, resting her arms on his shoulders. "I got my persistence from my father. If it really was him, he'll contact me again."

His hands at her waist tightened briefly. "Are you prepared for that?"

She answered lightly, although there was a heaviness in her gut. "How can anyone prepare for something like that?"

He leaned in closer to her, resting his cheek against hers, whispering in her ear. "I'll be here for you when it happens."

"I know you will."

And then she kissed him, letting him take away all her tension and anxiety, wrapped in his arms and his love for her.

She knew there would be ups and downs in their relationship, she knew hard times would inevitably come because of who they both were. But she also knew that they had each changed. They had changed each other. And in changing, they had found each other.

Protection for Hire

A Novel

Camy Tang

Tessa Lancaster's skills first earned her a position as an enforcer in her Uncle Teruo's Japanese Mafia gang. Then they landed her in prison for a crime she didn't commit. Now, three months after her release, Tessa's abilities have gained her a job as bodyguard for wealthy socialite Elizabeth St. Amant and her three-year-old son. But there's a problem or two ... or three .... There's Elizabeth's abusive husband, whose relentless pursuit goes deeper than mere vengeance. There's Uncle Teruo, who doesn't understand why Tessa's new faith as a Christian prevents her from returning to the yakuza. And then there's Elizabeth's lawyer, Charles Britton, who Tessa doesn't know is the one who ensured that she did maximum time behind bars. Now Tessa and Charles must work together in order to protect their client, while new truths emerge and circumstances spiral to a deadly fever pitch. Factor in both Tessa's and Charles's families and you've got some wild dynamics—and an action-packed, romantic read as Tessa and Charles discover the reality of being made new in Christ.

Sushi Series by Camy Tang

 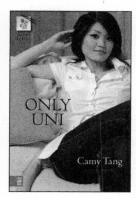 

Sushi for One?

Lex Sakai never had time for dating until her crafty grandmother insisted she bring a date to her cousin's wedding. The always-in-control Lex uses Ephesians to compile a huge list of traits for the perfect man ... but God seems to have a much more unlikely candidate in mind.

Only Uni

Trish Sakai is ready for a change from her wild, flirtatious behavior, so she creates three rules to follow from First and Second Corinthians. But with a persistent ex-boyfriend and a gorgeous coworker in pursuit, suddenly Trish's simple rules don't seem so simple after all.

Single Sashimi

Venus Chau is a high-powered video game developer. Now she might be working for the man she's always hated ... but what if he's no longer the man she thought she knew? The third book in the Sushi series offers romance with the spice of ginger.

Available in stores and online!

Share Your Thoughts

With the Author: Your comments will be forwarded to the author when you send them to *zauthor@zondervan.com*.

With Zondervan: Submit your review of this book by writing to *zreview@zondervan.com*.

Free Online Resources at
www.zondervan.com

Zondervan AuthorTracker: Be notified whenever your favorite authors publish new books, go on tour, or post an update about what's happening in their lives at www.zondervan.com/authortracker.

Daily Bible Verses and Devotions: Enrich your life with daily Bible verses or devotions that help you start every morning focused on God. Visit www.zondervan.com/newsletters.

Free Email Publications: Sign up for newsletters on Christian living, academic resources, church ministry, fiction, children's resources, and more. Visit www.zondervan.com/newsletters.

Zondervan Bible Search: Find and compare Bible passages in a variety of translations at www.zondervanbiblesearch.com.

Other Benefits: Register to receive online benefits like coupons and special offers, or to participate in research.